D1576954

PERILOUS JOURNEY

By the same author

THE HILLS ARE LONELY
THE RUNNING FOXES
THURSDAY'S CHILD
A CRY ON THE WIND
THE GUARDIANS OF STAGHILL

PERILOUS
JOURNEY

Joyce Stranger

SOUVENIR PRESS

Copyright © 1998 by Joyce Stranger

The right of Joyce Stranger to be identified as author
of this work has been asserted by her in accordance with
the Copyright, Designs and Patents Act 1988.

First published 1998 by Souvenir Press Ltd,
43 Great Russell Street, London WC1B 3PA

All Rights Reserved. No part of this publication
may be reproduced, stored in a retrieval system,
or transmitted, in any form or by any means, electronic,
mechanical, photocopying, recording or otherwise, without
the prior permission of the Copyright owner.

ISBN 0 285 63424 0

Typeset by Rowland Phototypesetting Ltd,
Bury St Edmunds, Suffolk

Printed and bound in Great Britain by
Creative Print & Design Group (Wales), Ebbw Vale

To Eryl Restall
with immense gratitude for being my lifeline at the
end of the phone while I was battling with a brand-
new computer I didn't understand; and also for
very nobly typing out seven chapters for me. I can
never thank her enough.

One

'Life is a perilous journey.'

Liese Grant could not get the words out of her head. They echoed in her mind and drummed through her dreams, so that she relived the funeral over and over again, longing to forget and yet unable to do so. She had felt at times during the last four weeks as if she had lost control of herself and was being blown, like thistledown on the wind, by events that piled up upon one another, overwhelming her.

She and the vicar had sat in this room. He was a big, heavy man, stolid and incapable of understanding other people, a drawback that had become worse with the years. His God was a jealous God, a vindictive God, promising hellfire for the wicked. His wife, who terrified the Women's Institute and the Mothers' Union and the Young Wives' Club, was even more intolerant, convinced that all his parishioners lived in mortal sin.

Large, grey-haired, dressed in heavy tweeds summer and winter, children ran from her, and the villagers crossed the road to avoid her.

'How do you know that Grant woman was actually married to him?' she had asked at breakfast with distaste. He had just commented that he would have to visit her to make arrangements about the funeral sermon. Liese had never attended his church services.

'I suppose you can't refuse to bury the man, but it ought to be in unconsecrated ground.'

Their newspaper headlines were not quite so lurid as those of the tabloids, one of which he had seen in the newsagent's when he went to pay his bill:

'Millionaire playboy dies after weekend in love-nest.'

When he visited the widow he wondered how she felt. He ought to comfort her, offer her platitudes, assure her that time would heal and her sorrow would pass, but the look that she gave him daunted him and he left the words unsaid. There was a wedding photograph in the room, so at least he could set his wife's mind at rest on that point. It had been taken in front of a church porch.

He had never visited before. The place shocked him. He hated the mercenary society in which he lived.

'Thou shalt not serve God and Mammon,' he thundered from the pulpit.

Here affluence proclaimed itself with every item in the room. The beautiful antiques were all, he was sure, extremely valuable, but not objects he would want in his own home, even if he could afford them.

Liese had been uneasy when the vicar called. She was sure that he had judged her and found her wanting. The past few weeks had shown her that she had no friends, and that she was more alone than ever before in her life.

Edward the millionaire had been a man to be courted; Edward the fraud and cheat and liar was a man to deny. There had not been one letter of condolence at his death; the only flowers on his coffin had been hers. The discussion with the vicar had provided little good that could be said about her dead husband. She could not find a single virtue, but she had kept silent about the past few years of misery, of harsh criticism, of sarcasm, of the constant belittling of her that had reduced her to inadequacy and fear.

She had only been happy when Edward was away, and as the business trips became more frequent, so she found more time in which to heal before his return. It had not occurred to her to try to escape. She had no will of her own left.

The words spoken at the funeral were induced by

despair. The vicar had no idea what to say. He would have liked to tell the truth: this our brother who was taken from us so suddenly was a wicked man who should have been in jail. Even though the church was almost empty, he had to say something.

'Life is a perilous journey. We do not know where it will lead. For some there is a haven at the end. For those of us who love God and obey the law, there is a just reward in heaven. Wrongdoers shall end in the everlasting flames.'

Liese, clutching at sanity, had a desire to giggle help-lessly when God and the law were bracketed together. The vicar had an unpleasing voice and she ceased to listen. She looked at the coffin and marvelled that it should contain the remains of the man whose life—part of whose life—she had shared.

It seemed unreal.

No haven for Edward. He had surely ended in hell, if there was such a place. Desolation overwhelmed her. An only child of a mother who had been an only child and a father whose bachelor brother had been killed and whose sister had never married, she felt utterly alone.

She was suddenly glad she had not borne Edward's child. Nothing to remind her. Perhaps one day she would look back on this and regard it with wonder, a part of her life that was reduced to insignificance.

There was an elderly couple with her. The vicar was glad to see she was not alone, but surprised when she was bundled into a small, battered car and driven away. He did not know that these were her gardener and his wife who were overcome by pity for her, and horrified to find that she seemed to have no living relatives, and no friends.

They took her to their home and gave her a meal and then brought her back to the house she hated. She ought to feel sorrow—however much she had dreaded Edward's home-comings, she had never wished him dead—but all she felt was anger and fear. How could she have been so ignorant all those years?

She shivered as she thought of the blank and unfriendly faces of the policemen who had interviewed her. Those who told her of the death had been kind, but then came more and more revelations. She had known nothing about his business affairs but she did not think they believed her: how could anyone be so stupid? She had been jolted out of a half-life into a reality that appalled her.

Life is a perilous journey. Her journey was now into unknown waters, and was just beginning. She was adrift in a rudderless boat. The house and furniture had to be sold; she would have nothing whatever left.

She should have been listening now to Edward's accountant, but could not concentrate. She wanted to escape, to run away, to hide and never be found again by anyone who knew her. She looked out of the window, needing to distract her thoughts. She fought for control.

Outside was the winter garden, no sign yet of waking life. There was a hint of colour on the huge heather rockeries that broke the wide expanse of green.

In a few weeks' time the beds would be bright with daffodils which she had planted in profusion. She would not be there to see them flower.

She felt like the princess who had slept for years and then been woken. But the fairy-tale woman had wakened to love, not to treachery and betrayal, not to this gnawing misery that seemed as if it would never leave her.

She wondered what the man opposite her would do if she screamed. Sam Laycock sat there, his files spread neatly over the antique table which had cost Edward a sum that horrified her, and spoke in a flat monotone that matched his appearance. He seemed unaware that he was destroying her.

You woke up from nightmares. But Liese was only too well aware that she was wide awake.

So many people had invaded her life in the past few weeks. Most of them were policemen, trying to sort out the aftermath of the accident that had killed her husband and the strange ramifications of his extraordinary lifestyle. Many of them were journalists, predators who reminded her of hyenas come to share the kill.

She felt as if she were performing one of the old forms of torture, reliving the same scenes over and over again. The policewoman held her arm as she looked at the face of the man she had been brought to identify. She was playing a part in a play, looking at the dead face of an actor.

She could say nothing. She felt nothing, only numbness and disbelief. She nodded her head and it kept on nodding as if she had no control at all.

They gave her hot, sweet tea. She hated tea. Mrs Hopkins, the housekeeper, also made her tea when she was brought home. She wanted to be alone. She went out into the sanctuary of the February garden, taking raisins with her. There was frost on the grass and frost icing the trees, but she did not feel the cold.

The robin flew down and fed from her hand. His small, bright, familiar presence was a comfort. The squirrel was nowhere in sight, although she whistled. He was curled in his drey with his nose under his tail, waiting for warmth. They were her only companions, her only realities. She longed, more than ever, for a dog or a cat, an animal that would give meaning to her life, would liven the house, and would bring excitement and unpredictability into the days that stretched endlessly, always the same.

Once she had bought a Siamese kitten. It had enchanted her for three days, but on his return Edward had taken it straight back to the breeder. What on earth was she thinking of? It would claw the furnishings and destroy their value.

She brought her thoughts back to the present. This

quiet man in a grey suit, with hair so fair that it was almost white and a neat, almost white moustache, with grey eyes that held no expression, was finishing what the others had begun.

'You do realise the position, Mrs Grant?' Sam Laycock tried to keep himself from showing sympathy. He was uneasy, aware that Liese's hold on her emotions was fragile. She must be a pretty woman, he thought, though now she showed signs of the major strain under which she suffered. Grief could not hide the smooth complexion, or the remarkable dark eyes that were shadowed by a blue that had not come from artifice. A haunted face that he would remember for a long time.

There were times when he hated his job and today was one of them. The senior partner should have come: he dealt with Edward's affairs. An unlucky movement had aggravated a slipped disc and Stephen was at home, probably in considerable discomfort, but at least he did not have to deal with an intolerable situation.

Sam knew too well from past experience that the least word of understanding could provoke a storm of tears. He had met Edward Grant on several occasions but this was the first time he had met his wife. He was afraid he would show the shock he had felt when he began to probe deeply into her husband's financial position. He had had no choice, as the firm had dealt with the man's more respectable business affairs for years.

He put a sheaf of papers in a file, nerving himself to continue the interview.

Liese stood up, desperate for movement, longing to get away from this room where she had spent so many hours alone during her ten-year marriage, hoping for . . . what? Time to spin backwards?

Now, free of Edward's influence, she found it hard to understand herself. She was only just beginning to realise that the man she had thought she loved had terrified her.

'The sale of the house and contents may cover the debts,' the grey man was saying. She wished he would leave her alone to curl up like a sick dog and try to live through her misery.

Edward had taken all her money; he had never invested it. He had never had any of his own. The business contacts and conferences were all lies. His time had been spent on racecourses and in casinos, losing a fortune, her fortune. He had borrowed indiscriminately, offering securities that proved to be forged.

There were men clamouring for money that her husband owed because he had gambled. Some of the messages frightened her, as did two of the men who hammered on her door. Once she had called the police, at which point they too had begun to unravel the mess that had been left behind. There seemed no end to the revelations.

Edward had left no will, which did not help.

Liese felt as if she were moving in a fog. It was impossible to take in what had happened to her. She had not realised, until the grey man began to talk today, just how Edward had betrayed her. Here she was at twenty-nine, widowed, homeless and penniless.

She could not sit still. She poured coffee from the percolator which had been plugged in over an hour ago.

'Milk? Sugar?' she asked. Drinking and eating were part of normal life. Had she eaten today? She couldn't remember.

'Black. One sugar.' Sam Laycock was watching her. She shivered, although the room was warm. How long did shock last? It was over four weeks since Edward . . . Don't even think it, she warned herself.

She took biscuits from a tin and put them on one of the Minton plates, taking an absurd small pleasure in using an object that Edward had insisted should be kept in a cabinet. She arranged them obsessively, as if the pattern were vital to both of them. The small routine was a comfort. She placed the matching delicate cup and saucer in front of him.

'Thank you.'

He was sitting under the picture that Edward had given her for her birthday—two farmyard cocks, brilliantly coloured, strutting among a bevy of small brown hens. She had been born in the Chinese year of the Rooster.

'So silly,' Edward said. 'You're too shy, too self-effacing ... anything but a strutting cock. I'm the cocky one in this family.' She thought he liked that, that it made him feel protective. That had been one of the good times, early in their first year of marriage. He had loved her then. Or had he? Had he ever loved anyone but himself?

She looked back at her nineteen-year-old self with disgust. How stupid could you be? He had carried her off, in spite of her aunt's opposition. All the excitement of an elopement at night and a special licence. He was a glamorous man with a glamorous job. He was an under-cover agent for the police, he told her. He worked for them and was often asked to take some secret role and infiltrate a group of men, to prevent a robbery, or even a bombing.

That was why he was away so often and she must never try to get in touch. He did not even leave her a contact number when he went away. She realised now that there would have been someone to whom she could appeal if he vanished, as he said he might, killed one dark night on some very secret assignment.

All his business activities were a cover, he explained, and she held his life in her hands. She must tell no one.

He was, he said, a financial wizard, a genius as well as a hero, and they would live like royalty—as they did. He could invest her money in such a way that it would bring in even higher dividends. She had inherited at eighteen, and had sole control of her fortune. There was the insurance money for her parents, who had been killed in an air-crash when she was sixteen. The house had been sold, producing more. She had gone to live with her father's sister. Within a year of her parents' death her mother's mother had died, leaving her even more money.

Edward had sacked the man who had looked after her affairs for three years, and persuaded her that Frankie, her aunt, was against the marriage as she wished to benefit from her niece's fortune. It was hard to accept he had never told her one fact that was true.

Frankie had been right: all he wanted was her inheritance. Why in heaven's name had she signed those papers giving him full power to deal with her finances? The gullible little innocent. She must have been mad. Now she realised he only came home when he needed more money and, once he had her signature, he went away again.

She drank hurriedly from her cup, scalding her tongue. The pain was a distraction, helping her overcome the terrors that haunted her. What am I going to do? she asked herself, and knew there could be no answer yet.

I was bewitched . . . besotted . . . I always believed him when he said that this time he would change; life would be different. How could a man who had so much charm be such an utter bastard? Which was the real man? She had no idea. For ten years she had lived from one day to another, from one moment to another, remembering the good times, the promises, the wild loving; choosing to forget the insults, the fear that he despised her, the knowledge that she could never live up to his ideals.

Becoming less and less of a real person; a timid echo of her former self. What would she have been now if she had never met him?

Outside the patio doors a blackbird sang from the rowan tree, his voice soaring into a blue sky that mocked her as much as did the expensive room. She did not belong in it. She never had belonged. For a moment the man in front of her, the garden outside, and the brocade curtains swam together. She put out a hand to steady herself.

Sam watched her, horrified. He could not cope with a fainting woman.

'Mrs Grant! Are you all right?' He tried to keep his voice brisk and unconcerned.

The sharpness in his tone restored her. She picked up her cup and saucer and walked carefully back to her chair. She sat and took a deep breath and a more careful sip of coffee.

'All right?' She needed to keep her temper and not show this man her feelings, but the explosion had been building for days and she had no control over her tongue. 'My husband is killed in a motorway pile-up. He's with his secretary who's ten years younger than I am and he spent three days with her in the honeymoon suite of one of the most expensive hotels in the country when I thought he was on a top-secret undercover mission. He paid with his credit card. I have to pick up his bill. For him and that . . .'

She had seen a photograph of her. Nineteen years old with the kind of beauty that made men foolish, while she was ten years older and had lost her looks long ago. Her marriage had destroyed her.

'I've been pestered daily by horrible reporters, by men from the BBC and ITV, by men offering me money to tell the widow's story. How did you feel about your husband's mistresses? Everyone knows how stupid I am. The tabloid Sundays had pages on Edward and his lifestyle. People stare at me when I go out . . . How the hell do they think I feel? You ask if I'm all right.'

She astounded herself. The anger that had fuelled her since she began to learn the truth was turning her into a different person. She took another deep breath. Relax, she told herself and almost giggled, hysteria rising. But now that her feelings were unleashed, she had to go on.

'The media have had a field day. They even had a copy of our wedding photograph on the TV national news the day the story broke. The playboy who pretended to be an undercover agent. That was what I told the police when they asked if I knew where he had been. I thought he had perhaps been found out and had died a hero's death. They knew nothing about him; they probably thought I was delusional . . . needing to invent a cover story to hide my own knowledge. They don't even believe I didn't know how he lived. Needless to say, no security organisation had ever heard of him.'

She laughed, a sound that mocked herself.

'I'm badgered and hounded, and now you tell me that even our wealth has been a lie. The newspapers didn't find out the half of it. I had no idea that he had massive debts. I knew he had some . . . men called here, or phoned. I was frightened and that was when I called the police. We never discussed money. We were rich, I thought. There was all my money. I thought it was still invested. He had invested it for me, he said. He never denied it to me if I asked, though my needs, compared with his, were very few.'

Sam, embarrassed, and not knowing what to say, took papers from a second file and aligned them carefully on the table as if their neatness would belie their contents.

Liese still needed to talk. She felt as if a dam had burst inside her.

'I bought this house with the money my parents left when they died. They were both heavily insured apart from the extra they took out when they went on holiday. There was over a million pounds. The house was free of all debt, and now you tell me that it's mortgaged, and when sold there'll be nothing left over to pay other debts. How could he mortgage my house?'

'He forged your signature. As he did on many cheques. We have at least the proof of that. No one is blaming you.'

Did that help at all? she wondered.

She did not like the house. Edward had chosen it. He ruled her life. He would not even let her have a car of her own, although she could drive and sometimes took the wheel when they went out together. There had been no shared excursions for more than four years.

'I thought that these antiques were to be my lifeline if Edward died . . . Who expects a man of forty to die? I'm so angry . . . if he walked through that door, I'd kill him!'

The absurdity struck her suddenly and she began to laugh helplessly. The laughter turned into tears and Sam, faced with the scene he had dreaded, went to the sideboard, looking for brandy.

No expense spared, he thought, as he picked up the elegant glass into which he had poured a stiff dose. Light glittered on a mass of crystal. She sipped, fire in her throat, warming her. She took a long breath.

'I'm sorry. It's just been too much. I don't know how I'm going to get through.'

'Haven't you any relatives or friends who would come and stay?'

'Edward detested all my friends. I lost touch long ago. His friends . . .' she shrugged. 'I learned to accept them. I didn't like them or the kind of life they led. They drank heavily; some took drugs. They slept around. I hated them. We needed them for business, he said, and also some of them were part of his undercover work . . . they mustn't suspect that he was watching them, waiting for an opportunity to report their activities. He was chosen because we had the money to keep up the same lifestyle. I provided camouflage. I had to be his hostess; it never mattered at first because I thought we had each other, and needed no one else.'

He knew how to reawaken love when he had gone too far; knew just what would make me sure of him again, and believe that it was I who was causing the problems, so that I tried to please him, abjectly, like a submissive she-wolf longing to placate the packleader. He flicked his fingers and I grovelled. I've been living on a roller-coaster . . . why didn't I see it?

The blackbird had been joined by other birds, and their singing was intrusive. Matt Davis, their part-time gardener, came suddenly into sight, pushing a wheelbarrow. She would have to find money to pay him and courage to tell him he had to go.

'I've one aunt . . . she lives in Wales. She's an odd bod, a crazy old crone Edward always said. They hated each other. She said I ought not to marry him. She said he was a con man, all charm on the outside and colder than Arctic ice within, wanting nothing except his own gratification. She said he was only after my money.' Her voice was bleak. 'She was right. I should have listened, but who does, at nineteen? We know the world is ours and that anyone older than us is out of touch, is unable to understand.'

Sam looked at the silver-framed wedding photograph standing on a little bureau that must be worth a fortune in itself. How could any man spend so much? That honeymoon suite, according to the newspapers, had cost £1,000 a night. A frugal man himself, Sam hated extravagance.

The photograph was a promise. A hope for a future life that would be happy ever after. Only the very young and the very naïve ever believed that.

Liese Grant . . . ten years younger, her expression radiant, the headdress framing ash-blonde hair that had darkened now to the colour of ripening corn. She was looking up adoringly at a man who might have made a fortune in Hollywood had he tried. The camera did not do justice to her amazing eyes. Not even her exhaustion could hide their beauty, though the deep brown had no light in it and the lids were faintly pink through many shed tears.

Sam looked at the image of the man, suddenly envious

19

of the handsome face, the thick mass of beautifully cut hair, one lock tumbled on to his forehead, the tanned skin, the body that women would always turn to see again. Few would notice the weakness in the mouth, the hint of self-indulgence that was already beginning to thicken his waist. The bride was looking up at her groom; he was smiling straight into the camera.

'How long is this going to take?' Liese asked, distracting him from his thoughts. 'Am I going to be dispossessed tomorrow? How do I organise it all?'

He looked at her, frowning.

'Have you any money at all in the house? You'd better not use your credit cards . . . The debts are greater than the assets, so far as we can judge. If the house hadn't been remortgaged . . . that was recent . . . only about six months ago.'

'I've been writing cheques on our joint account . . . I don't have one of my own . . . they'll all bounce. Edward always checked the statements; I never dreamed there could be any problem . . . I've been so stupid . . .' The undertakers . . . That had been a huge bill. She had a vision of a large dark man knocking thunderously on her door, demanding his payment.

What on earth was she going to do?

'Why don't you go and stay with your aunt? I'm sure she'd be pleased to see you . . . after all, the cause of your quarrel is no longer here.'

'I hoped she'd phone.' Liese sounded forlorn. 'She can't have failed to hear about it. It's been in every news-paper published.'

'Perhaps she was afraid of rejection. Ten years is a long time. But family is family, and your aunt sounds as if she could be trusted to be a good friend now you need one. She won't know your new ex-directory number.'

'I'll ring her,' Liese said. 'Can I still use the car? Will that have to be sold too? I'd really like to exchange it for something smaller.' If there was any money left over for that. Would the garage continue to give her credit? She didn't know. The reality was only just beginning to hit her.

I've never driven it on my own, she thought. Dare I try?

'I'll do my best,' Sam said, unprepared for the wave of pity that swept over him.

'It's so damnably unfair,' he said later that day when he visited his partner, who was unimpressed.

'Happens all the time. Can't afford to get involved.' Stephen grinned at Sam. 'Pretty woman, is she? Not much sense.'

'How could she go on for so long without even suspecting?'

'He was clever and plausible. I met him socially, at various dinner parties. He was sought-after. She rarely came, in these last few years, but he was never alone. He brought some stunning partners. Such a charming man, most people said. I always suspect charm. But I never dreamed . . .'

Sam's thoughts were haunted for days.

Liese, wandering aimlessly from room to room, ended in the kitchen, wondering when she had last eaten and if she could bear to make herself a meal. There was a tap on the door, and she stared blankly at Matt, whom she had forgotten.

He was an elderly man who had turned to gardening to eke out his pension. It had seemed ample when he retired, but now, with his wife ailing and in need of constant warmth, it did not stretch to cover all their expenses, frugal though they were.

'My Annie is worried about you.' Liese had lost weight and looked exhausted. He felt a wave of pity. 'She says I'm to make sure you feed yourself . . . she knows how it is. Have you eaten today?'

Liese looked at him blankly.

'I honestly don't know.'

He walked into the kitchen, leaving his wellingtons outside on the step. His grey hair had thinned, and his skin was weathered by the outdoor life he had led for the past five years. He had once been a policeman, but found retirement dreary. His own house had very little garden and he found satisfaction in helping those more fortunate.

Without asking, he took over her kitchen, finding bread which he cut for toast, hunting in the refrigerator for eggs and scrambling three of them; making fresh coffee, grinding the beans as if he had lived there for ever.

Liese discovered that she was very hungry.

Matt, trying to distract her, brought out photographs of his three grandchildren: two little boys and a baby girl.

Children . . . she had wanted them, but Edward had so hated the idea that he had a vasectomy. Which left him free of all fear of consequences when he chose to wander, she thought now with sudden insight.

'I don't suppose you'll be staying here,' Matt said. 'Do you want me to keep the garden in order for a bit? It's more likely to sell easily if the outside looks good.'

'I can't possibly take advantage of you. I can't pay you after today.'

'Don't worry about that. I can keep it going till the place is sold. I'll come in and tidy. I've no garden of my own and I'll miss this one. There's not a lot of work just now. Weeds shouldn't start growing for a few weeks yet and maybe it will sell quickly.'

Liese choked back tears.

'I can't thank you enough,' she said. 'Maybe one day . . .'

There had to be a future but she had no idea where that would lead her.

Matt left. The house was unbearable. She went out into the garden, taking bread for the robin, but he did not appear. There would be frost by nightfall. She shivered and went back into the empty rooms. Silence emphasised the fact that she was now alone. Though she and the housekeeper had never been friends, at least there had been another human presence when Edward was away. There had been movement and sounds.

She switched on the radio, but switched it off again after a few minutes, wondering why there were so many idiotic programmes. She put on a compact disc, choosing *Swan Lake*, but the music did not soothe her. Television was worse. She had enough problems of her own without agonising over those of other people, even if, as in this programme, they were real and not figments of someone's imagination.

She picked up a book, but the words meant nothing and she read the same page three times without remembering a single sentence. She was cold and turned up the heating. There was no one to phone; no one who had the slightest interest in her. She knew that if she did call any of her past companions they would find an excuse to ring off after a few minutes, anxious not to be involved. She felt like the fairy-tale queen whose heart had turned to ice, who infected everyone she touched with the same chilly remoteness.

She went to the telephone and dialled half her aunt's number, and then put the receiver down. Suppose Frankie said no, I don't want to see you? Suppose she just rang off without saying a word? Maybe it would be better if she set off and arrived unannounced. She wouldn't turn her away. Would she?

She could not make up her mind whether to go or stay. If Frankie turned her away . . . dear God, what have I done to deserve this? she asked aloud and then jumped as the doorbell rang.

The chain was on, and she undid the bolts and turned the key. She stared through the gap in dismay at the man who confronted her.

Most of the press interest had died away as the police had promised, but Reg Mavis was a freelance, who specialised in the women's viewpoint, writing it up for various magazines. The more outrageous the better, so far as he was concerned. He was apt to invent if the story was not sensational enough.

He used a number of pseudonyms. Some of the material he submitted as true was pure invention, with various of his female acquaintances only too pleased to share in the rich rewards and pretend to be the subjects of his articles.

'Price has gone up. Clever girl, aren't you?' he said, leering at her. He reminded her of a weasel, with a narrow face and disconcertingly small eyes that mesmerised her. 'They'll give you a small fortune for your story . . . must have one, mustn't you? They want it all: your lovers, the rich life you spent with your husband, and what you did while he was away . . . we can all guess . . . pretty woman like you.'

Liese felt sick.

'You can go to hell,' she said, furious at the intrusion. The police had promised to protect her and she had changed her telephone number, but there was always someone clever enough to outwit the watchers. Or maybe they had now been called off. Few stories persisted beyond a few days.

She slammed the door and stood against it, shaking, the renewed tears annoying her, because she seemed to cry at nothing these days. He put his finger on the doorbell again. She shot the bolts as noisily as she could and walked away. She had had enough. It was five minutes before he gave up. She watched him as he walked down the drive and climbed into his car.

He sat there, and she thought he would lie in wait, ready to pounce on her if she left the house. He would not accept that she had no story: there had been no lovers; the rich life had stopped some years ago. No more holidays and flying visits to Paris or Amsterdam. Just loneliness and despair. Although she had not known the depth of Edward's treachery, she had suffered his moods and been aware that she disappointed him.

She would, quite definitely, go to Frankie. No one would find her there.

She went round the house, drawing all the curtains, although it was not yet dark. She was afraid of prying eyes and hidden cameras.

A sudden new fear added to her worries. Suppose her aunt had died and nobody told her? Suppose she drove to the farm and met a stranger?

What on earth would she do then?

Two

It was the only home the German Shepherd bitch had ever known. She had been born there. It measured six feet by three feet, a compartment in a leaky barn where seven other bitches also had stalls like hers. She never saw them, though she heard them and at times, when life became unendurable, they lifted up their voices in a mutual keening, the sounds echoing over the foothills. Those who heard them thought the noise came from the hound pack that was kennelled three miles away.

Once a day each in turn was tied for an hour to the big tree in the place that had once been an orchard. It was now overgrown with nettles and thistles and the piled debris of last year's shed leaves, which rotted and died and formed a carpet on ground worn bare by the many bitches that had known a brief respite from their prisons for the past fifteen years.

Although they were tethered, they had twenty feet of chain to hold them and could roam, stretching their legs, sniffing at the ground, lying sometimes under a sun that warmed and comforted them and eased the ache in bones that knew only dirty straw, damp from the drips that fell through the leaky roof. Flattened-out empty baked bean tins were nailed over the many rat holes.

The bitch, like the others, feared the man and the woman who looked after them—never with love, never with kindness, though they were not actively cruel as these were their livelihood, their investment. They were groomed occasionally, when anyone remembered. They had water and they were fed. No one bothered about the fleas, though they were occasionally wormed.

Every six months, from her first season, each bitch was mated. There were always puppies in the barn. When one of the dams grew too old and ceased to be productive, she was shot and another bought to take her place. Death came too if one fell ill. Vets cost money and it was easy enough to replace her. The man had no compunction about using his gun: it was quick and cost nothing.

The pups fetched good prices. Even the worst were appealing small animals that tugged at heart-strings, and people were mugs. Punters didn't know the difference between a well-reared little animal and these pathetic creatures. So long as they survived a few weeks after they were sold, who cared what happened? The receipt said 'no responsibility taken after the pup leaves the kennels.' The new owners could be blamed for neglect.

The pups were removed at five weeks old, bathed and put in a wonderful run in the immaculate front garden of the house where the Smiths lived. Their future owners could see them from a passing car. The notice on the gate, 'Puppies for sale', brought in families out on picnics with the children, clamouring for a dog.

It was a good area, with Snowdonia forty miles away and Shrewsbury, Liverpool, Manchester and Chester all within easy driving distance. Their business was just off the main road, well signposted, and the little lane in which it stood was beside a clear stream that ran over rounded rocks, edging woods where children could play without harm with their parents near.

The buildings presented a smart appearance to the outside world. There were always a number of breeds as many litters were bought in. Puppies meant hard work and often first-time breeders were only too glad to pass on the responsibility of rearing them, at four weeks old, accepting a lump sum for the litter of £100 a pup. It seemed a fortune, and saved so much money and work as growing pups were expensive to feed and there would often be vet bills. They did not know that a week later each was sold for three or four times the price paid.

The German Shepherd pup with chestnut markings above his eyes had been nicknamed Eyebrows by Eve. He was bigger than his litter-mates and they hoped to charge more for him. By the time he was born his mother, only four years old, had already whelped seven times.

She was their best money-maker, always producing nine or ten puppies after each mating. Over sixty pups they had had from her, at £400 each—£24,000 from that one bitch, paid in cash and never declared. She was a major part of their private goldmine.

She had no name. She was just Number One, in the first compartment in the barn. No one ever stroked or petted or praised her. If she made any overtures towards the pair who fed her, she was pushed roughly away and the man kicked her. She learned not to ask for comfort.

She had loved her first litters, but by the time her eighth was born she hated puppies. She had suffered for years from the small mouths feeding from her. More than sixty sets of sharp teeth had worried at teats that grew more tender each time. All those puppies growing and fighting and teasing and pestering her.

She spent three weeks in season; nine weeks in whelp; five weeks with pups that were taken from her too young. She then had seven weeks' rest before the cycle began again; seven weeks which never gave her time to build up her strength after the long strain. She was gaunt and shabby and had no shape left. Her teats never had time to recover.

Beyond the barn was a wilderness, encouraged deliberately so that no strangers were ever tempted to walk through the overgrown bramble-thick woods that led to it. The house was a quarter of a mile away. The barn had once been part of a farm that now stood empty, bare rooms open to the sky, the roof a mere memory, stripped long ago.

There was a village belief that it was haunted. Every night, when the clock struck twelve, footsteps ran up the lane, a gate creaked open and a hand hammered on the cottage door, followed by screams and cries. But there was no gate, no path and no door, and no sign of footsteps in the long wet grass. The fear ensured privacy.

There were eleven pups in Number One's eighth litter. Ten were smaller than usual, and fretful, as there was not enough milk and it was never supplemented. Two died. The rest survived, fighting for the richest teat, but the eyebrowed pup, who was twice the weight of the others, always won.

He learned to be bold and he learned to be fierce, snarling at his mother if she tried to push him away, biting hard and with intent at any of his brothers or sisters who dared to challenge him. The bitch was too weary to discipline him. She did her best to keep away from him, but he had youth and persistence.

The pups were weaned at four weeks old, as by now the bitch had no milk at all. She had fulfilled her function and was useless. The next litter would probably not survive. One day she was taken away. The shot startled the birds in the wood and sent them flying, crying their warnings of danger. The pups had had no kindness from her and did not miss her. She was buried with the others in the woods.

They were a troublesome litter. It was soon plain that the eyebrowed pup was the cause, stealing more than his share of the food, pushing the others away, snapping and snarling at them. He was taken to the house and given his own crate, which allowed him space to turn round and little more. He was bored, and spent much of his time trying to escape. He missed the rough and tumble of daily life, of the other pups around him. He enjoyed bullying.

The eyebrowed pup grew used to hard hands that pulled him out of the crate by the scruff of his neck, to being lifted high and then planted hard on the ground after being carried a few yards to his food bowl, as he was fed outside, being a messy eater. He growled, but was shaken so thoroughly for his impudence that he learned not to do that again.

Once the man, dragging him out of a corner by his tail, hurt him so much that he turned in fury and sank his teeth deep into the hand that had seized him.

The instant thrashing he received left him bruised and painful for weeks afterwards. He learned that the huge two-legged creatures who walked the world were very unpleasant indeed. At night, alone in an empty room that had once been a large scullery, he whimpered to himself. He was cold.

In the days that followed fear became part of his daily life, as the man, now nervous of him, made sure that the pup knew who was master.

The family who called were shown the pup.

'Sweet, isn't he?' the woman said in a soft tone that the pup had never heard before. 'He's so beautifully marked, with that dark mask and those chestnut lines above his eyes.' Her husband thought the little dog had the appearance of a forlorn clown. He seemed aloof, and made no move towards them.

The breeder had her eye on the little girl. She was a pretty child, with enormous eyes that stared out of a too-white face. She moved as if in pain. The parents watched her anxiously, paying less attention to her more solid and rosier brother who, two years older, was thoughtfully weighing up the puppy.

'I don't think he's quite what we want.' The father was uneasy. He did not like the woman and did not trust her. The fat man, working outside, had grunted and gone away when he had been greeted. The pup did not behave as puppies should.

'I want him,' the little girl said. 'You said I could have a puppy ... I like his eyebrows. I'm going to call him Shadow, 'cos you had a puppy called Shadow when you were a little boy, and he was a lovely dog, you said. He'll always be there for me when I come out of hospital.'

Debbie looked up at her father, knowing very well how to get her own way. He put his hand on her shoulder, pulling her close to him, his eyes suddenly tender.

Eve Smith was good at sizing people up. She saw the anxious exchange of looks between husband and wife, the man's slight shake of the head, and the woman's suddenly set lips as the child went towards the crate and stooped down and began to talk to the puppy, who had not yet been released. He was lying on a snow-white rug, which had been placed under him as the car turned into the yard. He liked the softness and the warmth. He had never experienced either before.

The little girl put her hand into the cage and the breeder held her breath, suddenly afraid. The pup hated hands. The child spoke softly. The pup watched her, cautious. The tiny hand stroked him, a gentle movement that triggered an instinct in him to guard and protect. He licked the small fingers, which tasted of the sandwiches she had eaten for lunch.

'See, he likes me.'

'Debbie ... we thought a smaller dog, darling,' her father said.

'He is small.'

'In six months' time he'll be bigger than Auntie May's Sabre and you know how big he is.'

'I want him.' Her mouth was beginning to quiver, and the breeder took the pup from the cage and put him gently into the child's arms. 'He's mine.'

An hour later they were on their way home, the father

wondering how on earth he had managed to buy not only one of the most expensive puppies he had yet seen, but a couple of soft white rugs, a polythene bed and a sack of dog food, as well as a bowl for food and a collar and lead and a remarkable toy that spun and twisted like a live weasel and was guaranteed to give hours of fun.

He had been assured that the crate in which the pup had been penned would be invaluable.

'It gives the puppy a safe place away from the children. He'll consider it his home,' the woman said. She charged him £150 for it, assuring him it would be big enough even when he was fully grown.

It seemed a very good idea.

When they were gone, Eve Smith and her husband looked in glee at the astonishing cheque and celebrated that evening with a bottle of expensive wine.

'The easiest sale I ever had. I was sure we were on to an easy touch,' Eve gloated. 'There's something wrong with the child. I knew by the way they treated her she'd only to ask and they'd give.' She was well satisfied with her own shrewdness. She might be accused of all kinds of things but nobody could deny that she was a good business woman.

The pup did not like the car. He lay in his crate, forlorn and anxious, listening to the engine, hating the sudden stopping and starting and the unfamiliar smells that surrounded him. He felt lost, seeing too many new sights all at once, and unable to understand what was happening. The journey seemed to go on for ever, but then it stopped and he was carried out into a house where a large tabby cat spat in fury at him, and flew from the room.

He was released in the kitchen and at once puddled, desperate. The man bent to pick him up when he had done, intending to put him in the garden. The pup snarled, afraid of large male hands. The hands insisted, and he bit, meaning to hurt. The man released him, and went to the tap to wash the injury, wondering how they were going to cope with this small demon. If he took him back now . . . Debbie was not to be stressed under any circumstances, the doctors had said.

'He's scared. Come on, silly.' Debbie had no fear at all. 'You have to learn.' She opened the garden door and led the way outside.

The kitchen had been big but the garden was enormous. The puppy cowered by the door. He had never seen so much space, nor had he seen trees that rustled, or felt the wind pushing against him, ruffling his coat. There had been no view from the kennels or the house kitchen. He had never been outside, except in the yard. He knew the sound of wind in the branches, but the sight terrified him.

He fled indoors, to crouch in a corner where he felt safe, protected by two walls. Nobody could come behind him.

The crate was on the floor. He crept towards it, remembering that in there he had felt secure and also there was the soft rug which had felt so comfortable after lying on hard wood or damp straw. He climbed inside and lay down, wanting only to be left alone. There were so many big people, all crashing around, their feet thumping on the floor, which vibrated. The immense cat, far bigger than he, scared him too.

The voices did not bother him. He was used to angry noises, as the breeder and her husband fought continuously. They shouted at each other and they shouted at the bitches and the puppies, always in a hurry as there was so much to do.

There were other voices in this new place. They seemed to go on all the time and to emanate from a strange object on the window-sill. The pup had never heard a radio before and it puzzled him, especially if it was quiet when he came into the room, and then suddenly blared. For the rest of his life he intrigued people by making a wide detour round any box at all, lest it suddenly shout at him.

Sometimes there was music and that he enjoyed, so long as it was soothing and not a clashing cacophony that irritated him so much that he lay growling softly to himself, wishing the sounds would cease. He did not like the box with flashing pictures, though sometimes he could make out a dog or another animal. He preferred to lie behind it, where he could not see the screen.

The days passed, and he learned that he must empty himself out of doors and not in the kitchen. He learned that the little girl was gentle and loving, and he began to follow her around. He allowed her to pet him, but he avoided everyone else, walking away if they tried to touch him, and he growled at the man if he came too near.

He allowed no one near his bed. He liked to lie at the top of the stairs and look down on everyone, and he often lay in the doorways, so that people had to walk round him. Nobody was ever allowed through a door before him. He was always first, racing to make sure that he was not foiled.

He worked out a way of living that suited him very well. Nobody realised that he had made rules and so long as the family obeyed there was no trouble. Within days, he was sleeping in Debbie's room, having decided that he preferred her company to being alone in the kitchen. They tried to shut the door on him so that he could not get out, but he scratched so hard at it that they gave way. He tore up the lino, and in the morning they found about six feet of it had been ripped into tiny pieces.

No one dared go near him while he ate. He had had to fight for his food all through his first five weeks, and he was afraid that someone might take it from him now. At four months old he decided that he had to protect the family from everyone who came, no matter who they were. The postman and the milkman lived in dread that he

34

might escape. Friends chose not to visit. Those who passed the house walked on the other side of the road.

When the father walked him he lunged and snarled at every dog they met, pulling on the lead. In the end they gave up trying to take him out and let him exercise himself in the garden, doubling the height of the fencing and enclosing him as if he were a zoo animal.

He had not yet learnt to come to his name. Only Debbie could call him. Only Debbie could groom him. No one realised that he thought her the packleader, as she was fed so often, tiny meals carefully designed to tempt her almost non-existent appetite. Everyone treated her with immense care.

The rest of the family endured him for her sake, but hated him. He learned that here no one hit him, though they might scold him and that he did not like and made sure they knew it. The mother was afraid of him and he recognised her fear, which rewarded him with a sense of power.

He learned that his small mistress was rarely scolded, but her brother was treated in a very different way. He was gentle with Debbie, who sometimes coaxed him into the big wire kennel they had bought to replace the crate which he had soon outgrown. Those were the days when a strange man came to see her and examined her, and looked grave. After he had gone and the children were in bed, the woman cried.

That worried the dog and he went to her and put his head on her knee, wanting to comfort her, but not knowing how or why. It was the only time he made contact with anyone other than Debbie. When he was eight months old, the little girl went away. He missed her dreadfully, and mourned for her, and waited for her return.

He did not understand the sorrow in the house, or the boy who was so much quieter, or the woman who often sobbed when she was alone, not regarding him as company. Then he did go to her and look at her, as if asking her what was wrong and why his presence did not help.

They had never seen him so subdued. Whenever a car stopped near the house he ran to the door, hoping Debbie would return. He spent the nights on her bed, burying his nose in the covers, half-comforted by the memory of her that lay everywhere in the room.

He became unpredictable. Nobody dared touch him. He needed grooming and, being full-coated, was soon shabby and unkempt. He growled at anyone who came near and showed no sign of making friends with anyone else in the family.

'It's no use,' the father said, some weeks after the child's funeral. 'He's dangerous and will be more so when he's full-grown.'

'He's our only link with Debbie,' the mother said.

'We can't risk it, love.' The man's voice was regretful, but his hand was scarred in several places. The dog was a villain.

There was no room for him in the RSPCA kennels, but there was a kennels that always kept a few empty places for dogs in need of homes. Roger Dane, contacted by the inspector and asked to give the dog a temporary home, came with his van to take Shadow, and did not like what he saw. The dog retreated to his indoor kennel. Anyone who touched him risked a bad bite. The two men decided the only thing to do was to close it, and then lift it and the dog into the van. He roared his displeasure and flung himself at the door. Luckily the wire was very strong.

They put it in with the door facing towards the driver's seat. Shadow was released into the compartment specially built for travelling dogs. The cage was removed and the door shut before the dog had time to turn round. Roger had become expert over the years.

Driven away from the only real home he had known, and an existence that suited him very well, Shadow rent

36

the air with a long, forlorn wolf howl. That did not produce a result so he attacked the mesh between him and
Roger, determined to get rid of this man who had stolen
him and was carrying him away from the one person he
had loved more than anything else in his short life. He
still waited for her to come home.

When the van stopped in the yard he decided to take
root. He was not going to leave the security of the compartment in which he had travelled. There were two sections.
The empty one contained his equipment—his bed and
blankets, his bowls, his lead and his grooming tools which
were almost new. Roger thought he had seldom seen such
a coat. He would probably need the vet to sedate the dog
before he could comb out the matted fur. The hair was
longer and denser than that of most of his breed.

It took him and two of the kennel men to manage, at
last, to bring him out with a dog catcher which consisted
of a noose on a long stick. It did not help quieten Shadow.
They dragged the dog out and, after a struggle, he
slammed the door on an animal that appeared to have
gone berserk.

There was only one kennel in which he could possibly
be confined, well away from the boarders. It had a good
wooden hut, and a big run which the dog would need as
it did not look as if anyone would be able to walk him, at
least for the time being. There was a polythene dog bed
lined with a rug, on a platform made to keep out any
draughts.

Shadow had only one idea and that was to escape and
find his way home again. He spent the next hour flinging
himself at the wire door, tearing with his teeth, scraping
with his paws, until his mouth and claws were bleeding
and he was so exhausted that he gave up and lay with his
head under his tail. He refused to touch the food in the
bowl that had been put in with him.

Don Payne, Roger's partner, looked at the dog when

he came off duty. His police dog, Venn, lay in the yard, watching the newcomer. Shadow attacked the mesh, wanting to get at his rival who dared to catch his eyes. Don put Venn in his cottage, realising what was wrong.

'A hound from hell,' he said. 'You didn't pay for him?'

'What do you think? They couldn't wait to be rid of him.'

'We can't re-home him. Vet for the last injection?'

'He's only nine months old.'

Don looked at his partner. Roger, twenty years older than Don, and placid where his colleague was fiery, sometimes regretted the impulse that had led him to suggest they should team up. Don never knew when to stop pushing.

'And he's healthy and we might be able to change him . . . you never learn, do you?'

'He went to the wrong people.' Roger had fought this battle before and had no intention of losing it.

'And was bred by the wrong people. Got his pedigree?'

Shown it, Don pointed to the breeder's name.

'That one spells trouble. We get offered dogs for the police bred by them. They're always useless. Not had a good one yet.'

'I hadn't looked at it. They were too anxious for me to take him away. He needs a chance. Every dog does.'

Roger looked at Shadow, who had stopped snarling and sat, staring at them, as if trying to dominate them. He was a very handsome animal and would improve immensely once that coat was groomed. There was misery in the brown eyes.

'Give him a month,' Don said. 'We can't sell him or even give him away. He's too dangerous. He'll be costing his keep and he's in need of a lot of attention. If he shows no sign of civilising by then, he goes. Besides, no one but you will be able to handle him. We daren't let any of the men touch him. Certainly not Sue. Maggie will almost certainly leave. She's afraid of the boarders: imagine what she'll do when she finds this one when she comes back from her shopping trip.'

He frowned.

'She has too much time off. And she doesn't do her job properly. I wish we could replace her.'

'She's been the best of a bad bunch.' Roger rarely criticised other people. He looked uneasily at Shadow who had recovered his strength and showed no sign of giving up his attack on the gate of the run. 'He's going to exhaust himself.'

'Then we'll all have some peace. One day I'll be sending for the little yellow van for you. Only an idiot would bring back a dog like that. And just look at our staff . . . they've all got problems.'

'Who hasn't?'

'I feel like a nanny at times,' Don said, and walked off, leaving his partner staring at him. That was the last description he would have applied to the man. Once more he regretted having offered him a home and a future. But he had no idea how he could dissolve the partnership without far more grief than he could stomach. Soft in the heart and in the head, his mother had always said.

Don, on his way to his cottage, was hungry for his evening meal. The radio at his belt chattered inanely. The newcomer pricked his ears, puzzled by the man who seemed to make strange noises as he walked. He did not like the big dog that was free while he was caged, though Venn had only been in sight briefly on his way to the cottage. Shadow hated his new quarters.

He refused his evening meal. He wanted Debbie. He wanted to sleep on a soft bed. Left alone at night, he tried again to break the mesh, but failed. He spent the long hours of darkness taking the kennel apart, plank by plank, until there was nothing left but the roof, which he began to chew.

By morning his shelter was a mere memory and he was surrounded by loose planks and torn-up wood and roofing material. He licked the blood from his mouth.

On his way out to work, Don found Roger staring at the debris.

'I'd take him to the vet at once,' he said. 'How in the world are we going to civilise that?'

Shadow was looking at them with considerable dislike. They were responsible for his plight and he had no intention whatever of making any overtures of friendship. 'I've seen some bad ones,' Roger said at last, 'but never one like this.'

'Over to you. On your own head. I know what I'd do.' Don whistled to Venn and put him in the dog van. Shadow challenged.

There were other dogs to feed and exercise, and kennels to clean. The untouched food was still in the bowl. Roger walked away, and was bedevilled all morning by the knowledge that he would probably be defeated. This time, he suspected, he had little chance of helping the animal.

Maggie, the receptionist, coming in late, with an incipient headache, was maddened by the constant barking. She showed her irritation by refusing to hear the phone, and going back to her own rooms for forgotten items at least ten times, so that she was missing when a client came to take home her dog.

Throughout the morning Roger was aware of Shadow lying in the rain and knew that he had a decision to make. Tony Brier, his vet, calling in with worming powders, took a long look at the devastated kennel.

'You're going to need a gun for that one,' he said.

'I hate giving up.'

The dog's eyes haunted Roger all day. Each time he passed he was treated to a threatening growl, and several times, when he had to walk by with dogs that he was exercising, to a full-throated angry bark.

He put an old door from the barn against the mesh so that Shadow could not see out. He and two of the men managed to drape a roofing tarpaulin across the top of the run. The dog would at least have shelter from the rain and sun. There was no way anyone could go into the kennel without being harmed. Yet he did not want to use the catcher again.

By teatime he had made up his mind: he would try for a month as Don had suggested. It was a poor choice, but there was no other. Roger never gave up on a dog until it was certain that there was something physically wrong that could not be cured.

He knew that he had given himself problems. The weather had worsened during the day. Shadow could not be put in the main block with the other dogs, as they could see one another through the mesh that divided them and that would cause major trouble.

He spent the evening in an uneasy argument with his wiser self. He had never met a dog like this before and had no idea what to do.

Three

Rising early after a restless night, Liese felt as if she were in limbo. Should she risk visiting her aunt? Should she phone first? Whatever she did, she could not stay here. The weasel face had haunted her dreams, the man offering her astronomical sums of money for her confessions of frequent love affairs in her husband's absence. She woke dry-mouthed and feeling sick.

Everything seemed pointless. She started once again to ring her aunt, but did not complete the number. She might not be welcome . . . how could she be?

She left the curtains drawn, but looked out into the back garden. There was no sign of watching eyes and she went out to the bird table, putting down more crumbs. If the robin came she would go to Frankie. He was very tame and often perched on her. She loved the feel of his tiny body on her hand.

There was a sudden chirrup and he was standing in front of her, his pert little presence a welcome sight, his bright breast glowing in the faint sunshine. He cocked his head, his sharp eyes watching her, and then, when she made no move, he began to feed.

She knew it was absurd but she felt she had been given a sign from Heaven. She had often asked herself in the past days if indeed there was a God. Perhaps she was being punished for her own foolhardiness and idiocy. If only she had a companion . . . a dog to greet her, his tail wagging. There had been dogs at her aunt's . . . she had once thought she would make a career with animals. Where had all that hope gone?

She roamed from room to room, wondering what to pack; wondering if there was anything she could rightfully sell.

Her valuable jewellery was in the bank. She did not want that. Too many memories. Was it hers? Was she liable for her husband's debts? She stared at the clothes in her wardrobe, marvelling that she could ever have worn them. They belonged to another existence. Edward had chosen them for her, insisting on designer labels. Could she sell them, or could they too be taken as part of the settlement?

Nobody had as yet made an inventory. Who was to know what she had bought? She began to lift them out and pack them into bags, keeping only those suitable for casual wear. The suede jacket . . . she loved that and set it aside. The pile of clothes on Edward's bed reminded her that he would never sleep in it again. She had put them out, wondering if the Salvation Army might like them, but when she looked in his wardrobe she realised that many more were missing than could be accounted for by a long weekend. He had intended to leave her.

She was shaken by anger. How dared he? Worse, how dared he die and leave her with all his problems? She beat her hands against the pillow. It wasn't fair. The tears that had been threatening since she woke suddenly overwhelmed her, so that she lay sobbing helplessly.

At last the paroxysm ceased. She had to face life, somehow. She washed her face. The emptiness mocked her. She looked at the books. She had a vast store of paperbacks, which helped to fill the long hours of each day. None of them was worth much, but the local bookshop carried a second-hand section and would give her fifty pence for each copy.

They were hers, not Edward's, and surely no one would include them in any valuation. That was due next week. She had given Sam Laycock a key and he had promised to supervise.

There were more than she had realised, in cupboards, in the bookcase in her little sitting-room, beside her bed and, when she nerved herself, stored in boxes in the loft. She collected them, filling numerous carrier bags, then took them out to the car. There were three hundred . . . £150. Would the shop take them all? She had never needed money so desperately in her life. No one could live on air and there could be no widow's pension. She was too young. But she was unemployable.

She packed for a country weekend, dressing in pale blue slacks, an Aran jersey and the suede jacket. She stood for a long time, summoning her courage. She manoeuvred the car out of the garage, parked carefully in front of the house and closed the big doors, wondering if she would ever come back to live here, even briefly.

Frankie, Frankie . . . will you welcome me, or do you hate me? She drove slowly, seeking confidence, wondering how she would fare by herself. It was years since she had driven alone. Edward always took the car, and she used the village taxi service if she needed to go out while he was away. The housekeeper had had her own car.

The bookshop owners hesitated . . . there were so many. They would, in the end, only take half. Perhaps she could find another shop when she reached her aunt's home. Seventy-five pounds felt like a fortune. It would cover the cost of petrol and a meal and leave a little over.

The rest would bring in as much again if she could sell them.

Guilt stung, nettle-like, as she drove. She could have visited Frankie. Why had she let Edward dictate to her? Why had she never stood up for herself? Because she had not the energy. Because his constant criticism had made her doubt her own abilities. He was a leech, sucking me dry, she thought, wishing she could avoid the motorway and the thundering lorries that made her feel like a rabbit beside an elephant.

It was years since she had driven this road. Edward, at the start of their marriage, insisted on frequent holidays in exotic places, so that airports and planes were more familiar than cars. There had been no holidays at all in the last few years . . . she had not even thought to ask why. She had been relieved, hating being torn from her safe home and her garden, disliking foreign food and foreign customs.

There had been changes since her last visit. She remembered country lanes where now there was a three-lane highway, and even the scenery seemed different. Their home was near Prestbury in Cheshire, though not part of the village itself. Their house was modern. She would have loved one of the old Tudor cottages. She was near enough to walk to the main street. She had so much time to spare, and no absorbing occupation.

The village remained a time capsule, though now most of the shops, in spite of their architectural age, catered for tourists. The bank fascinated her. The building was seventeenth century, the furnishings unchanged. Outside the black and white timbered front blended with the rest of the village. It took very little time to drive through, and leave it far behind her.

She was thankful when the M56 gave way to the A55, her mind retracing the long-ago journey to Wales. The road ran beside the coast, foothills bordering its edge on the other side. The distant mountains were cut-outs against a pale sky almost devoid of all colour. Their lower slopes were shrouded in mist, but as she drove the sun emerged, a ghost of itself, and shone on patched fields and stone walls and sheep that were white shapes without outline.

The sea was a dull grey, the rolling waves white-flecked. It was high tide, a wind blowing, and once a wave broke high against the wall and splashed across the car.

She felt as if she were going home.

45

How would her aunt greet her?

Frankie Morrow was totally unlike her brother, who had been self-contained and very hard to know.

The new tunnel under the river saved so much time. She remembered the queues at Conwy. She turned off the main road towards Betws-y-Coed. The hills enclosed her. Snowdon wore a white cap, but there was no snow on the other peaks.

The hedges were much higher in the well-remembered lane. They cut off the view. No one cared for them now. Once there had been a vista of mountains, with the sea in the far distance.

The journey had been much quicker than she expected and once she settled to driving alone, she was far more at ease than when Edward sat beside her, gritting his teeth or driving his feet into the floor. Change down, can't you . . . his voice echoed.

She was suddenly afraid. She needed time. Frankie might not live at Bryn Mawr any more. Or might turn her away. Or greet her with anger. Or might be so old that she had become senile, and would not even recognise her niece.

She drove into a layby by a gateway that led to a field, where placid cows gazed at her incuriously. She had not stopped for a meal, but bought a small carton of orange juice and a packet of sandwiches from the shop at one of the garages, feeling the need to husband her small resources. She ate without tasting the food. The drink was refreshing. Driving had made her thirsty.

She was coming back to life and it hurt. She longed for numbness to return, because she felt fury. Much of it with herself, for being so blind.

A tractor passed, the driver waving. An errant ray of sunshine pierced the clouds and shone on the flank of the hill nearest to her. Time to rally her wits and drive on. Frankie could only tell her to go away.

46

She reached the farm. There were still wise heads looking out over the half-doors of the row of stables. Only six. She had a sudden lump in her throat and tears in her eyes which she brushed impatiently away. There had been twelve when she left. The tears would not stop. What was wrong with her? She did not usually succumb like this.

She dried her eyes and tried to distract her thoughts. Was Frankie still breeding dogs? She was suddenly afraid again. She should have phoned. Suppose their meeting was hostile? What right had she to expect a welcome? She sat in the car, summoning up courage.

There was no sign of anyone about, and the kitchen door was closed.

A vagrant piece of verse teased her:

'Tell them I came, and no one answered,
    That I kept my word,' he said.

She swallowed, and nerved herself to climb out of the car and open the gate.

The place showed signs of the passage of time. The windows and doors were in need of paint, and there was grass between the cobbles. There was an air of desolation. It had been so busy when she was young, with people coming for riding lessons, or to hire a horse and hack the lanes. And there were the dogs, with which Liese had fallen passionately in love. She ached for a dog of her own again.

She sighed. The heads that watched over the stable doors were unfamiliar. Or was it just that they were now old? There had been Jedda and Sula; Bracken and Bramble. Some of the others had gone while she still lived at Bryn Mawr. They were retired at twenty and lived on, still cherished, with tears shed when they died.

Even ten years ago the encroachment of the town had made the lanes unsafe for riding. When Liese married there had only been those horses that Frankie called her

47

Oldies, retired, living with her on an income that made it hard to cope.

An old Golden Retriever, grey muzzled and a little gaunt, was staring in amazement at one of the stables. Surely that wasn't Mac, who had been a lively two-year-old and her treasured companion? She had missed him so much. From inside the stall came the sounds of a terrified horse and a desperate pleading.

'Come on, Merlin, it's for your own good. I didn't mean to frighten you. It was supposed to make you better. Do get up and shut up. Please!'

There was a sudden shout and a crash, followed by a desperate voice.

'Oh, God! I can't get up either. We'll both die here, you old idiot.'

Liese ran. Mac saw her and gave a token bark and a token greeting, too absorbed in whatever was happening inside. He had never seen anything like it and nor, when she reached the door, had Liese. She looked in amazement at the figure that turned to confront her. Merlin was struggling to his feet, head hanging, the woman beside him trying to pull herself up by the manger, and covered, as he was, in a mess of grey slime out of which brown eyes peered.

Liese, bracing herself, held out her hands and her aunt took them and managed to stand up. The grey slime was slippery. Liese sighed as she looked at the patches that marred the suede jacket.

'Liese! God did hear me. For heaven's sake, girl, go and get me a bath towel.' She might never have been away.

'A bath towel?'

'You're not auditioning for that damn silly play. The woman says "a handbag" in just that tone. Get it, do. I didn't choose to spend the day like this.'

Liese covered the farmyard in record time. The kitchen

door opened at a touch and barking came from some-where inside the house. Her feet remembered the way. She returned with the biggest towel she could find, an exotic specimen depicting a jungle scene in which unlikely-looking parrots flew above an equally improbable-looking tiger standing among palms and strange flowers that took up every tiny space.

She choked back an explosion of laughter as her aunt emerged dripping, but clean, from the horse trough and proceeded to remove all her clothes in the middle of the yard.

'My dear aunt!'

'How many times do I have to tell you I don't mind being aunt to a cute little girl with pigtails but don't feel old enough to be aunt to a twenty-nine-year-old woman. Don't stand there staring. You look like the vicar's daughter who's just seen the statue of David for the first time.'

'I just wondered what you'd do if anyone walked through the gate. And the horse trough is an odd place to choose to bath, especially in February.' She was over-come by the absurdity, laughing for the first time in a month.

'I expect they've seen worse sights. I couldn't walk through the house like this, now, could I? I needed to clean my clothes as well as me. Merlin needs hosing. Find some overalls and get him presentable, poor beast, while I have a hot shower.'

Liese grinned at the spectacle of Frankie ducking into the kitchen clad only in a bath towel, her hair dripping. She decided to shed her own trousers and jersey before putting on dungarees that were too short in the legs, and adding a waterproof jacket which was too large in the body and too short in the sleeves.

Merlin had been a cherished part of her life before she left home. Once his head was clean she recognised him. He, like Mac, was showing his age. He tried to rub himself against her in greeting, which did not help matters at all. He must be nearly thirty now.

He objected to the spraying water and Liese had to take care to keep herself out of the way of his sudden plunges. She spoke soothingly, afraid he might injure himself. Or damage her. It was so long since she had handled a horse.

She thought of Kipling.

'Whoa, whoa, who's going to kill you?'

As she said it aloud, she was answered by an excited whinny from one of the other stables. Starlight, my first real love, she thought, with a sudden lift of excitement. He's still alive, too. The Welsh Cob had been hers. Merlin had belonged to Frankie, but Liese often groomed the horses.

There were signs of lack of money in the stables too. Three were unoccupied and almost derelict. Post and rail that had once been bright with new paint was dingy and untended. She had offered her aunt part of her insurance money as a thank-you for the care and attention lavished on her, but had been turned down.

'You need it, girl. I don't. I can manage. You may find yourself without a job one day.' That day has come, and there's no money left either. Damn Edward.

In those days, busy thinking about her own future, she had seldom wondered about Frankie. She was a constant background, but they never exchanged confidences.

Starlight whinnied again.

'I can't come now,' she said, but the horse persisted. Anyone else would get rid of them, Liese thought, as she worked on. She was warm for the first time for years. This was the life she needed; not the luxurious prison she had inhabited for all of her married life. You could trust animals. They never deceived or betrayed you.

Though they could bully, she thought, and grinned. Merlin, aware of her drifting thoughts, had nipped her ear with gentle lips, pinching but not damaging.

She finished hosing him. The late afternoon air was chill, a bitter wind, newly risen, promising a cold night and maybe frost by morning. Liese took the horse into the stable to dry with balls of straw. She hoped it made him warm; the effort certainly heated her.

Her aunt arrived when she was halfway through, carrying a small bottle. She tipped the contents down the horse's throat. He gasped, swallowed and breathed fumes of brandy.

'For heaven's sake!' Liese said, wondering whether they would have to cope with a tipsy animal.

'Treatment for shock.'

Liese doubted it, but there was no point in arguing. The brandy had already gone down.

Frankie took up straw in her turn and began to rub. Merlin, somewhat fuddled, lost his fear and decided that, after all, these idiotic people were trying to help him and not torture him. He stood quietly at last, though swaying slightly, enabling them to finish the job.

'They're all over twenty, would you believe,' Frankie said, rubbing with a will. 'I wonder what they learn about us; whether they think we're utter idiots, doing such silly things, or just live in a blankness. I'm quite positive Mac thinks I'm deranged. He definitely thinks. He dreams too, and sometimes has nightmares, poor old boy. He's nearly twelve now.'

'He's good for a few years yet,' Liese said. The old dog was sitting watching them, his eyes bright and amused.

By the time Merlin was reasonably dry it was too late for their tea and evening stables took precedence. Liese, back in a routine she had forgotten—feeding, mucking out, and putting down fresh bedding—felt as if she had never left the farm. Starlight whinnied joyously when she came to him, butting at her over and over again, begging for attention. They had all aged so much. Only now did she realise how many years had passed.

'They all look like Nicholas Nye,' Frankie said forlornly as she shut the last door. 'Knobble-kneed, lonely and old. Like me.'

'They might be bony but at least they're not ownerless.' Liese laughed. Frankie hadn't changed at all. For a few days at least she might be able to forget her fears.

Frankie led the way into the kitchen, both shedding their overalls in the porch.

'Coffee, and then puppies, and then we'll eat.' Frankie busied herself with the kettle. Agas were wonderful, Liese thought. Always hot. The last rays of the sun glinted on the stone walls. The farm had a history when Victoria came to the throne.

She sat in her old chair, feeling it hug her close, comforting her. Nothing had changed yet everything had changed. Frankie's hair was white instead of flaming red, but the brown eyes, so like her niece's, were as bright and the quirk of amusement still came through. She had forgotten that.

She took the steaming mug that was offered her, and stroked Mac, who now found time to remedy his remissness and was greeting her as if she had only just arrived.

'He remembers me,' she said, surprised.

'You lived with him for two years. They don't forget.'

'May I ask what, in the name of sanity, you thought you were doing in the stable?' Liese asked.

'Merlin has laminitis,' Frankie said, as if that were all the explanation needed.

'So?'

'I don't like bute, and the vets nearly always seem to give that. Or ours do. In any case I prefer natural remedies as you know. I asked Herbal Joe and he gave me the clay. It's special stuff. His own recipe. You make up a wallow and stand the horse in it, and keep him standing there for some time. Only Merlin decided that I was about to use a new form of torture on him and plunged, and since the stuff is slippery we both went down. I was holding him so went into the trough with him.'

'You were lucky he didn't break a leg and you didn't break your neck,' Liese said. 'Or vice versa. Suppose he'd fallen on you? What's the vet going to say?'

'Graham? He knows me and laughs at me. Says I'm a stupid, gullible old woman, but I can mystify him at times. Mac had a bad ear and I asked Trish to put him on her black healing box, as antibiotics and ear drops didn't seem to cure it. It did clear. Graham said it's all rot and I asked him how he thought TV arrives in our homes, with no wires or anything else. So why not healing rays? I don't suppose the clay will work anyway.' Frankie grinned, and Liese was suddenly and totally at home again, remembering laughter over the animals and over her aunt's occasionally extraordinary healing methods. 'You know me. Try anything once.'

'Who's Trish?'

'Herbal Joe's mother. She'd probably have been burned at the stake in the old days, but she's a wonder with animals.'

It was peaceful in the kitchen, a peace she hadn't known for many years. The grandmother clock ticked insistently. A lamb bleated, sudden and urgent, and was answered by its mother's deep baa.

'Do you have sheep?' Liese asked.

'The field's rented. They belong to a farmer down the road, who needed more land. It helps pay the bills.'

The door between the kitchen and the hall drifted open, almost as if it had been pushed. Mac turned his head and his tail beat on the ground.

'Allie, don't shove,' Frankie said. 'I know you're there.'

Liese looked at her aunt, a worried frown on her face. Allie was a long-ago dog, dead before Liese came to live here . . . she must have died over eighteen years ago.

'Allie?' she said, not wishing to make a plain statement.

'She comes back,' Frankie said, as if it were the most usual thing in the world to have a ghost dog visiting her. 'She nudges me, hard. She always was a bossy bitch. She came when you were here, but you never sensed her.'

She glanced up at a photograph on the wall. Allie had been a magnificent Red Setter, the only one of her breed Frankie had ever owned. She had been a present from an old friend, in return for a spell of looking after a litter of pups while the owner was ill.

'You never told me about her,' Liese said. Age must be addling Frankie's wits.

'You'd never have believed me. I thought perhaps now you're older . . . Mac sees her. Didn't you see his tail beat? She always comes through that door. She still comes with me when I go shopping, but leaves the car at the Adams' house. I always left her there so she wouldn't be cooped up on hot days. Mrs Adams sees her . . . he doesn't.'

Liese looked at the door. It had always had a tendency to come open, due, she was sure, to the draught from the front door, which fitted badly.

'You were always going to do something about the catch,' she said.

'You were a very down-to-earth child . . . you haven't changed. But your guardian angel is still protecting you . . .'

'Oh, Frankie!' She had forgotten her aunt's insistence that everyone had a guardian angel to care for them throughout life.

'How many times have you hesitated at a blind junction and been startled by a speeding car that would have hit you had you driven out a few seconds earlier? I find it more and more in my driving these days with other people so ruthless on the roads . . . I am sure I only come home safely because I'm protected.'

'What happened to Edward's guardian angel?'

'Maybe he forfeited his care by his behaviour towards

you . . . maybe yours was stronger, and knew only that way to free you for what lies in your future . . .'

Ten years seemed to have added to her aunt's oddity. For the past few minutes Liese had been aware of background noise, of small squeals and cries that were mounting to a crescendo.

'Come and see the puppies. Judging by the din, they're sure it's high time for their evening feed.'

Frankie led the way into the kitchen annexe where a chocolate Labrador bitch lay on a bench, looking at six pups desperate to feed from her. She jumped down, scattering them, ignoring the shrill protests, greeting Frankie as if she had been away for weeks.

She fondled the soft ears.

'She's seven now, would you believe? This is her last litter. She's due for a happy retirement and no more little mouths biting at her and making her life a misery once they're semi-weaned. She hates them then, don't you, Bonus?'

Champion Chocolate Treasure wagged her tail.

'Why Bonus?'

'I always meant to rename her but it would have confused her. She was a bonus. We . . . the vet and I . . . thought there weren't going to be any pups. The stud dog cost a bomb, too. Then Belle produced just this one, and she's done me proud all along the line. One of her pups went to the States for over three thousand pounds. This litter is going to command the highest price of any I've ever had.' She bent her head to Bonus's face, and the bitch licked her cheek. 'Best gundog I ever bred.' Frankie stroked the bitch. 'Wonderful mother, aren't you, my treasure? If these pups are half as good . . .'

'Keeping any?'

'One little bitch to keep the line going. The rest were sold before they were born; in fact I had to disappoint three people. She usually has nine, but these are bigger than usual. The sire was on the large side.' She picked up one of the pups and cuddled him against her. 'Just coming to the busy time. I've begun weaning. They're five weeks old. Need to supervise their feeding as I don't like them all eating out of one bowl. You can't tell who isn't getting enough.' She put him down and took up another. 'This little female gets her food stolen so you can take her into the kitchen and feed her there.'

Frankie handed the tiny animal to her niece. The pup nestled against her, totally trusting. People, she knew, meant fun and games and love. Liese took her and the bowl of scrambled egg and puppy biscuit well moistened with goat's milk, and set the mite on the hearthrug where Mac lay watching her, a protective gleam in his eye.

'Outside as soon as she's eaten,' Frankie called through the door.

Mac followed them into the now dark yard. The stable doors were closed for the night. Security lights along the back of the house flashed into action. Liese grinned as she watched the dog shepherd the pup back into the warm, her duty done. Bonus and her litter were now in the kitchen. The bitch put a heavy paw on her youngster and washed her thoroughly. Released, she crept into the pile of pups already sleeping contentedly and closed her eyes.

'Don't you ever feel like selling up and retiring?' Liese asked later when all the animals were settled for the night. It was nearly ten before the chores were finished and they sat down to a hastily concocted sandwich meal.

'To do what? Sit in a sheltered flat and spend the day reading, looking at television, wishing I were back here among my dogs and horses, or on my way to a show? I'm only sixty-six. I was younger than your father. I'd be dead of boredom within six months. This is my home. I'd hate to have to relocate.'

Liese looked at her aunt. Except for the white hair she

didn't look a day older than she had long ago, when a small girl came to stay and fell in love with dogs and horses. How old had she been on that very first visit? About three, a mite in a world of giants.

I'm a Morrow too, Liese thought, surprised by seeing almost a reflection of herself; unusually large brown eyes, dark lashes and dark eyebrows, amazing against the white hair, a nose she would have liked redesigned to remove the hump in the middle; and a wide, generous mouth.

'Do I pass?' Frankie asked.

'Sorry?' Liese was baffled.

'You were looking at me as if I were a not very attractive horse and you were wondering whether to buy me.'

'On the contrary. I was thinking that you don't look much older than you did when I was small and that if I wear half as well as you I'll be very happy.'

Frankie laughed.

'The Adams next door were convinced you're my illegitimate daughter as we're so alike,' she said. 'Your father and I were often mistaken for twins though there were two years between us.'

'I never made out how you both had the same parents. Dad was always so much more solemn.'

'He was born old. He was six years older than Simon, who was tremendous fun. My baby brother. Do you remember him? You were only seven when he was killed. I hated his job. I can't understand why anyone should want to be a war correspondent.'

'I remember him swinging me up in the air and laughing up at me. He brought me a Russian doll, dressed in national dress. I wasn't keen on dolls but she was pretty. He also brought me a woolly dog. I loved that and took it to bed with me till it fell apart.'

Frankie yawned.

'Tomorrow's nearly here. It's after midnight. Let's have some sleep.'

She stood up, moving stiffly. Age was showing, Liese thought with sudden compunction and had to choke back tears when her aunt came over and hugged her hard.

'I'm glad you came,' she said. 'I've been so worried. I nearly rang when I saw the headlines ... they made a meal of it all. I was so angry.'

'Why didn't you ring?'

'I wrote to you when you married; I rang you. You never replied, and if anyone answered it was always Edward, or someone I assumed was a servant, who said you didn't want to talk to me.'

'Mrs Hopkins, the housekeeper. Edward said they were nuisance calls, and I mustn't answer; it would upset me.'

Anger suddenly overwhelmed her. Why had she not even tried to ring, just once? She had never thought of going out to a public phone booth. She knew the house-keeper monitored her calls on an extension. All those wasted years.

Lying sleepless, she wondered if perhaps Edward had told the woman that his wife was in need of care; maybe mentally afflicted, needing supervision. The ground beneath her feet was no longer solid. It opened unimagin-able abysses at every step she took. She wondered if she would ever be as content as her aunt.

The bed was familiar, islanding her in a security that she had not felt for years. There was a snuffle beside her, and a wet nose pushed into the hollow beneath her chin as she turned over. For a moment she was afraid that Allie had come to haunt her, but ghost dogs didn't have cold noses. Or did they? She switched on the bedside light.

She was relieved to see old Mac, looking at her hope-fully, sitting on the rug. When she lived there he had often stolen an illicit cuddle as Frankie didn't approve of dogs on beds. He was stiff with age now. Liese helped him into the place he had always chosen, letting him lie against her so that she could hold him in her arms.

He put his head on her shoulders, sighed deeply and licked her face with his smooth tongue. She wiped the slobber off with the sheet. His body was hard and bony but his fur was soft and warm.

Oddly comforted, she fell asleep.

Four

Liese was at a party. Everyone was dressed in the most wonderful clothes and all she had on was a transparent nightdress. Edward's mocking laughter echoed in her ears.

He turned suddenly into Sam Laycock, offering her a live rooster that looked exactly like the one in her picture. He was shouting at her, telling her she was to kill it and cook it for the evening meal.

She woke, to find Mac had his front paws on her chest and was barking desperately, trying to wake her. She sat up, shaken into action by the sound of another shout and a shot. Dear heaven! What on earth was going on? The luminous hands of her little portable alarm said four-thirty.

There was brightness in the cobbled yard outside her window where security lights flooded the ground. One of the horses was kicking against the partition of his stall, a monotonous, rhythmic sound.

Bonus, shut in her annexe, was also barking furiously, scratching at the door. As Liese pulled on trousers and jersey, thrust her feet into her shoes and raced into the passage in a succession of swift movements, Mac exploded down the stairs and into the kitchen, rushing through the open door into the yard, his age forgotten.

Frankie, her hair on end, her feet thrust into worn black slippers with holes in the toes, her body encased in a red dressing-gown pulled tightly round her by a piece of string instead of a cord, lowered the shotgun she was holding. In the lane an engine blared into life and a hidden vehicle took off, tyres scouring the road, almost skidding.

'I think they were after the horses . . . there've been so many injured around here . . . at least I frightened them away.'

'I'll ring the local police.' Liese looked at the gun. 'I hope you didn't injure anyone? You shouldn't have that thing.'

'I use blank shot . . . and even then fire into the air. I'm not an idiot,' her aunt said, her voice testy. 'I have to shoot rabbits or we'd have no grass at all. I wish to God we could sleep in peace. I worry all the time.'

Liese, talking into the phone, could give little information. Some sort of van but she hadn't seen it. Two men, her aunt thought. She hadn't seen them either. She had only been aware of them when one of the dogs barked. Bonus, reassured by silence, was lying with her pups cuddled closely around her. She lifted her head when Liese looked through the door, and wagged her tail but did not move.

Mac, who had explored the yard busily, his nose registering the presence of strangers, came into the kitchen and flopped by the fire, his attitude saying that it was unreasonable to drag an old fellow like him from his comfort. Frankie threw logs into the Aga which flared fast into a comforting blaze.

The kettle, always sitting on the hob, provided them with instant hot drinks.

'The police will be here.'

'Fat lot of use that'll be. There's nothing to see, and whoever it was is long gone. They didn't even get out of the van. Bonus warned me and I was at the window as they drove up to the yard. She hears vehicles at the end of the lane and always gives me ample notice of people around. Mac's going deaf.'

Liese had forgotten just how isolated they were. The nearest neighbours were a quarter of a mile down the lane. Suppose her aunt was ill? How did she manage on her own?

Bonus's bark startled both of them. Mac added an echo. He could still hear the other dog, and that triggered him. Footsteps sounded outside the door. Frankie and Liese stared at one another, both unnerved.

'Who's there?' Frankie called.

'Police.'

'I ought to have dressed. They'll think you've brought in a scarecrow,' Frankie said as Liese opened the door into the yard. Two uniformed men stood there. Mac ran to greet them as if they were old friends, his long tail waving happily.

'Just wanted to check that you were OK,' the younger said as they walked into the kitchen. 'Not much hope of catching your callers.'

He was a red-headed man with a freckled face and blue eyes that danced with frequent amusement, as if he found life a tremendous joke. His companion, smaller, darker, black hair capping an angular face with astonishing flaring eyebrows, had a more sombre expression.

'Bill Adams,' Frankie said. 'I told you the Adams always look out for me, and Bill still does though he doesn't live at home any more. And that's Colin Clark, my favourite fellow . . . always cadges a cup of coffee when he's passing, though he pretends he's only come to keep an eye on me. Coffee, boys, or do you have to get on?'

'No sign of any van,' Bill said, putting his cap on the dresser. 'I reckon we can spare a few minutes and have a warm.' Liese, looking at him, laughed with sudden recognition.

'Carrots,' she said. 'Carrots Adams. I'd never have recognised you. You were thin as a bodkin, all long arms and legs that never seemed to be in control, and had a mop of hair that almost hid your face. And you pulled my hair.'

He stared at her for a moment and then grinned.

'Liese Morrow, by all that's holy. Scrag, they called you.

All skin and bones and big eyes and almost white hair that was never tidy, and a way of saying things that hurt if you'd a mind. Wouldn't have known you either. You've improved with keeping.' He took a long sip of coffee.

'So you didn't become a fireman,' she said.

'No. You converted me to the police after a debate on law and order. One day I might become a dog handler. You got me interested in that too. You changed my life, ma'am, and here I am.' He grinned at Liese again, his eyes showing that he liked what he saw.

Liese, startled, wondered how many other people she had influenced and if that was good or bad. What happened to me? she wondered. Where did that girl go with all her enthusiasms?

Mac had his head on Frankie's knee, looking into her eyes, a long, loving gaze that he held as she stroked his ears.

'He's grown so old since I worked with him,' Liese said, regretting the lost years.

'You lived here?' Colin asked.

'Frankie's my aunt. My father's sister. She took pity on an orphan when I was sixteen. Probably regretted it ever since.'

'We had our moments.' Frankie laughed. 'I think Liese's always been much more conventional than I am . . . I can still manage to shock her.'

'Have you ever met anyone who bathed in a horse trough?' Liese asked, glad to turn the conversation away from herself.

'I was covered in clay. I couldn't do anything else.'

The two men looked at one another, amusement in their eyes.

'Clay?' Bill asked.

There was a sudden chatter from Colin's radio.

He answered it and then sighed.

'Problems. I don't suppose there's a short explanation, is there?'

'Don't ask,' Liese said. 'It would take for ever.'

The kitchen seemed remarkably empty after they had gone.

'Where's your gun?' she asked. The thought of it worried her.

'Behind the door. I keep it handy in my bedroom at night. I wasn't going to let them see it, though. They might try to take it away. It scares intruders off. They don't know it's only blanks. It's never left loaded anyway.'

'Have you had night-time visitors before?'

'Once. Last year.' She yawned. 'Scared them off too. Suspect they were after machinery. I've a much too portable generator in the outhouse. We get power cuts here when it snows. Those are two nice lads. Colin's only been here six months.'

Liese rinsed the mugs under the hot tap.

'Bill started off living at home but went into a hostel for unmarried men. Colin's there too, but I don't think he likes it. Not sociable, like Bill, who wanted more freedom.' Frankie sighed and stood up, easing one leg. Liese knew better than to comment. 'Not worth going to bed now. We'd better get on.'

The morning sped by. Liese walked Starlight, feeling once more the old pull. She had forgotten how it felt to be with animals, to know certainties again; not to wonder what they were thinking, or if she would cause a problem by speaking her mind, or if they would go away and mock her and laugh at her when she was not there.

'I don't know how I endured the last ten years,' she told the horse. 'I must have been crazy.'

I lived in hope, she thought, looking across the fields to the thin streak that was the river. One day, I used to think, it will all change. One day, Edward will be the man I thought he was when we married . . . one day . . .

Above the grey ribbon of water, briefly, a rainbow shone, arching over the trees.

'God's promise after the flood. The hope left in Pandora's box. That must be how all of us survive.'

Starlight, enjoying the human voice, and blissfully unaware of its meaning, dipped his head and flicked his tail, happy to be out of his stable.

She wondered if she wouldn't be wise to come back and live with Frankie. But she couldn't pay her way and was not going to accept charity. Nor could her aunt afford to keep her. Though she had not complained that life was difficult, there were small signs. She rarely used the phone, and was careful with the electricity. Clothes obviously came very low on her list of necessities.

Liese, watching, knew she too would have to learn to be very frugal indeed. She would have to look for work; any kind of work. She needed to educate herself. But for what? And how?

It was peaceful in the lane, no sound of traffic to drown the birdcalls. The distant woods were winter bare, stark against a leaden sky. There were rooks' nests in the nearest trees, huge black untidy bundles. A pheasant gonged suddenly and angrily as one of the outdoor cats leaped the bank into the little wood that bordered the farmyard.

She might never have been away. The peace was restoring her to a fragile content, which only lasted until she reached the farmhouse and found a car that she knew parked outside.

She had had less to do with their solicitor than with the accountants. Michael Dutton was the older of the two partners, a large man with a shock of white hair and an unnerving habit of prefacing every sentence with a raucous throat-clearing.

Frankie, her expression worried, had offered him coffee and home-made scones, while he waited for her niece.

'Mr Dutton. Is something more wrong?' Liese dared not hope for any good news.

'Hrrr. Hmmm. Laycock told me. I went to your house,

but though the milk is on the doorstep and the paper in the letter-box, nobody answered. I rang them to see if they knew where you had gone.'

'I never thought of cancelling them . . .' Liese was dismayed by her lack of organisation. 'I just left . . . there's been a journalist hounding me for my story. He came the day before yesterday again. I ran away.'

'I'll see to it. How long are you staying here?'

'I'm not going back.'

'Hrr. Hmmm. I see.' He sipped at his cup, frowning. 'Something else has come up.'

What could come up? What could be worse than the facts she already knew? Liese sat in the chair that had once been her refuge every evening. Mac put his head on her knee, sensing her distress. She waited, unable to speak.

Before the solicitor could answer, the kitchen door opened and Bill Adams walked in.

'What are the police doing here?' Michael Dutton asked.

'Someone tried to break in last night. Liese and her aunt were both very shocked. I wanted to make sure they were OK. My parents are neighbours.'

'Mr Dutton is . . . was . . . Edward's solicitor,' Liese said. 'I suspect he's brought more bad news.'

'I'll come back later.'

Bill walked towards the back door.

'No. Please stay.' Liese needed familiar faces. 'Whatever it is, it's sure to get into the papers eventually . . . they find out everything, including things that never happened.'

Her appeal to Bill sounded desperate.

He sat the wrong way on one of the wooden chairs, astride, leaning his arms on the back. His normally cheerful expression faded and he frowned, waiting for the solicitor to speak. Michael Dutton, overcome by pity for a woman he knew to be an innocent victim, wished he were anywhere else. Seldom at a loss, he did not know how to begin.

'Hrr. Hmmm. Did your husband ever speak of a woman called Anita Lester, Mrs Grant?'

'No. But he rarely spoke of any women at all. Why?'

'She called in at the *Daily Paragon* offices, claiming that her son was fathered by your husband and that she is entitled to money from the estate. According to her, Edward was paying her £1,000 a month and she wants it to continue.'

'Edward said he had a vasectomy. How could he have a son?' Liese felt suddenly sick. Had that too been a lie because he did not want to give her a child?

'Hrr. Hmmm. He did, eight years ago. The boy is nine, and according to her is the reason for your husband having the operation. His name is Simon Edward.'

'Do I have to pay for his upkeep now?' Liese felt as if someone had punched her. She was shaking. 'Will money have to be taken from the estate before the debts are paid? Mr Laycock says that there will be nothing whatever left; that there might even be money owing when they try to pay off.'

'You need proof first,' Bill said. 'It's very easy to cook up a case, especially if the woman thinks a lot of money is involved and that she could inherit the vast fortune that your husband is supposed to have accumulated. Nothing has been said in the papers about debts outstripping assets.'

It was the first he had heard about the state of affairs which Edward had left. A pity the man hadn't survived the crash to deal with his own affairs. He suddenly wondered if the accident had been deliberate . . . a way out of an impossible situation. Others had taken that path.

'Hrr. Hmmm. I have a photograph of the boy.' Michael Dutton took it out of the file in front of him, and passed it to Liese. 'Do you think he is like Edward?'

The child was dark, laughing up at the camera. The woman beside him reminded Liese of the girl who had died in the crash; long-legged, blonde, with an attractive face whose slanting eyes suggested an oriental ancestor. The boy had inherited his mother's eyes. Liese could see no resemblance at all.

'Have you seen his birth certificate?' Bill asked.

'Not yet, but I expect it will be the usual format for a child born out of wedlock . . . without the father's name.' The solicitor's mouth showed his distaste. In his late sixties, due soon to retire, the modern world often shocked him, in spite of his involvement with so many sordid cases.

Liese did not know what to say. She wanted to run away, this time to a distant island, where she could be alone for ever, and not have to make conversation or pretend to be part of a world that had not, it seemed, finished harming her.

'What happens now?' she asked.

'As . . .' he hesitated, frowning as he looked at Bill, unsure of the policeman's position in this household. 'As your friend says, we need to investigate. Hopefully, it will turn out to be an attempt at extortion, rather than the truth.'

'Will you stay for lunch? Both of you?' Frankie asked, wanting to dish up and feeling food might help Liese.

'Thank you. I must get back.' Michael Dutton shook hands with both women, hesitated as he looked at Bill and nodded. They sat in silence for minutes after he had gone.

Liese was fighting tears. Frankie looked pleadingly at Bill.

'Are you on duty?'

'No. I finished an hour ago. Came here before changing . . . I was bothered about you two.'

They ate in continuing silence for a few minutes, nobody knowing what to say. Liese found it difficult to swallow.

68

'I can get inquiries made,' Bill said. 'It ought to be easy enough to check on the woman; find out her lifestyle; how she's been living. It might be possible to find out if she had any links with Edward. £1,000 a month would set her up very nicely. But if she proves to have come from a squat, or be in a stable partnership and there are no signs of such payments, then we've got her.'

The meal continued uneasily. Bill helped with the dishes and, when he went, took Liese's hand and put his other hand under her chin, forcing her to look up at him.

'Don't worry, Scrag. I had a yen for you at school, did you know that? Don't think I ever quite got over it, and now you're back in my life, you're not leaving it. I can be remarkably persistent, remember?'

Liese, desperate for friendship, smiled up at him, though there was no smile in her eyes.

'I've been hating the police. I was sure they thought I knew all about Edward's business deals and was a willing partner ... It's easy to prove guilt; how do you prove innocence?'

'I'd think they know the truth about you by now. We aren't stupid. They had a job to do. There's no easy way of doing it. Chin up, girl. I suspect in spite of everything you'll be a lot better off with your husband out of the way.'

Liese stared at the door as it closed behind him, totally bemused.

'I don't think he's changed a bit,' she said. 'He always was overwhelming.'

'You hurt him badly when you married Edward.'

Liese stared at her aunt.

'Bill? I hurt Bill? But he was just a big brother ... he's a year older than me. There never was anything ...'

'You were both young and he was sensible ... ready to wait. Young marriages rarely turn out well. If I'd married my first love I'd probably have murdered him within a few years. Bill was always here, always waiting for some sign from you . . . and then you met Edward and lost your wits.'

'Hasn't he married?' Liese asked, contemplating a past that she had never understood.

'No. He's had girlfriends but they never last more than a few months. Policemen aren't reliable partners for the sort of life most girls seem to want nowadays. Work intervenes. Few women are mature enough to cope . . . Thank God I'm past all that.'

Work certainly took precedence here, Liese thought, aching after helping clean up the stables and groom the horses. How had she let herself become so unfit? She could have gone to a gym; or taken up jogging. Filled in the useless hours somehow.

'The horses do add to your work,' she said that evening. Frankie was exhausted and lay back in her chair, too weary even to feed the pups. Liese had done it for her.

'I couldn't do without them. I'm OK normally. I fell over in the clay, remember, and Merlin knocked me. I'm black and blue. Don't heal like I did when I was your age.'

She paused and eased herself into a more comfortable position, looking thoughtfully at the rosettes on the wall, memories of her past successes. The door came open and Mac beat his tail. Frankie smiled.

Liese had forgotten the demands of puppies. Frankie had a routine that seemed to involve every hour of the day. They came into the house, the floor well covered with thick polythene sheeting and then layers of newspaper. There were toys to tempt them, space to move around, and either radio or TV constantly in the background to ensure that household noises did not scare them.

The pups were therapy. Their small importance made Liese laugh. She had forgotten the wonder in those little faces, the astonishment as they met some new object, their endearing assurance that everyone loved them. The world was so new to them, and so astounding. They made discoveries every minute they were indoors.

Cocoa, who had more privileges than the others as she was to stay on the farm, explored the yard. Merlin, curious, came to the half-door of the stable and put his head over and huffed at her. She fled in terror to beg Liese to pick her up and cuddle her and save her from the monster. She was little bigger than one of his ears.

Holding her close, Liese walked over and patted the horse. Within minutes the pup relaxed. Frankie had chosen her well. She showed initial wariness at strange sights and large animals, but soon overcame her fear.

Next morning, when the big head swung towards her, the pup tried to lick his nose, an effort doomed to failure, as she was too small to reach him.

'They're more fun than anything I know,' Frankie said. 'Far more therapeutic than any box of pills. They make time pass in a flash. I spend hours just watching them, seeing which is boss, seeing new skills develop. It happens so fast.'

'I'd forgotten what fun they are,' Liese said.

The little bitch came to her and climbed her trousered leg, struggling until she was helped. She turned round, seeking comfort, and then lay in the crook of Liese's arm and was, quite suddenly, deeply asleep, exhausted by her busy explorations.

The tiny body was warm, the fur soft. Liese wanted a dog of her own again. She needed a dog. It was a sudden desperate craving. Maybe she could take one of these pups. But they were all sold. She sighed.

Life would go on and she had to find a new direction. She took the pup back to the annexe and busied herself with making a meal. She switched on the radio, hoping it would drown her thoughts, which were bleak. Was this boy really Edward's son? And if so, how would it affect her? Would she be expected to find money to help bring him up?'

Her head ached. At least while she was here she could take care of the cooking, though that also was something at which she had not had much practice. She had to learn a whole new way of life.

Frankie seemed to exist on sandwiches. Liese found meat and vegetables for a casserole which she put in the Aga. It could simmer all day.

Each pup had time alone with them in the house, so that being separated from the litter would not be too stressful.

'By the time I sell them they'll know their names. I call each one to be fed, which also teaches them to come when called, and starts something that will stand them in good stead for the rest of their lives.'

Liese watched in amusement as her aunt, returning a single pup to the annexe, battled at the door every time, trying to prevent the rest of the litter and their mother from spilling into the kitchen.

*   *   *

Three weeks later they were again in the kitchen. Now all the pups had gone the house seemed unbelievably quiet, in spite of Cocoa's efforts to liven them both. There was so much less work, but much less fun.

'I've a thought,' Frankie said as she offered the inevitable mug of coffee. 'Shoot me down if you don't like it.'

Liese looked at her, wondering what was in her aunt's mind.

'There isn't really enough work here for two; I don't want to start more brood bitches at my age. Roger Dane is a friend of mine. A good friend. We might have married once . . . I don't really know why we didn't. He has boarding kennels. He has just lost his manageress. She walked out without working her notice, after a row. He rang while you were walking Starlight. He's frantic for reliable help. There's accommodation; he lives in a converted farm-house, which has been divided into apartments. You'd have full keep, a flat of your own and a small salary. How about it?'

'Would I be able to cope? I've forgotten all my dog knowledge.'

'It'll come back. Answering the phone. Keeping records. Roger's hopeless at that. He's no time sense either and needs someone to keep him up to the mark. Walking dogs. Cleaning kennels, preparing food; giving food. You've been doing all that here. Meeting owners when they come to bring a dog in or take him home again. Collecting the money. That's one of his weak points. People can walk out with a dog and not pay at all and he doesn't notice.'

'Where is the kennels?'

'About fifty miles from here. Not far from Chester. There's a cottage in the yard as well where Don Payne, Roger's partner, lives. He's a police dog handler. He moved there last year when his wife died. He's a sleeping partner now, but when he retires, which policemen do relatively young, he'll be opening a school for training dogs. Roger hasn't time for that.'

'Does he have any staff? Or is it a one-man job?'

'Far from it. He can take up to sixty dogs, and he has several men, and a girl who I gather is a bit of a liability.' She laughed. 'We got back in touch after his wife walked out on him. She objected to coming a bad second to all the dogs. I think it's put him off matrimony for ever. He visits or rings when he wants to moan.'

A strange place, among strange people. Living in a group. Liese felt a sudden flood of panic. She could never cope. Frankie was still talking.

'His wife had a good job and paid most of the bills. He

was often away from home, dog trialling, or judging at shows. I don't think he realised how little he put into the marriage. After she left he had to make a living.'

Frankie watched the door open, and her eyes followed an invisible object as it walked across the floor. Liese sighed. Her aunt was becoming increasingly odd, and maybe needed someone to look after her. Frankie continued talking, oblivious of her niece's worries.

'Old Joe Cotter died, and Roger bought his kennels cheaply as it had been run down. He has to spend most of his time now with his work. He's made a very good job of it, but I think he'd really like so good a manager that he could go back to competing regularly again.'

Her eyes watched again, following what appeared to be a progress across the room. She stood up and walked slowly to close the door.

'I wish Allie would learn to do that,' she said. 'There's a draught under the front door.'

Which is why the door keeps opening, Liese thought.

'I'm not up to it. I'm not the woman you knew . . . my confidence has vanished over the years. I'm scared to say boo to a mouse, let alone a goose.'

Liese could not imagine living in close contact with people again. She was used to being alone. The thought of such proximity terrified her. She would not be able to escape, even for days out, as there was no money to spare. Also, would her wages be impounded to settle unpaid debts . . . or to look after that wretched child?

Frankie laughed.

'Anyone saying boo to a goose is either remarkably brave or very stupid. They're horrible creatures. I don't know which is worse, a gander or a goose with goslings. Wonderful guards. Maybe I'll invest in a few to keep intruders off the premises.'

A job . . . a lifeline . . . yet all Liese felt was terror. She was useless; she had been told that so often over the past

74

ten years that she believed it, seeing herself through Edward's eyes.

She tried to overcome her fear. She needed work: work was being offered to her, also food and a roof over her head. She would be independent and need not worry even if there was no money left over after all the debts had been cleared. Surely they couldn't take her earnings? Panic surged back, and she walked over to the window to hide her expression.

Frankie looked at her niece. It was difficult to conceal her own worry. She knew, only too well, that Liese was churning with emotions that baffled her, and would need a considerable time to recover from shock, grief and fury at betrayal.

'I honestly don't know . . . I'd make a mess of it . . . I'm not in the least efficient . . . I left everything to Edward . . . he made me feel . . . I'm not much good with people either. He always complained that I could never hold a sensible conversation about anything.'

Frankie drew a deep breath and stifled a sudden desire to shake her niece.

'I often found it a good idea to say yes when I meant no, and plunge in. I made mistakes, but I learned as I did so. Now, I'll still give anything a go.'

'Like clay wallows,' Liese said, with a laugh.

'Made Herbal Joe laugh too when I told him,' Frankie said. 'I was supposed to put the clay in heavy-duty polythene bags and tie them round Merlin's hooves. The trough was just for mixing it. Will you think about Roger's offer?'

Bonus barked as a small blue van drove into the yard, halting with a squeal of tyres.

'Talk of the devil,' Frankie added as a remarkably tall man climbed out of his seat, his grey hair, badly in need of a cut, flopping over his forehead. He banged on the kitchen door and walked in, fending off Mac who became a puppy again and greeted him with fervour.

75

'Calm down, you old ass,' he said, laughing and pulling at the long floppy ears. Mac leaned against him, his expression blissful.

'Roger,' Frankie said, taking the kettle at once off the Aga and putting three mugs on the table. 'What are you doing here?'

'Begging.' He turned to Liese. 'I don't want to seem intrusive, but it's difficult not to know what's happened. Rang Frankie to ask if you'd be interested in a job. I'm desperate. My manageress walked out on me at a moment's notice.'

'Just like that?' Frankie asked.

'She and Don had a set-to. You know Don. He needs careful handling since Marie died.' He took a bun and then turned again to Liese. 'I need someone desperately and I don't suppose you've changed much. You were good with dogs, and reliable.'

'How do you know that?'

'Watched you with them. I was at every show you ever went to, either competing myself or judging. Always thought it a pity you married so young. Waste of a life.'

And now I regret it. I hope it's not too late. A sudden desire to show her aunt that she could cope on her own made up her mind for her. She hoped that those working at the kennels had not read the tabloids. Maybe she could go back to her maiden name and become Liese Morrow again. But there had been those photographs, mostly of her wedding picture, which Mrs Hopkins had allowed to be taken from the house and copied. Liese had dismissed her as soon as she found out.

'I'll come. I don't know what else to do. I can't go home; and I don't want to find Frankie tires of me. We fought at times when I lived here; we probably still would.'

'Start next Monday. Frankie will give you directions.'

There was nothing more for her to do at her old home. She had taken the car back and returned by train. Sam

76

Laycock had everything in hand. She did not intend to go to the auction. Could she trust the solicitor? She had to . . . she had no choice. If only Bill could discover that the child and his mother were imposters.

The nights were always worst, when she was alone with time to think and sleep mocking her. That was when the past ten years seemed to repeat themselves again and again. That night she wondered if she had made a bad decision.

Sleep refused to come.

She sat up, arms clasping her knees. The bedroom was cold. She shivered, staring at a misshapen moon that peered through her window. Mac sighed and turned over. Lucky dog, she thought. If only I could sleep like you.

A clock struck five. Frankie would soon be up and this endless night would be over.

She longed suddenly to stay with her aunt, to go back to being young and protected, and loved. That would merely set her in the same pattern, with someone else taking the decisions. She had to work. She had no desire to return to her past way of life even if she could. I'll try, she thought. I'll never know if I don't.

'I think I'm crazy,' she said to Mac who curled himself more tightly against her, licked her hand and went back to sleep, snoring.

She ought to be grateful to Roger, but all she felt was fear of an unknown future which might be even worse than the past and hold as many hidden hazards.

Five

The bus dropped Liese at the end of a long lane, where uncut hedges and overhanging trees made a dark tunnel. March was halfway through but it was still bitterly cold. Her cases were heavy. The anxiety she could not cast off was worsened by a thin rain dropping from a dismal sky.

She wished she had refused Roger's offer and was now safely back in the warm, friendly kitchen with Mac beside her and Allie pushing open the door. Her fear of the future had not been helped by a phone call the day before from Sam Laycock, telling her that as well as the mountain of debts, there was an astronomical sum owing to the Inland Revenue.

She was exhausted after two sleepless nights worrying about her situation, and sure that she would be an abysmal failure in her new job. She had visions of a long prison sentence, and was now certain that she would be liable for Edward's misdeeds even though she had been totally ignorant of them.

The heavy cases were pulling her arms out of their sockets. She put them down on the ground and stood, wishing herself anywhere but here. A cow huffed at her over the hedge. Somewhere in the distance two horses called to one another. A bird sang, a sudden joyous trill that seemed out of place on such a wet day.

An absurd tag came into her head:

> I loved him not; and yet now he is gone
> I feel I am alone.

She picked up the cases and trudged on. She longed for someone to come down the lane, for a tractor to pass, with a friendly wave from the driver, for a man on a bicycle who would say good-day. She felt as if no one else existed in all the world. She skirted the puddles, wishing she had had the sense to wear more sensible shoes. Some of her tiny store of money would have to be spent on wellingtons.

She ought to have taken a taxi, but had been appalled when the driver told her the cost. It would have taken more than half of what cash remained after paying her train and bus fares. She did not want to start a new life by begging.

Frankie had treated her to a trip to a good hairdresser, which had boosted her morale. Even so, Liese felt guilty spending money on herself. She had an absurd suspicion that she was stealing from Edward's creditors.

The board announced 'Cotter's Boarding Kennels'. It was a well-kept place, the white woodwork newly painted. The yard was immaculate. Tubs of multicoloured winter pansies bloomed in brilliant profusion, brightening the sombre day. Against the stone farmhouse was a bed of wallflowers, promising more colour very soon.

The place was far bigger than she had expected, a jumble of odd buildings which appeared to have been added to the main block at random, as the mood took the owners. There seemed to be three separate dwellings. The tiny one-storied building at the end with its sloping roof had two fanlights, and curtains in the single window, though it did not look big enough for a dwarf. Once it could only have been a store-room, but had been converted.

Next to the outhouse a high wall hid a flight of steps which led to a front door, sited, improbably, beside the first floor window. Beyond that, its roof at a higher level, twisted chimneys proclaiming its age, was a third block, half-hidden by the largest part, built at right angles. The stone slab set in the wall read 1704. The walls, judging by the inset windows, must be over two feet thick.

Liese walked round the farmhouse, emerging into a larger yard, on either side of which were huge barns. Her presence startled all the dogs into barking. A girl who could have been no more than eighteen came out of the nearest, and grinned at her.

'You must be Liese. Rog is busy helping with the feeds. Sixty dogs in. We're full. Takes time. I'm Sue. Rog said to show you where you're living, and then get back pronto. You can make yourself a cuppa . . . he'll come and see you later.'

She was an untidy girl, her mop of startling orange hair spiky and badly in need of cutting and shaping. Her jeans raw-edged, slit at the knees, her jersey far too large for her small frame.

'I live in the doll's house. You're next door, up the steps.' She was leading the way as she spoke. Liese picked up her cases, wishing she had been offered help. She followed her guide up the worn stone flight. They must be lethal when it's icy, she thought.

'It's open. Keys on the table. Food in the kitchen. All mod cons. It's a better pad than mine.' She hesitated, and Liese suddenly realised that she was probably shy, and having to make the best of being told to greet the new-comer. 'Can't stop. Rog needs me. Greg's day off. Ev gets mad if I skive off.' She was gone, flying down the steps and across the yard as if pursued by demons.

Liese walked into a small sitting-room. The leaded windows let in little light. Dingy walls and drab furniture did nothing to raise her spirits. The beige-covered settee had a broken spring protruding through its cover. The wicker armchair looked as if it had been bought from the clearance sale of an impoverished household. The worn carpet had holes. It would need covering with rugs, or she'd trip. Maybe she could remove it and put down rugs on the bare boards; maybe sandpaper and polish them, if she only knew how.

But she wouldn't be staying. Roger had said a month's trial, on either side. She would never be able to satisfy him. Bleakness overwhelmed her. Her feet ached. She dropped the cases and sat down in the battered chair. If only she had been the second victim in the car crash. She couldn't face the future.

She had to pull herself together. Maybe coffee would help. She hoped the kitchen was less shabby than the sitting-room. A picture or two on the walls would have brightened it, but there was nothing to mask the dreary distemper.

She kicked off her shoes. She could never work in them. The rest of her clothes were probably as unsuitable. The door had been open when they arrived. She padded over in stockinged feet and shut it, though that did little to add warmth. There was an electric fire, a card-table with an old chair tucked beneath it, and a small clock that had stopped at eleven. She glanced at her watch, it was almost four.

The tiny bedroom was uninviting, though the bed, when she sat on it, did offer comfort, and the busily patterned bedlinen was clean.

There was a sudden bump. Liese stared around her uneasily, wondering if the place harboured a ghost. I'm getting as crazy as Frankie, she thought. She and Allie . . . She smiled at the memory. The odd sound that followed the thump did little to reassure her.

It came from beyond the sitting-room door which, she presumed, opened into a passage, only to find, when she opened it, that it led directly into an unexpectedly large kitchen, where a small Rayburn was already lit to welcome her.

The touch on her leg made her jump, and she bit back a scream. Looking down, she found herself being regarded by amazing blue-green eyes that stared at her out of a chocolate-coloured face. She smiled, totally enchanted. The warmth of the room and her new companion went a long way to restoring her spirits.

'So who are you?' she asked the cat. He rubbed against her legs, purring. 'You can't be mine, but you would be company. I hope you'll come calling, often.'

She filled the electric kettle with water and plugged it in. The cat jumped on to the table and curled his tail neatly round his legs, staring at her, apparently fascinated. He reminded her of a Siamese, but must, she thought, be a cross. Did he belong to the last tenant of her apartment? Had he been left behind? Nobody could abandon such a lovely animal. He must be part of Roger's household.

He was certainly not a stray. His compact body was well fleshed. He was so elegant. He continued to stare as if wondering whether she would fall victim to his charms. The soft coat was shaded, cream blending to gold while ears and nose and paws and tail were the colour of honeyed fudge.

She lifted the cat and buried her face in his fur. He cuddled against her, the noisy purr dominating the room.

The armchair in front of the Rayburn looked far more comfortable than that in the sitting-room, though it needed a new cushion. At least the place was clean, the walls obviously very recently painted. The top of the breakfast bar gleamed. The red-topped stool was new, as were the gaily coloured curtains, which were blue with a pattern of tiny tropical fish. The calendar on the wall, depicting a chilly scene of snow and a frozen lake, insisted that it was February.

She turned it to March; daffodils massed beside a pool. Corny, she thought, remembering hours spent learning the Wordsworth poem at school.

Both she and the cat jumped when the phone rang.

She had not noticed it, tucked away on a shelf in a dark corner.

'You've arrived,' said Frankie's voice. 'Settled in yet?'

Liese sighed.

'I've only been here a few minutes. It's a long way from the bus stop down the lane lugging two heavy cases.'

'Didn't anyone meet you?'

'If they did, I didn't see them. I've met a girl called Sue who lives in a tiny annexe next door to me, and been told that Rog is feeding the dogs because it's Greg's day off, and Ev gets mad if she skives off.'

'She's doing work experience. I gather she's the bane of Roger's life. A triangular peg, all corners, in a round hole. And whatever you do, it's Roger and Gregory and Evan if you want to stay friends. I expect she'll call you Lee.'

'Heaven forbid. I already have a companion, though I don't suppose he's mine. A most wonderful cat; he's been purring to me and he talks. I've been hoping the last tenant deserted him.'

'That'll be one of Roger's specials ... they're Tonkinese. It's probably Kaos. He's the friendliest of them.'

'I've never heard of them.' Liese looked at the cat, who appeared to smile at her. He flicked his tail, before concentrating on washing his ears with a well-licked paw.

'They're a fairly new breed. Originally they came from a cross between a Siamese and a Burmese. If it's Kaos visiting, watch your best woollens; he eats holes in them. Roger bought himself a very expensive cardigan for best; he left it on the table before putting it away and it lasted about half an hour. I put in some very badly darned elbows for him.'

When her aunt rang off she felt more alone than ever. She made herself a mug of coffee and unwrapped a packet of chocolate biscuits that she found in a cupboard.

Unused to having cats around her, she left the opened

packet on the table. A moment later it was on the floor. Kaos used an expert paw to dislodge one for himself, which he ate, watching her warily in case she confiscated it. She laughed and put the temptation away.

'Eat many of those and you'll lose your figure,' she told him. He seemed to enjoy conversation. His answering mew might well have been an indignant denial.

The kitchen contained a refrigerator with a small deep freeze on top of it, an electric stove, a washing machine, and a microwave oven. The deep freeze, when she looked inside, was well stocked with dinners for one.

After she had stowed her clothes in the rickety chest of drawers and the wobbling wardrobe, with Kaos commenting on every item she handled, she grilled bacon and fried two eggs. The bread was unexpectedly good, and was, she thought, home-made.

The only books on the little shelf were romances. She was restless, moving from room to room, unable to settle. Television offered a choice between a football match, a talk on maladjusted children, or a comedian whose humour did not appeal to her. The clock, now adjusted, ticked busily. She had never known time pass so slowly.

She rolled a piece of paper into a ball, and amused herself by playing with the cat who chased it, shook it, tossed it in the air, and brought it to her lap to throw again for him.

It was nine o'clock before Roger knocked on her door. Kaos ran to greet him, keeping up a busy commentary that sounded as if he were describing everything that had happened since Liese arrived.

'So you've met my vagabond,' the kennel owner said, caressing the small body that was now on his shoulder, leaning forward confidingly to look into his eyes and continue the saga. He made the room seem minute.

'He scared me,' Liese admitted. 'I thought I had a ghost when I first heard him.'

'He loves visiting. He often calls.'

'I'd hoped he belonged here. That my predecessor had abandoned him. He's good company.'

'He'll commute. He visits Sue often, but Maggie hated cats. Dogs too, I think. He's been dying to get in here and explore. She always chased him off. But please don't feed him or he'll get fat. I hate tubby animals; they have such lovely shapes that it's a crime to spoil them. Watch him; he's a thief. And he eats wool.'

'So Frankie said. She rang to see if I'd arrived.'

'And had you?'

She stared at him, and then laughed.

'I must have done, mustn't I?'

'I meant to meet you, but I had an emergency. One of the boarders had a fit. They didn't warn me that he was epileptic and the idiots didn't send any medication with him. Luckily they're local and our vet knew the dog and I'm now provided. Then when Gregory started out for you, the van broke down. He's a maniac driver and I daren't lend him my car. I'm sorry.'

'It didn't matter,' Liese said, reassured by the fact that they had not meant to desert her. She was not sure that she would have appreciated Gregory's driving anyway. Edward's death had left her wary of drivers other than herself.

Roger had moved into the kitchen.

'This is warmer and more comfortable. I'm sorry about the furniture. Maggie had her own and Don and I had to make hurried arrangements for you. Sue painted the kitchen and her mother made the curtains. We hadn't time to do the rest. You have our throw-outs, but we'll get something better once you've settled in.'

He stretched himself, having appropriated the arm-chair, leaving Liese to perch on the stool. She longed to take scissors to the hair that flopped above startlingly arched eyebrows. Blue eyes appraised her, making her feel like a dog being assessed by a very meticulous judge.

'Who made the bread?' she asked, wondering how to keep up a conversation, and wanting to deflect that gaze.

'A splendid woman in the village who ekes out her pension with wonderful home baking. She also has a little café. One day you must sample one of her gourmet meals.'

'Coffee?' Liese asked, feeling some hospitality was necessary.

'Thought you'd never ask. I like it black, strong and two spoonfuls of sugar.' He looked across at her, and jumped out of his chair.

'You look all in. I was forgetting. Used to Maggie, not that I ever visited her. She was fit as a flea . . . why are fleas fit, I wonder? Do they never have illnesses? Come to think of it, a sick flea must be a very sorry sight.'

Liese stared at him, not realising that he too was shy and trying desperately to make conversation.

He had taken the kettle from her and was pouring boiling water into mugs.

'Milk and sugar?'

'Milk. No sugar.' Liese was rapidly becoming convinced she had agreed to work with a madman. Not very mad, but certainly borderline odd. She had an idiotic vision of a miserable flea unable to jump.

'So many questions,' Roger said musingly, wrapping his hands round the green mug. 'Does Kaos understand what we say? Do dogs mind having fleas? Is it just humans that are fussy? We take the attitude that only domestic animals have illnesses, yet those in the wild can have them too. Lions get distemper. The King of Beasts, out in the jungle, is often a mangy animal.'

He looked at her and laughed.

'I'm too much alone,' he said. 'Can't have a real conversation with Sue; she's no interest except in the latest pop star; Gregory's fine if you talk about motor bikes. He hankers after a Harley Davidson. He lives in a bedsitter and collects one girl after another and never seems to find one to suit for more than a couple of outings. Evan is desperately shy with new people; he'll take time to unwind.'

He foraged in the cupboard for the chocolate biscuits.

'He's not absent-minded; he's suffering from a brand new baby who thinks the nights are meant for crying. Don't worry if you don't get answers. He only speaks when absolutely necessary. But he's a miracle with the dogs. You might think he's not listening, but he does his job well.'

Life might be posing more problems than she had expected. Liese felt even more apprehensive.

'Sue's a typical teenager, and often it's a case of God help us all as she's capable of producing more chaos than Kaos, and that's saying something. Spike's a tease. Don't take much notice of him. His mother has Alzheimer's and he can have some very peculiar nights too.'

Liese stared at him. A more unlikely assortment of people would be hard to find.

'My much too rare visits to your aunt are my lifeline; we share the same interests, and go back some thirty years. I went abroad soon after you left her. After my wife left I tried emigrating to Australia, but I missed my old dog scene and came back four years after you married. You can come over to Frankie with me if you want.'

'What time do you start in the morning?' Liese asked, wondering if her duties began at the break of day.

'About seven when we're full, which we are just now. A lot of people seem to go on winter holidays.' He sighed. 'I should be so lucky. I always hope a fairy godmother will turn up and say, 'There, there, you shall go ski-ing.' Only so far no one ever has. I often wonder why I do this job. Other people's holidays are our busiest times. August, Easter, Christmas; bank holidays. Seven-day week and no time off for good conduct.'

'Why do you?' Liese asked.

'No good at anything else and I do enjoy dogs. I tried a variety of things—barman; merchant navy, only I'm seasick, and never got over it; I thought of the police, but I don't like being bossed around. Then I struck lucky: my uncle died, and had never married and left his estate to me.'

He flicked one of Liese's paper balls across the floor for Kaos, who leaped off his lap and began to pat it round the room.

'It isn't a mouse but it's a good substitute,' he said, grinning as he watched the cat's elegant contortions. 'Uncle didn't leave a fortune but when this farmhouse and dog business came on the market I was able to buy it and have a bit left over. I didn't change the name as it was already known.'

'When do you want me?'

'Nine o'clock will do. Books need sorting. It's nearly time for those infernal tax returns. Maggie couldn't do arithmetic, or much else. But beggars can't be choosers and there aren't many people who want this kind of job, so I was grateful when she applied.'

It wasn't the most tactful of sentences, Liese thought, sensitive to meanings that were perhaps not intended. Was Roger criticising her? Saying he had no choice but to take her, just as she had no choice but to accept?

'You'll work mostly in the office—at first, anyway. I'd like you to check the dogs out when their owners come. You'll give a better impression than Sue. I do it if I'm not busy, but I deliver dog food, and have to fetch it from the wholesalers; and that's some distance away, so I can be out for most of the day.'

He patted his knee and Kaos leaped up, circled four times, and settled. He began to purr, kneading Roger's legs, and then sucked at the thick jersey.

'Oh no, my lad. You'll go out in the cold if you do that,' he was told. The cat stared at him, and settled his nose on his paws.

Roger took another biscuit, fielding Kaos expertly as the cat leaped up eagerly, at once wide awake, attempting to snatch.

'He ought to be a pig, not a cat. Watch him. He's cunning.' He frowned, as if trying to recall the conversation.

'I need someone I can trust to make sure the owners get the right dogs. Maggie confused two Westies and Gregory was only just in time to prevent a young couple taking the wrong one. They thought he'd grown! He was a friendly little soul and greeted them as if they were his real owners, only too pleased to have some attention. The little fellows *were* very alike. It's not always convenient to have the lads interrupted to bring out the dog and make sure the bill is paid.'

Exhaustion suddenly washed over Liese. She longed for Roger to leave, so that she could go to bed. The dogs seemed to bark constantly.

'Are they always so noisy?' she asked.

'No. The main block is sound-proofed and you hear very little from them. You only hear them if the door's open. I've one in an outside kennel due to be rehomed, if it's possible. He's miserable and unsettled. I'll tell you about him tomorrow. He's only just arrived. Time I went. You're tired.'

The place felt singularly empty after Roger and Kaos had gone. Liese washed the mugs and put the biscuits in a tin that she found in the china cupboard. Later, lying in bed, she wondered whether she was going to cope in her new life. Her surroundings could be improved, and she realised how her ideas had been altered by living for so long with so many beautiful objects. This apartment was utterly spartan, except for the kitchen, but she was grateful for the effort that had been made to prepare the place for her in such a short time.

Her wages were minimal and the little money she had brought with her would be gone in a couple of weeks.

She would have to think twice before making any purchase. Luckily her clothes were top quality and would last a long time. If she wore trousers she wouldn't need tights, and cotton socks lasted for ever.

She had a place to live; she had a job. She was free for the first time for ten years, to be herself, to find out who she was. Edward would never hurt her again.

Shadow, exhausted by his barking, was lying in his run, whimpering softly to himself. No one yet had been able to get near him. Food had been pushed in through a minute gap in the door, which he attacked as it opened. Roger, anxious not to disturb the dog, went into the lane and round to his own front door, carrying Kaos. If the cat ran free, Shadow would bark.

Liese slept until two, when Sue's moped roared into the yard, setting the dog off again. The girl ran to her door, whistling, and slammed it shut. How in the world, Liese thought irritably as she got up and made herself a hot drink, could one person made so much noise? It was so long since she had lived with neighbours. Not since she was sixteen, when she had lived with her parents on a small, very secluded and expensive estate. The people on either side had been considerate.

The strains of one of the most recent pop songs swelled on the air. Did the wretched girl never sleep? It was nearly four o'clock before the sounds from next door ceased.

Eventually Liese fell asleep, to dream of policemen telling her she owed millions of pounds and would go to jail if she did not pay.

She woke exhausted, and made up carefully, using rouge to brighten her pale cheeks, and covered the darkness under her eyes. After a token breakfast of toast and coffee she took a deep breath and went out to face her new world.

Six

It was not a good beginning to her first day. March had turned sullen and rain sheeted out of a leaden sky. The two young men who passed Liese, both holding leashed dogs, looked thoroughly miserable, in spite of their heavy-duty wet weather gear. It was just after eight o'clock.

Beyond the kennels was parkland; huge trees shaded the fields where cattle grazed. Out of sight lorries thundered, changing gears for a slight incline. She found herself aching for the interrupted skyline, the high hills with their ever-changing horizons as the sun shone and shadowed clouds drifted over them.

This landscape reminded her too much of her own home. Her days there always began with solitude. Edward, if not away, was up and out early and she rose later, savouring the quiet, anxious to find peace in her garden, where growing plants enchanted her and the necessary chores diverted her.

Aloneness had only changed to loneliness in the past few years. It had crept up imperceptibly. She was not sure when it began. She had found conversation increasingly difficult with strangers, and wondered now how she would manage.

She needed to discover the routine. She was restless, and as there were already others working she walked into the office. It was easy enough to find as she only had to follow the arrows directing owners bringing in their dogs. She looked around her, feeling dismayed. She would never manage to be efficient. She could see herself, like Maggie, giving out the wrong dog, or charging the wrong price.

Shadow was quieter this morning, though the sight of Liese had started him barking again. He had flung himself at the mesh of the gate as she hurried past, praying that it was strong enough to hold him. What on earth were they doing with a dog like this? Were all dogs like this nowadays? She had had nothing to do with them for so long.

Roger was in the office and nodded to her, making notes as he spoke on the telephone. He sighed as he rang off.

'I can't imagine why it's necessary to ring so early in the morning to book in a dog for September. She's one of our more difficult clients. Maisie is a Welsh Terrier. She comes in with a bar of chocolate for every day plus her bed and her toys and carpet for the floor of the run.'

'I hope she's house-trained,' Liese said, contemplating a future filled with oddities. 'Do you give her the chocolate?'

'Human chocolate's bad for dogs. It contains theobromine which is poisonous to them in quantity. The lads enjoy it. Actually, she's quite a nice animal in spite of being thoroughly spoiled.'

'I don't really like human names for dogs,' Liese said. 'I prefer dog names, like Patch and Fly and Colonel. It's less confusing.'

Roger laughed.

'We've had in a dog called Justa, because he did everything just a minute before they expected him to. He was also Justa Nuisance. Training changed him. He's Justa good dog now. Another was Soona, because he did everything sooner than they expected.' He passed her the envelope on which he had been making notes.

'Put it in the book now, or we'll lose this. I always mean to have a proper notebook beside the phone and I never get round to putting it there. Nor did Maggie. We've had the odd disaster as a result: someone coming in who we hadn't written in the booking diary and no kennel available. It doesn't enhance one's reputation.'

Roger walked across to a table in the corner and plugged in the coffer percolator. He laughed, struck by a sudden memory and wanting to relax Liese, whose expression betrayed her tenseness.

'We had one dog named Haddock. He was a Labrador who was one of our regulars some years ago. He's dead now. There's nothing like standing in a field calling 'Haddock, Haddock,' and having new clients arrive with a dog. They probably decide you're mad!'

'Why Haddock?'

Roger laughed.

'They had a fish and chip shop. I suppose it was better than calling him Kipper.'

Liese began to relax, and Roger sighed with relief. Oversensitive to mood, he had been reminded of a nervous bitch coming into kennels, afraid of everything around her, and needing to be coaxed before she would settle.

The two dogs that had been taken out were back again, now as wet as their handlers. Shadow was once more determined to reach them and teach them a lesson they would not forget. A third man came out of the farthest barn, being towed by a large Great Dane who appeared to have only one idea, which was to bolt.

'That one needs a spot of discipline,' Roger said, turning his attention to the mail which lay unopened on the desk. 'Can you type?'

'I can learn,' Liese said. 'I won't have much to do in the evenings. Perhaps I can take the typewriter over to my rooms and practise? There must be books which help.'

'I'll ask in Smith's when I go into town this afternoon,' Roger said. 'I've a small portable in the house; you can borrow that. This one's electric and heavy.'

There was a sudden crescendo of barking.

'That dog . . .' Liese said, watching Shadow throw himself again and again at the mesh.

'I thought you might like one of your own. He's for you.'

Liese looked at Roger in horror. The man who had just come in through the door laughed.

'You must be Liese. You'll learn. Roger's apt to pull our legs till they drop off. He can see as well as I can that you could never cope with a dog like that.'

'What's made him like that?'

Roger answered.

'Came from a puppy farm. Went to a family. Nobody could control him and he did as he chose; he made the rules and they obeyed him. Nobody has ever tried to teach him to be a dog; I'm not sure that anybody can. So far none of us has been able to get anywhere near him.'

'Haven't wanted to. I'm Spike, by the way. Roger never remembers to introduce people. I need some sweetener for Sukie. She's doing her usual and refusing to eat.'

Roger went to the cupboard, brought out a tin containing a brown substance, and broke off a large piece.

'Liver cake. Dogs go mad for it as a rule. I'll swear Sukie does this every time she comes in because she knows that Spike or Evan will sit with her and hand-feed her, and offer her really wonderful treats to stop her fretting.'

'Do many of them fret?' Liese had not thought about the dogs' feelings before. Frankie never had many brood bitches and they were always house-kept. She rarely took boarders; only sometimes a pup she had bred herself might spend his holidays with her, but to them it was just a matter of coming back to the place where they had been born and meeting their mothers again.

'Very few. Those that have been here before seem to regard it as a treat to come back, and rush to greet us and then go to their old kennels, so we make sure they always have the same one.'

Spike left, and Roger brought out the appointments book for Liese.

'Name, address, telephone number. Breed, sex and age of dog as well as its name. If it's a bitch find out when its season is due. I've special quarters for them or we end with a kennel full of moaning dogs, all mad with desire. Date of arrival and date of departure, and do make sure when they leave their dogs that they know our hours are nine to five; there's nothing more annoying than having people turn up at daybreak having got off a night plane, or come late at night when we're all in bed.'

Liese looked at the book in horror. Lines had been drawn without a ruler, names scrawled so that they were barely readable, dates crossed out and altered. She felt a sudden lift in spirits. She could at least do better than that.

The office, sited in part of one of the stone barns, was furnished with a revolving chair, an armchair, a couple of padded benches, a large table and a metal filing-cabinet. The walls were covered with photographs of dogs. The fax machine beside the telephone worried Liese: she had never used one. She was relieved to see that there was no computer. Roger kept that in his own home.

A side-table contained an electric kettle, the percolator, a jar of instant coffee, a box of tea bags, six named mugs, a bottle of milk and a packet of sugar. No time for frills, Liese decided, but knew that she would have to bring a jug and a bowl; the untidiness irritated her.

There was a small sink. The tea towel was revolting, and so was the towel. She threw the cloth that had obviously been used to wash the cups into the waste bin. She went across to her own rooms and brought back clean replacements.

As she sat at the desk, something poked at her leg. Startled, she looked down, to see a large German Shepherd curled into a tight ball, regarding her with anxious eyes.

'That's my fellow, Rake. He was going to be a police

dog, but he thinks he's a teddy bear, not a dog. He enjoys being cuddled. He likes tea when we have our coffee. His bowl is on the shelf above the electric fire. If you're cold put it on. The fire, not the shelf.'

Roger, who seemed to lead a somewhat Jack-in-the-Box existence, popping in and out, vanished through the door, leaving Liese feeling bemused. There were letters piled on the desk. Did they need an answer? Had anyone read them? Was that part of her job or were they private? The first four were bills—for feed, for cat litter, for the telephone and fax machine.

There seemed to be no order, and she sorted them into neat heaps, according to date, and whether they were due to be paid or payments. Several had cheques attached. She clipped these together and listed them.

There seemed to be no method at all in the way Roger dealt with his correspondence. A post-book to log in everything sent out or received would be a very good idea. She began to make a list of her own requirements. If Roger jibbed, she would buy them herself. Were notebooks expensive? She didn't even know.

There was a blank notepad beside the typewriter. She listed the staff names: Sue. Spike. Gregory. Evan. Had Roger mentioned anyone else? Presumably Don did not come in for coffee, but went to work every day. She matched the names with the mugs. She needed to replace Maggie's with her own. That too went in the bin. She hated the thick china. Those in her rooms were daintier.

Shadow's barking worried her. She had never met a dog like him before. It was impossible to ignore and it unnerved her. She began to go through the appointments book, and sort out which dogs were actually in kennels now, and when they were due to go out, and which could be coming in during the next week.

Maggie's writing was atrocious and she was concentrating so hard that, when the door opened, she jumped.

'I'm Don, Roger's partner,' the visitor said. He was one of the biggest men she had ever seen. His uniform made him bulky, yet his size did not prevent him looking extremely smart. Though obviously much younger than Roger, his dark hair was greying at the sides. The slate-grey eyes that regarded her had a cold and uncompromising stare. His full mouth was tight-lipped.

She smiled at him uncertainly, wondering whether he expected her to shake hands. He remained in the door-way, frowning. Shadow's barking caused him to raise his voice.

'I'm on nights at present, so I thought I'd look in and introduce myself as our meetings are likely to be unpredictable.' He towered above her, making her feel small, then Rake emerged from under the desk, waving his tail, and greeted him as an old friend.

'Shame he has no courage.' The police dog handler pulled the dog's ears very gently and was rewarded by a licked hand. 'He does everything else so well, but introduce him to a loud noise, or a man shouting, and he's off.'

'He's a lovely dog.' Liese felt more inadequate than before. The feeling of unreality returned. She was an alien in this strange place.

There was an angry shout from Roger, just outside the window, accompanied by a renewed noise as Shadow hurled himself against the mesh of his kennel run, telling everyone how much he hated his surrounding.

'Sue! Will you stop galloping around like a demented goblin! You're upsetting all the dogs. How many times have I told you . . .' The voice died away as he moved across the yard. Sue, wearing a long flowing skirt and an off-the-shoulder jersey, with no outer protection in spite of the rain, followed him, a sulky expression on her face.

'That girl has no idea.' Don was at a loss. Never at ease with women, and even less so since his wife had died, he found Liese as unnerving as she found him. Abruptly, he nodded to her and went outside, meeting Roger. Neither man noticed that the office door was ajar. Shadow had exhausted himself and was lying quiet.

'I told you you're crazy,' Don said, irritation in his voice. 'She reminds me of a bird that's always lived in a gilded cage. She's wearing a fortune in clothes. She'll never fit in here, any more than that damned dog you've taken in, or Sue. That girl's going to get bitten, or injured by a dog that pulls her over.'

Liese wanted to close the door and shut out the voices, but knew if she did so the men would realise she had heard them. Misery swept over her. She'd pack up and go away. Don, never tactful, gave vent to his exasperation.

'When are you going to let your head rule your heart? You might as well suggest she takes on that damned dog you've saddled us with and works him as well as running the office. She'll be worse than Maggie . . . and that would be difficult.'

He walked off to his own quarters and Roger went to the other barn which, Liese now knew, also contained a number of kennels. Sliding doors led to outside runs which were too wet to use today. Liese, stroking Rake, who had put his head on her knee, felt near to tears. She made herself a mug of black coffee and drank it, scalding hot.

She inserted a piece of paper into the typewriter. How did the wretched thing work? There was an instruction book in the desk drawer, and she sat down to absorb it. Gradually, as she read, anger took over from misery. She had nowhere else to go and couldn't face job-hunting. Who would take her, anyway? Frankie had probably engineered this. Her mood changed abruptly, as it had done so often in the last few days. She felt as if she had been on a helter-skelter, her mind out of control.

She could already see ways of improving the office procedure. She would make both men change their opinions of her.

By afternoon she was alone. The dogs, all exercised, were resting in their kennels and the staff had two hours in which to relax. Sue, more suitably dressed, went off on her moped. Spike took Roger's own dogs for a long tramp on the moors. Evan and Gregory both vanished, the first in a battered car, the second on a powerful and very expensive motor bike borrowed from his brother, his unreliable car being in for repair again. Roger was delivering dog food, which he stocked in quantity and sold to his own customers at slightly lower than shop price.

The sky had cleared and a warm sun brightened the day. Liese looked out of the window at the dog. He was lying, his nose on his paws, and seemed so forlorn that she felt sorry for him. He was as unhappy as she, and probably finding his surroundings just as strange, if he had been house-kept by his former owners.

She could see why they did not want him. Perhaps he would not bark at her if she went across to him. In any case, there was nobody about to hear. She opened the tin of liver cake and took out a large piece.

She walked across the yard to Shadow's run. When he exploded, she threw a piece to the ground in front of him. She stood quite still, remembering Frankie with a horse bought long ago from a man who had treated it abominably.

'No one here will hurt you,' she said softly. 'Be a good lad. You could be a splendid dog, do you know that?'

The soft voice astonished him. He listened, wanting to hear it again. This stranger in front of him reminded him of his small owner. There was a scent on the piece of food she had thrown him that was very familiar, for Liese used the same brand of soap as that used by his former owners.

He watched her, wary, not yet prepared to be friendly. He sniffed at the cube on the ground, and his ears pricked. It smelled wonderful, quite apart from the lingering traces of soap. Nobody had offered it to him before. He ate it and waited for more, snapping up each piece as it came.

Nobody yet had spoken to him, as he barked so loudly when the men approached, and he barked also at Sue, sensing her fear. No one had had time to do more than try to feed him. The run needed cleaning. Maybe they could entice him out of it into a cage, and give him a decent environment. Or sedate him. He needed grooming.

She felt a sudden kinship with the animal. They were both in a strange environment; they were both unhappy; they both needed to come to terms with their new situations. Shadow was now sitting quietly, listening to her, his eyes puzzled. She began to recite poetry, nursery rhymes, anything that came into her head, aware that he was paying attention.

She chose the longest poems she could remember. Time ceased to matter. The dog needed her and she needed him. Half an hour passed. He was now far more relaxed.

> 'Stands the church clock at ten to three,
> And is there honey still for tea?'

The sound of a passing car in the lane outside triggered his barking again. All rapport was lost. Liese went back to the office, not wishing to be seen with the dog. She was amazed to discover it was after four. Spike returned, followed by Evan.

She had not seen Gregory arrive and was surprised when he passed her with a young and very attractive Samoyed on his lead. She did not intend to mention her session with Shadow. Roger might be angry with her, and she could not afford his displeasure.

Why hadn't she listened to Frankie, or to her headmistress, who had both wanted her to go on to college? She had been accepted in the biology department at York University. She might have found herself a decent job if she had had any qualifications.

The ringing phone rescued her from her increasingly gloomy thoughts.

When she disconnected she looked with satisfaction at the booking, for three weeks ahead. Name. Address. Telephone number. A twelve-month-old Golden Retriever bitch named Honey. No problems. She was spayed. They had four vacancies on that date so she hadn't double-booked. At least she had justified her presence during the afternoon.

The appointments book was almost full. She found an unused duplicate in one of the desk drawers, and copied out the details of the dogs in the kennels in a neat print, that anyone could read. Each dog had its owner's surname added to its own name, together with any exceptional details. No dog was due to go out today.

Four were going at the end of the week. Two appeared to be semi-permanent residents, returning every three months for four weeks. One was in for a year while his owner worked in Brussels.

Cassie Blake was on a special diet. Major Davies had to have drops in his ears. Bruno Paul was on medication for a heart condition. Twelve years old. The other two from the same home were youngsters.

Rake was out with his master. He had jumped into the van with delight, loving his rides. Everyone else was busy.

She began listing the day's post on sheets of A4 that she found in a drawer. She washed up the mugs again. None of them looked clean, the earthenware was stained. She emptied the coffee percolator, washed it out and refilled it. The brew had tasted horrible. The tin containing home-made cakes was old and battered and rusty. She would replace that one day. She cleaned the sink.

She dusted the shelves and replaced all the items on them. Some seemed very odd. A large torch: that was reasonable. A book on astrology for the current year. Roger's? Or Maggie's?

She didn't believe in it but opened it at her own birthdate out of curiosity. She had been born on the third of March: Pisces. She appeared to be a curious mixture of characteristics—capable, practical and reliable, yet she also suffered from a lack of confidence in herself, and a conviction that she would not live up to other people's expectations.

That at least was true, she thought with a wry smile. People might find her standoffish, because she was very shy and reserved and selfconscious. In time she would relax and become a very loyal friend.

She looked at the forecast for the week ahead, and read that difficulties she had were raising worries, but that these would pass; the door had opened to new and exciting opportunities.

If only, she thought, as she turned to the other contents of the shelf. Three out-of-date women's magazines, which certainly had to be Maggie's. All three were top-quality glossies, which did not seem like Sue. There were also a number of catalogues of dog equipment, of herbal veterinary remedies, of dog foods, which she tidied and put together under a large flat stone on which was painted a green woodpecker. It made a good paperweight.

There was a book labelled 'Rescue Organisations' which contained only five addresses. There must be more than that. Someone seemed to be great at starting things and never finishing them. That, too, she could alter.

The office looked much cleaner and far tidier than it had that morning, but there was nothing left to do. Could she go home now, or had she to stay? There was no one around to ask.

It was a relief to have a small cat jump in through the

window and push his solid little body against her leg. Kaos was bored and looking for adventure. He tapped at the typewriter keys, one eye on Liese to see if she would stop him.

She watched with amusement. He explored the waste-paper basket, hooking out pieces of paper with his claws. Liese rolled one of them into a ball and tossed it. He spent an ecstatic few minutes chasing it, throwing it in the air and catching it, only to send it spinning across the floor again.

Exhausted, he jumped into the armchair, curled himself into a tight ball and within seconds was fast asleep. How could cats sleep and purr? she wondered. It was so long since she had lived with a cat. Frankie always had several, but they seemed to spend all their time out of doors.

She had not yet explored the filing-cabinet, which presumably was also office equipment and did not contain private papers. It was almost empty, but in the top drawer she found a few photocopied sheets labelled 'Mix n' Match', with a picture of a cat that might have been Kaos on the front with another, darker, behind it.

She began to read. The Tonkinese. A cat that went back to the dawn of time, and then was rediscovered. She was intrigued to find that it had in fact been known in the fourteenth century, as manuscripts pictured a breed that could be nothing else.

Breeding looked impossible as two Tonkinese did not produce the right type of kitten. If a Burmese was mated to a Siamese then true Tonkinese kittens resulted. These when mated produced all three types. The genetics looked complicated, and she did not really understand them.

But some of these kittens were called variant types, and if a Burmese variant mated with a Siamese variant, then the kittens were again all Tonkinese. She would have to ask Roger. She wondered where he kept his queens, and also how they reacted to the dogs. Kaos seemed to have no fear whatever, and was apt to startle some of the boarders into barking as he approached them.

The day had been brightened by encounters between dogs being walked and the little cat, who had made no effort until now to come in. It was some days before she discovered he had a rigid timetable, visiting his particular friends and appearing so predictably that the men claimed they could tell the time by him.

'He's changed his routine. He hated Maggie,' Spike commented, coming in briefly for a cup of coffee. Kaos was on Liese's knee, being singularly unhelpful as he tried to catch her pen. 'He only came in here when she was out.'

Liese now realised that the office routine would not keep her busy. She would have to find more to occupy her. Perhaps she could wash up the dog bowls, as the kitchen for the kennels also had a phone. That chore must take hours, as all were fed twice a day and there were also water bowls to clean and refill.

She was thankful when the day ended and she was free to return to her quiet rooms and make herself a meal. Although she had not been busy, she felt exhausted. She concocted a prawn omelette, which she ate with salad. A local farmer, Gregory said, came round each week with organically grown vegetables, and they were excellent.

Whoever had stocked her larder had thoughtfully provided an enormous bowl of fruit.

Kaos loved oranges; they had immense possibilities if knocked on to the floor. He called in briefly, amused himself for an hour and then asked to be let out. She sat watching television, too lazy to finish her chores, but when the programme ended and a games show began, she decided it was time to tidy up.

She had just finished washing the dishes when the doorbell rang. She was surprised, when she opened it, to see Spike standing there, holding his crash helmet.

'I thought you'd gone home.'

'I had. But . . .' he hesitated. 'You may think it a bit of a cheek, only I can't think of anyone else.'

'You'd better come in,' Liese said, puzzled.

He had to duck his head as he came through the doorway. She was suddenly glad of his company: she had been feeling sorry for herself.

Spike was diffident, hoping he was not intruding. Maggie would have sent him away, furious at having her evening interrupted. He would not have gone to Maggie anyway.

'Coffee?' Liese asked, wondering why he was there. To complain? Had she done something wrong that day?

'If you've time . . .' Spike was clutching the helmet as if it was part of him.

'Do put that down,' she said, as she poured water into the two mugs.

'Black, one sugar.' Spike lowered himself into the armchair, still holding on to his helmet, as if afraid it might vanish if he let go of it. His chestnut hair was flattened. He was the youngest of the men, his face still boyish, although he looked tired. Brown eyes watched her, as if trying to sum her up.

'I found this,' he said. 'Look.'

Curled up on the padding of the helmet was the smallest kitten Liese had ever seen. It stared at her from wide blue eyes. The tiny body was soaked. Pity and anger mixed as she lifted it. It mewed feebly and nuzzled her hand, trying desperately to suck at her finger.

'I came round a corner just in time to see some lads throwing something into the ditch,' he said. 'They raced off on bikes so I reckoned they were up to no good. I hadn't a hope of catching them and anyway I didn't know what they were doing. Could have been a coke can. I went to see what they'd chucked there.'

He watched Liese who was afraid of hurting the tiny animal. There was nothing of it but skin and fragile bones, the sodden fur clinging to its frame revealing how desperately thin it was.

'I didn't expect this. I couldn't leave it there, but I live with my mum, and she couldn't cope. It's going to need feeds every three hours day and night at first. Roger won't mind you having it in the office . . . only . . . I don't know what to do with it if you won't take it on.'

'Little beasts,' Liese said, angered as always by cruelty. She caressed the wet little animal. A minute rough tongue licked her hand.

'Just as well I couldn't catch them. I hate kids like that.' Spike suddenly looked dangerous. 'They deserve beating, but nobody ever does anything about the little brutes these days.'

Liese had taken a large pad of paper towelling and was rubbing the kitten dry. Spike opened the Rayburn and added more fuel.

'Poor mite. How old do you think it is?' Liese, working on it, wondered if it would survive. He was so tiny, and might have been anywhere before they threw him away. Maybe born in a ditch.

'Four weeks, perhaps, or a badly fed six weeks. He doesn't seem to lap yet. Roger suggested I bring him to you. He said you fell in love with Kaos.'

'I did. He's wonderful. But what will he do with an intruder on his patch?'

'There's cats all over; not just Roger's pure-breds. He's a soft touch for any animal and this isn't the first we've had here by a long chalk. There must be about eight around the place; they sleep in one of the little sheds at the back of the biggest barn. Roger has five other dogs in kennels in another of the outhouses . . . all strays brought in and never claimed. He can't bear to have a healthy animal put to sleep and none of these would make a good pet.'

'Wouldn't your mother like it?'

'Mum's got Alzheimer's. She doesn't know the time of day. Can't get used to it; she had a good job, was bright and funny and dressed well . . . and now . . . I have to make sure she does dress, or she'll be out in her night things or maybe in nothing at all.'

Liese was shocked.

'How do you manage? You surely don't look after her alone? What about daytime?'

Spike shrugged.

'No choice. Roger's good if I do have to take time off. No room in the council places; she's not ill, so she can't go into hospital, and we can't afford a private home. The vicar's made a rota of ladies who'll come in during the day. The church has a volunteer organisation of its own. It's wonderful. Helps all kinds of people caught like me.'

He sighed.

'I'd left home. Had my own flat and a girlfriend. She couldn't take it. She's married now to someone else. My sister's married now, too, with three small children. She does what she can. Washing and such and cooks cakes and pies for us. She's with Mum tonight. Her husband's baby-sitting. I was going to the cinema; it's my night off. Only I found this . . . and I couldn't leave him.'

He pushed his hands through his mane of hair.

'Roger felt you'd like some company . . . even if it is only a cat. He's a thoughtful bloke, in spite of his weird sense of humour. He'll probably keep Shadow. Drives Don crazy, he's much more down to earth.'

'Have you eaten yet?' Liese asked, suddenly realising that it was well past Spike's clocking-off time and that he had not yet been home.

He shook his head.

'I could murder a sandwich.'

Liese cut thick slices of bread, offering butter and cheese to go with it. Whoever had stocked her pantry had done so lavishly. Or had Maggie left the food?

The kitten needed milk. It lay on her lap almost motionless as she prepared the sandwiches, sitting at the table. It was so small that it fitted into the palm of Spike's hand. She looked down, worried, afraid it had stopped breathing, but the small chest was still moving in and out. An odd little morsel, she thought. The disproportionately large bat ears were set almost sideways, and the impish black and white face had an elfin look about it.

She jumped as the door-bell rang again, and the door was pushed open. No one seemed to stand on ceremony here.

'Can you cope with it?' Roger asked, as he ducked his head to come into the room. 'I've brought kitten milk and a feeding bottle; I doubt it's lapping yet. I've filled the first one. Ever done this before?'

He filled the room, reminding her of Kaos who was equally sure he was welcome.

Liese shook her head and sat, somewhat bemused, watching the big man lift the tiny animal gently, settle it against his thigh, and dip the doll-sized bottle teat into its mouth. At first it did not seem to understand and then began to suck vigorously.

'He'll do,' Roger said. 'Not much wrong with an animal that feeds so strongly. But if you take it on, it's three-hourly feeds for at least a week; which will mean midnight, three and six. I've brought you an alarm clock. You're going to be tired.'

'I can help out,' Spike said. 'Do the evening six o'clock feed. You can sleep for a spell.'

'I'll do the nine o'clock.' Roger was massaging the tiny body and cleaning it gently with a tissue.

'I don't sleep very well anyway,' Liese said. 'I'll be glad to have an occupation. The nights seem very long. I'd love to keep him.'

'He's all yours.' Roger continued to massage the small body with expert hands. 'You need to do this after every feed. His mother licks him to make him eliminate and he won't do so without it. He's younger than I thought; he's not learnt to do this for himself yet. He can't be a day over three weeks old. I was hoping Rani would accept him but she spat when she saw him, and I can't risk putting him in with her. She's a bit unpredictable when she has kittens of her own.'

He finished cleaning the damp fur and put the tissues in the Rayburn. Spike had put the helmet on the floor and the kitten, released, did his best to climb back into it.

'I think I'll call him Helmet,' Liese said, laughing at his determination. 'He'd like to keep it.'

'Afraid I need it,' Spike said. 'Thanks for the grub. I'd best be off or my sister'll be convinced I've a had a spill. Don't much fancy my helmet, though. It's damp inside. But got no choice, have I?'

'Give it to me.' Liese brought out her hairdrier. 'It'll need a spot of cleaning, but at least it's dry,' she said, handing it over. The kitten, deprived of its goal, had clambered up Roger's trouser leg and curled on to his lap.

'He's strong and has plenty of spunk. I think he'll do,' Roger said, holding the tiny body against his chest. 'It might be an idea to tuck him inside your jumper now and keep him in your bed this evening. He needs warmth and comfort from another body; he's far too young to be thrust out into the big world.'

'I'll bring a shoebox tomorrow,' Spike said, as he went out into the darkness. 'Make him a bed in that.'

Liese glanced at the noisily ticking alarm clock. It was

just after ten, so she would need to start her routine very soon.

'There's enough for four bottles there,' Roger said, indicating the little plastic box he had brought with him. 'I'll make up another set for tomorrow. Warm them in hot water. They're best kept in the fridge.' He glanced at her and seemed about to add something more, but then changed his mind.

Sue's moped buzzed into the yard. She ran into her house, slamming the door, and at once the air was rent with the sound of loud jazz. Roger walked over to the wall and thundered on it with his fist.

'Don't let her get away with it,' he said. 'That one has a lot to learn, and she doesn't like learning. She doesn't like work either, which is tiresome, as it means the lads are always doing her jobs and sometimes covering for her.'

When he had gone Liese showered and put the alarm clock beside her bed. She wondered if the kitten would settle and took him with her into the bedroom. He curled into the hollow beneath her chin, his small body warm now, a rusty, unpractised purr shaking it.

She seemed to have been asleep for only moments before the alarm bell shrilled, waking both her and her new protegé.

Half-asleep, sitting in the big armchair, Helmet sucking lustily, she wondered how life could change so suddenly and completely. The tiny black and white scrap of life was her only possession.

He was more than company: he was a promise. Looking around her she felt a small stir of hope for the first time since Edward had died.

'Perhaps I'll find out who I really am,' she said to the kitten, but he only curled closer against her and purred. Three-hourly intervals, she realised, did not mean three hours' sleep, as it took nearly half an hour to feed and clean him.

When she slept again she dreamed of Edward, standing above her and laughing at her, enjoying her discomfort. After the six o'clock feed she showered and dressed, thankful to begin a new day.

Seven

There was frost in the air and frost on the ground as Liese went outside. It was almost seven o'clock. She negotiated the steps carefully and then jumped as Shadow barked and then gave vent to the most extraordinary sounds she had ever heard a dog make.

She turned the corner of the farmhouse into the kennel block yard and found a scene that appeared to her straight from Hell. She did not recognise the figure in front of her as human; he seemed a visitor from another planet, dressed like an astronaut, padded beyond recognition. He held a long pole with a noose at the end and there, pinned by his throat, was the big German Shepherd, twisting and turning like an eel on a line, trying to attack his tormentor.

Panic had overtaken the dog. He was held prisoner, trapped by a monstrous figure that bore no relation to anything he had ever seen before. He had to escape. He had to defend himself. He was choking, unable to fight free of the remorseless grip that held him. Don had no intention of letting go.

Liese, feeling sick, watched the battle, knowing that the dog could not win, and sure he was terrified beyond sanity. Tears pricked her eyelids and she longed to run out and intervene. Was this a preliminary to a last visit from the vet or even to a shot from a gun?

Roger, in overalls, armed with bucket and scoop, walked through the open door of Shadow's kennel area and Liese realised that this was the only way they could possibly deal with the dog and get his run clean. They couldn't leave him in total squalor, and no one had yet dared go near him without the protection of the mesh. His food was put inside swiftly when he was at the back of the run. He always raced to the gate.

There were four empty dishes, as he chased them around the ground when he was eating, and they were out of reach by the time the next meal was brought.

His water bowl was fastened to the door on a bracket and could be filled from outside, but that too needed cleaning. Roger replaced it. Don needed all his strength to hold the dog and prevent him escaping. Shadow was terrified by the restraint and also by the appearance of the man who held him; although he smelled human, he did not look it.

The security lights that were turned full on lent a surreal appearance to the scene. Roger's own dogs were barking now, triggered by the desperation in Shadow's tone. Liese stood helpless, wondering what would happen to the dog in the days to come. He did not look as if he would either settle or behave himself in a way that would enable them to help him.

Sue had heard the din. She arrived at speed, in slippers, wearing nothing but a brief pair of knickers and a tee shirt. She looked as if she were about to run at the two men and yell at them. Liese grabbed her by the arm.

'No. They have to do it. You can't interfere. You might cause a disaster. Come in with me and let's have some breakfast. We're not needed.'

To her surprise, Sue followed her meekly.

'I'd better dress.'

'Then come back. A real fry-up? Good old English breakfast, full of all the wrong things to eat. I'm amazingly hungry.'

It was a lie, but Sue needed distraction, as did she.

Amazing was the word, she thought as she grilled bacon and dipped bread in beaten egg, frying it with tomatoes. The smell triggered an appetite she thought had vanished for ever. Frankie loved eggy bread. Liese hadn't eaten it for ten years. She had forgotten the old name for it, a memory from her aunt's own childhood. One of her grandmother's economies.

'Made one egg serve us all,' she explained. Eggs had been rationed in wartime when Frankie was small.

Sue appeared wearing her long skirt, with a large baggy jersey on top that made her thin figure look bulky.

'That's surely not very practical for working with the dogs?' Liese said, wondering too why her companion chose to dye her hair that brilliant and unbecoming orange. She wore three gold rings in each ear.

'Rog won't let me walk dogs dressed like this. I hate walking.' Unexpectedly she slipped off the sandals that she wore on bare feet. 'Look.'

Her soles were a mass of blisters, some of them burst and one at least infected.

'I'm not very surprised if you try to walk in those,' Liese said, putting a heaped plate in front of the girl. 'Does Roger know?'

'No. And don't tell him. My own fault but I can't afford any decent shoes.'

'You'd better bathe those feet, and cover them, and find jobs to do that don't involve walking. You'll have to tell him.' Liese frowned. Couldn't afford shoes? 'You do get paid on work experience?'

'Yeah. But my Mum and Dad need the money.'

Liese was rapidly revising her opinion of the eighteen-year-old.

'There are nine of us, see,' Sue said. 'I've got eight brothers. Mum and Dad weren't very clever . . . another baby kept coming along. Put me off them for life, I reckon. Babies, I mean. You won't catch me getting caught. Put me off men, too. Nine in the house . . . you don't have any romantic notions left.'

She was eating as if she were half-starved.

'Tone's the eldest. He's two years older than me; he works in a garage. That's how I got my bike. He's good at putting bits together from old ones to make something that works.'

'How old are the others?'

Liese, as an only child, had often wished she were part of a big family.

'I'm next. Mark's seventeen; he's a packer at Tesco's. Johnno comes after him; he's sixteen. He's the clever one. Wants to be a doctor, so we have a Johnno fund; we all put a bit in so when he gets to college he won't have to borrow. My dad hates borrowing. Won't even have a credit card. Then there's Sam and Dan, and Merv and Matt and little Ry. Dad and the lads chose his name after their favourite footballer. He's only two.'

Nine children. Liese could not even imagine how they lived.

'Where do you go when you go out at night?' she asked. She had been imagining pub crawls and wild raves, and a boyfriend in the background.

'Home. Mum's not that strong since Ry was born and none of the boys ever lifts a finger, nor does Dad. Merv isn't strong either; he's only eight and often ill, and Mum needs a break. Most nights there's work to do—ironing; preparing food for next day; baking. She's a great one for baking, my Mum. Lovely cakes she makes. The boys eat like vultures.'

She stopped talking and mopped her bread in the runny egg left on the plate. She ate it with relish.

'Tuesdays we go to bingo. Mum's night out. If we win anything it goes into the Johnno fund. His Head reckons he'll make a great doctor.'

Helmet had been curled on Liese's bed. He woke and, with a small mew, climbed down the hanging cover to the floor and put his tiny bat-eared face round the door, which was ajar.

'Hey. Who's that? It's not one of Rog's.' Sue was entranced. She dived across the floor and scooped him up, holding him against her face. The rustiness in his purr had vanished. She laughed. 'He sounds like a tiny engine. I like cats much better than dogs.'

'Spike found him. Some boys chucked him in the ditch. Luckily Spike saw them and went to see what was there.'

'He's all bones. Are you keeping him?'

'Yes,' Liese said. She was already attached to him. He was totally adorable. She took the tiny animal and held him in her cupped hands. He stared at her through wide blue eyes. He had been fed at six, and his next meal was not due until nine. The noise in the kennel block yard had died away.

'You're not a bit like Mag,' Sue said, as Liese put the kitten on the floor and teased him with a piece of ribbon. He tapped at it and caught it, tugging at it happily.

Liese was not sure whether that was an insult or a compliment. In any case, she could not think of an answer.

'He's a lot of ground to make up. He's more than half-starved, but today he's lively enough.' Liese rolled the ribbon and tucked it in her pocket as Helmet had lost interest. She cut bread and put two slices in the toaster. 'What was Maggie like?'

'She treated me like I was ten. Always criticising. Nothing I ever did was right. Made me feel useless, stupid, no good. I hated her.'

'That was what my husband did to me.' Liese felt a jolt of misery at the memory. 'I'd never do it to anyone else.' She looked back to herself at Sue's age. 'I married when I was nineteen.'

'Daft. Lots of girls I know have. They think it's the white knight in shining armour, or the prince himself come to save and adore them, and find it's just the same as ever: washing, cooking, cleaning, shouting.'

She picked up the dirty plates and carried them over

to the sink, raising her voice to talk above the sound of running water.

'Off with the lads and coming home drunk, off to football every Saturday or hogging TV, to watch the match. Would you believe some of them video it and watch it again, night after night?'

Liese picked up a tea towel and began to dry the dishes. There seemed little need to talk when Sue was around.

'All most men want is another mum to look after them. Stay little boys all their lives. Want to be waited on hand and foot; want the moon and want it now. Who said patience is a virtue, have it if you can, sometimes in a woman, never in a man? Reckon they lived with men. If you'd lived with nine of them you'd not have been in such a hurry to marry. Slave to the lot of them, my Mum is.'

Liese had never heard the rhyme, but it described Edward. We go out, now; we go away, now; I want my food, now. If there was a queue in a shop, he'd walk out. She wanted, suddenly and passionately, to forget him.

'What do you want to do with your life?' she asked.

'Thought I'd like to be a model, but not with a face like mine. I'm skinny enough. Then maybe act . . . only I'm no good at learning things. I don't want to work with dogs, that's for sure. Wouldn't mind a cattery but Rog doesn't board cats.'

She put her sandals on again, wincing.

'You need to do something about those feet,' Liese said. 'They'll only get worse.'

'I'll see the district nurse tonight when I go home. She lives next door. Mel. She's great.'

Melinda? Melanie? Liese wondered. Sue was still chattering, and Liese suddenly realised that she probably had little conversation at work. None of the men seemed very talkative, except for Spike, and even he was not likely to listen for long.

'Didn't want to fuss. I hate people who fuss. You should

see my brothers if they have a sniffle; think it's the end of the world and they're dying of double pneumonia.'

'What time do you start work?' Liese asked.

'Eight.' Sue stood up, making a face as she put weight on her feet. 'Time to be going. You're lucky. You don't need to start until nine. People don't usually ring before then. If no one's around there's an answering service. Cheaper than an answerphone, Rog says, and it can't go wrong.' She grinned suddenly. 'Mag wouldn't have had me darken her door when she lived here . . . she always behaved as if I had fleas. Well, she behaved as if we all had fleas. Too posh for us really, Mag was.'

'Why did she work here, then?'

'Jobs don't come easy. You *have* been out of the real world, haven't you? Was any of it good, the way you lived? You don't sound as if you had much fun really. I always thought if you were rich, then there'd be no more problems.'

Liese looked out of the window at the beginning of a brighter day.

'At your age I thought I'd found my dream man. Instead I had a self-seeking crook with so much charm that every-one thought he was Mr Wonderful. They didn't see him when we were alone. I had all the money in the world and a lovely home by most people's standards . . . and life was completely empty. No one cared about me, or really wanted me.'

Sue looked at her, and then startled Liese by hugging her. The fierce grip of the thin arms was remarkably com-forting.

'Reckon you need that,' Sue said. 'It does my Mum a power of good when I do it to her. It's just to say thanks for the grub. I have toast, or muesli.' She laughed. 'And for not being like Mag. I couldn't have stood another one like that. And thanks for not telling me how I ought to dress, or do my hair, or live.'

At the door the younger woman turned and looked back.

'I'll keep the noise down at night. I used to do it because it annoyed Mag. I don't want to disturb Helmet, do I? And why Helmet?'

'Spike brought him home in his crash-helmet and he thought it ought to be his bed,' Liese said.

Sue laughed and was gone. The room seemed very empty after she had closed the door.

Liese tucked the kitten into the crook of her arm and walked across to the office. A row of filled bottles stood on the table, together with a small box lined with part of an old jersey. Rake, creeping out from under the desk, greeted her like an old friend and then sniffed the kitten. Helmet fluffed his fur and spat.

Roger, coming in through the door, grinned at her.

'Astonishing how that reaction comes when they're so young,' he said. 'He'll soon get used to Rake. He thinks cats are dogs, and most of the cats here are sure they're dogs too. Kaos is a retriever. Throw him anything and he'll bring it back. Bad night?'

'Not as bad as I expected,' Liese said. 'I went back to sleep fairly fast after feeding him. I'm enjoying his company.'

Roger poured two mugs of coffee from the percolator, which must have been started as soon as the men came in. He passed one to her. It was considerably better since the percolator had been washed and she wondered if anyone had noticed. He dropped into the armchair and stretched out his legs, occupying most of the floor space.

'Thanks for deflecting Sue this morning. She might have caused a real problem if she'd come forward. That's something I hate. We very rarely have to do it, but you can't leave a dog in a filthy kennel. Don wasn't in the best of moods, which didn't help. He knew how much it would upset the poor brute. He thinks I ought to have him put down.'

'And you won't?'

'I agreed to a month's trial and I'm keeping Don to that. You can't tell how these dogs will settle. Some are much slower than others, but most come round in the end. Come and see my own dogs. Every one of them has a bad history, but they're none of them too difficult now.'

He led her to a huge pen attached to an outhouse which seemed to have been built as an annexe to the second kennel block.

'We need heat for them in the winter. Easier if they're all under one roof rather than a lot of separate ones. Come on, dogs. Let's have you out for the lady to look at.'

He opened the door of a roomy compartment, in which were five plastic beds, lined with immaculate white rugs. For a few minutes there was a wild reunion as dogs raced out, leaping at Roger, each vying for his attention.

'I tell everyone else not to let their dogs do that and never cure mine,' he said, laughing as he fended off frantic paws and eager bodies.

'OK. That's enough, gang. Now sit and let's see you properly.' All five sat in unison, brown eyes alight with life and the joy of being free and with their master.

'This is Tyro. He's a greyhound, as you can see. Someone dumped him on my doorstep. He's permanently lame and probably stopped winning races. He's a sweetie.' He stroked the dog on the head. 'Midge was found tied to a tree in a wood, with a muzzle on her so she couldn't bark. Luckily some boys came across her. She had cigarette burns all over and a badly healed fractured leg.'

Midge was a small dog, who looked like a collie with short legs. She wagged her tail happily when she heard her name.

'Shala was chucked out because she was past breeding

age. She must have had a litter that died, they thought, when they found her. Full of milk, and totally exhausted. She'd been dumped from a van, and ran after it till she dropped. She's a lovely old lady, and adores the kittens. We think she's about eleven now.'

The German Shepherd was grey-muzzled and shapeless, but she too sat quietly, and lifted her head to Roger as he petted her, her eyes adoring. Her tail brushed the ground happily.

'This is Knight. Probably a cross between a bearded collie and a working collie; he certainly likes herding and is apt to force his companions into a neat group and not let them move till I come and release them. His owner had twins when he was just a year old and couldn't cope, which is hardly surprising. He's the only one that came with a name.'

'And here's my old Grandee, which is short for Grande Dame. She always thought she was a cut above the others when she was young. Pedigree Red Setter, no less, with a very regal ancestry. They called her Glory but I changed her name as I felt it might make her happier. She committed a crime.'

'What crime?'

'She stopped winning first prizes at Breed shows when she was nine months old, and was left in the kennel and never taken out at all. You go off people. She had so little exercise her muscles wasted. Don saw her when he went to her home to investigate a break-in. In spite of his tough attitude, he's not much better than I am: he persuaded them to let her go for nothing provided he didn't report them.'

He put his hand in his pockets and five eager heads looked towards him. He called each in turn and laughed as the dog sat in front of him, eyes on his hand, and was rewarded with a small biscuit.

'They have shelter, food, companionship and a riot

each day with me for about an hour,' he said. 'Spike takes them for a long hike during the afternoon as it's too far for him to go home for his break. It may not seem much of a life but it's a sight better than any of them had before.'

'And what he doesn't say,' said Spike who had come up behind them unseen, 'is that they all come into the house with Rake at night, and are spoiled rotten. I believe they sleep on his bed.'

Roger laughed as he shut the pen door behind him. They were followed by whimpering.

'That's Midge. She hates it when I leave her. She stops as soon as I'm out of sight, as she knows it won't work. Come and see my other treasures.'

'He means visit the Cat Palace,' Spike said, grinning, and ducked his head to avoid a playful punch.

The breeding queens lived in an annexe attached to the farmhouse. It opened on to a large enclosed space, where trees and bushes grew, and kittens watched them from the lower branches of a rowan that protruded through the mesh. It had once been a walled garden, but now all that remained of that were the fruit trees.

'I can't risk having them free to explore.' Roger knelt to stroke a cat that looked more like a Siamese than Kaos. She lay on her back, legs in the air, waiting for his hand to smooth the fur on her tummy.

'She's due to kitten in a few days,' Roger said. 'It's a very tricky business, sorting out how to mate them. Novices often get the oddest animals; nothing like they expected.'

'I saw the pamphlet about them,' Liese said. 'It looks very easy to get it wrong.'

She looked down at the little cat. She was dark brown, with black points. The silky fur on her stomach was the colour of pale caramel. Green eyes watched the stranger.

'I can't show her because of that white diamond on her chest,' Roger said. 'But she does produce the loveliest kittens, though they're never show quality. She's had two litters. This is her last. I have to watch her: she's addicted to eating plastic bags.'

'Are those Tonkinese?' Liese asked. Three of the kittens were nothing like any cat she had ever seen.

Roger grinned.

'We had an intruder and heaven alone knows how he did it, but they have a healthy background of ginger tom who had no right at all to be anywhere near the place. I kept them; wouldn't do my reputation much good if I let them go, and be seen and talked about. My dark secret.' He laughed.

'How did he get in?'

'My own theory is that it was a piece of mayhem: somebody let him in on purpose. I could be wrong, but there are funny goings-on at times round here. Evan, who sees ghosts and talks to them, reckons somebody cursed us. I told Frankie and she sent Herbal Joe's mother over to take away the bad luck.'

'Frankie's sure her old dog is still there and comes nightly,' Liese said. 'I got used to her talking to thin air, and Mac wagging his tail at nothing.'

'I know all about Allie,' Roger said. 'Rake sees her too, according to Frankie. Me, I'm on the fence . . . maybe, maybe not. Like believing there are aliens out there, or maybe even here already waiting to take over.'

Liese looked at the cats.

'Little green men,' she said. 'I never could believe in them. Did you say you had a cat with kittens?'

'Yes, but she likes privacy and I don't let anyone near them till they're six weeks old. Then we play with them when she's out of the room and hand-feed them and get them used to people, or they'd be disasters when they were sold. One of your jobs: play with kittens. Maggie wouldn't. She was far too dignified.'

'Message from the Fox and Grapes,' Spike said, as they returned to the office. 'How many for your celebration?'

'I'd forgotten all about it.' Roger picked up the mail which lay on his desk. 'I take all the staff out for a meal on my birthday. This year I'll be sixty ... something I suppose I should celebrate in style. Want to join us?'

'I'd like that,' Liese said, hoping this meant that she was accepted and could stay on after her month's trial.

'Maybe Sue will change her mind and come if you come,' Spike said. 'I don't know where she gets to in the evenings, but she can surely miss out just once.'

'She goes to help her mother who seems to have eight sons and a husband at home, none of whom help,' Liese said. 'Only don't tell her I told you. And, by the way, the reason she doesn't want to walk the dogs is that her feet are a mass of blisters.'

Roger raised his eyebrows but said nothing. He and Spike went out together. It was feeding time, and judging by the clamour when the kennels door was opened a lot of very hungry dogs were protesting that it was late.

Liese, entering appointments in the book, suddenly wondered if Sue felt homesick. Here she was among men all day, but they seemed to despise the girl. Spike had little to do with her, Gregory was curt with her and Evan, so far as she could see, was incapable of speech.

By mid-morning, Helmet had abandoned his box and was curled up against Rake, who was warm and comforting and maybe reminded the kitten of the mother he had lost. The big dog lay with a patient look on his face, as if afraid to move lest he disturb his small protegé.

Kaos, visiting during the morning coffee break, took one look at the newcomer and marched off, his tail in the air. Sue giggled.

'He looks just like me when my Mum told me we were about to have another baby,' she said. 'God, how I hated those babies. Every time one came my Gran, that's my Dad's Mum, would visit and say, "Another mouth to feed. You'll never manage, my girl." Cheered Mum up no end just after giving birth, I don't think, but I didn't realise it then.'

'How many babies were there?' Roger asked, not wishing to reveal that Liese had already told him. Sue had never spoken about her family before. Liese suspected that their earlier conversation might have changed the girl's attitude. She did not seem nearly so defensive.

'There are nine of us. Then Mum went to be filleted; best thing that ever happened to her, she says. She had a growth, but it wasn't malignant. Taking her ages to get over it, though, as the baby was only six weeks old when they did her.'

'Coming to my party?' Roger asked.

'Is Lee?'

Gregory grinned at Liese. So I was wrong, and Frankie was right, she thought, and grinned in her turn.

'She's coming,' Roger said.

'OK. Save me being the only rose among the thorns, won't it? I'll wash the dog bowls.'

'Miracles can happen,' Roger commented after the girl had left them. 'She's never offered to do anything before. Give her a lecture, did you?'

'No. I just listened. I think she misses her family, even if she does complain about all the babies. She thinks a lot of her mother. One of the boys wants to be a doctor. All the family is saving so that he can start college with some money in the bank. Her dad doesn't approve of credit cards.'

'Why didn't she tell me about her blisters?'

'She hates moaning. She doesn't, does she?'

'Not about herself. She might moan about the dogs at times.'

Outside the day had brightened and the sun was warm. The snowdrops and crocuses in the tiny patch of garden beside Roger's part of the farmhouse were almost over. Daffodils promised bloom in the near future. Shadow was lying quiet, his head on his paws, his eyes forlorn, gazing into nowhere, as if he did not feel part of the world.

Liese spoke softly to him and threw him pieces of the liver cake she had purloined from the tin. She went back to him in the afternoon when everyone else was out, and brought the stool from her kitchen. She sat on it, reading aloud from a magazine that Sue had lent her. It was surprisingly warm in the sunshine.

The dog began to watch her, but whenever she looked at him he turned his eyes away, refusing to meet her gaze. He was quiet until a van drove into the yard and a man climbed out, handing her a large parcel for which she had to sign.

'Dear heaven,' the driver said as Shadow threw himself frantically at the wire, roaring his fury. 'I hope that one can't escape. I wouldn't like to meet him on a dark night . . . or a bright day for that matter,' he added, raising his voice above the din.

'Oh, Shadow, Shadow,' Liese said. 'What are we going to do with you?'

The kitten had followed her. It was time for his next feed. Three hours seemed to pass remarkably fast. She lifted him and took him back into the office.

Shadow settled down again, his nose on his paws, longing for his old home. He felt desolate. He knew now that his prison was escape-proof, but the scent on the air called to him. Had he been free, he would have followed it until he reached the place he still thought of as his sanctuary. Although his small owner was gone, the people there were all he had known after he left the kennels where he was born.

Eight

When Liese went into the office next day, Roger handed her the enormous package that she had taken in.

'For you, not for me,' he said.

She had not been expecting anything for herself and had left it on the desk without even looking at the label.

She opened it that evening, with help from Helmet who found the rustling irresistible and jumped in and out, enjoying the noise. His small body dived beneath the paper, his bat-eared head appearing to look up at her, and vanish again, finding tunnels and recesses in which to lurk and leap out, pouncing on nothing.

She was surprised that anything so small could be so active, although his pounces were not yet steady, and he sometimes fell over, his expression making her laugh. By now, if still in the nest, he would have been interacting with his littermates.

Liese relaxed, watching him, enjoying laughter, which had been rare in her married life. She was content to linger, to ball up pieces of discarded wrapping and throw them for him to dash at and tap at. He adored the box and sat in it, investigating its corners as if he hoped to find some hidden trophy.

The contents reduced her almost to tears. Frankie had sent her a huge throw covered in jungle animals, obviously a match to the bath towel that had so amused her niece. It transformed the drab settee. The cushions were in more sober colours: one featured horses' heads; one was embroidered with cat faces; a third was covered in dogs. She put them on her bed.

Owls looked out at her from the tea towels, which were

wrapped round something that proved to be the spotted money pig.

'Just thought that it's the silly things that make a place home,' Frankie had written in her almost indecipherable scrawl. 'Thought you'd like pig. He always made you laugh. You'll be able to buy a few more bits and pieces when Roger pays you. I don't suppose your new home is at all cosy. It must be such a big change.'

There was another package at the bottom of the box. She unwrapped it and then grinned. Layer after layer of paper came away, revealing in the end a very small bar of chocolate. It had always been one of Frankie's jokes. Just such a package had lain on her bed when she felt blue. If she spent time away, there was the little overwrapped parcel at the bottom of her holdall, a reminder of home, of affection, of Frankie herself.

There was so much she had forgotten about her aunt.

The room was brightened by the decorative gifts.

Liese rang Frankie to thank her. She told her aunt about Helmet and added that she found it odd that her present role in life was to be mother to a little animal.

'I never dreamed it could be so demanding and time-consuming,' she said.

'Luckily kittens grow fast. This part of it won't last for more than a week or so. He's probably a bit retarded due to an appalling start in life, but he sounds healthy and he'll soon pick up.' Frankie's voice was comforting. Liese smiled as she rang off and she looked again at her gifts, feeling cosseted.

They were expressions of love. She had never felt that about Edward's presents to her. They were not only too lavish but had always been followed by a request for more money for a wonderful new scheme.

Spike and Roger helped with the evening feeds while Liese slept and she did not find her new charge too taxing. The days passed surprisingly fast. She developed her own routine, discovering that if she immersed herself in work she forgot her worries.

She was busiest at weekends when dogs went out and new boarders came, sometimes having to juggle while one of the men finished cleaning the kennel. Each was thoroughly washed before a newcomer took up residence. If owners had to wait, Liese gave them coffee and cakes and chatted to them, Helmet providing a wonderful conversation piece.

Time hung heavily on other days, but when Sue rang in at the beginning of April to apologise because there was trouble at home, she found new occupation in adding the girl's work to her own. Helmet had grown fast and was now almost as large as Kaos, who was small for his breed. The other cat disliked the newcomer and they were kept apart. Kaos resented being deprived of his visits to the office, and soon Helmet stayed in Liese's apartments and was allowed exercise when his rival was indoors.

Sue, who had begun to return earlier from her evening visits home now that she had a companion next door, had often called in before going to bed and Liese missed her. She returned one night during the second week in April at 2 a.m. Liese woke to the sound of the moped and Helmet sat up, his tail wrapped neatly round him, his ears listening. Liese switched on the light to supplement the moonshine that lit the room.

A few minutes later there was a soft rap at her door. Liese slipped on her dressing-gown and invited the girl in.

'I saw your light ... I ...' She looked at Helmet who was perched on Liese's shoulder. The orange hair was a bush in need of a comb; mascara, applied too heavily, always reminding Liese of a forlorn panda, had run down her cheeks. She reached out for Helmet and held him against her and then began to cry, helplessly, unable to stop. She buried her face in the soft fur.

'I'm sorry,' she said at last, when the paroxysm was reduced to an occasional sob.

She went over to the sink and bathed her face. Liese made tea for both of them, adding several spoonfuls of sugar to Sue's mug. Helmet, unused to being held so tightly, jumped down and curled himself on the rug in front of the Rayburn. Liese, dismayed by Sue's misery, put her arms around her and the younger girl relaxed, continuing to sob like a small child for some minutes.

'I'm sorry,' Sue said at last. 'My Dad . . . he's had a stroke. Mum can't cope with the boys as it is; if Dad comes home and can't do anything for himself . . . I'll have to give up work and help her. I won't have a place of my own any more. It's so noisy. And I oughtn't to be thinking of me.' Tears threatened again.

'How bad is he?' Liese asked when Sue had managed to control her sobs.

'His speech has gone. He can't move his left arm or leg. We don't know if he even knows us. His face is all lopsided. It isn't my dad. He'll hate it. He's always so active, rushing everywhere, out most nights, going to football matches with Tone and Johnno; playing rugby with them. He dashes up the stairs two at a time; he's always laughing. He's noisier than any of the boys.'

Liese, feeling helpless, resorted to practicalities. She had a sudden memory of the policewoman making cheese sandwiches, brewing tea and insisting that she ate and drank. She had felt better afterwards.

'Have you eaten this evening?'

Sue shook her head.

'I've been at the hospital with Mum. She spends as much time with Dad as possible. My Gran's with the boys. They only have tea and coffee in those ghastly machines. There is a canteen but we never found it. There's miles of corridors. I hate hospitals.'

'Will your mother cope?' Liese asked.

130

'Got no choice, has she? Just came back for a bit on my own. I wanted to think. Felt I ought to tell Rog they need me at home, but Mum says no. She says there's nothing I can do and Gran's moved in for now. She lives alone. She's pretty active and says she'll stay for the time being. I called in at home before I came here. She was making Tone iron his own shirt. Meek as a lamb, too, he was.'

She made a noise that was halfway between a sob and a laugh.

'He thought the world had come to an end. Mum always does it for him . . . and for his girlfriend. She was getting an earful!'

Liese knew little about strokes, but she had read of people who made full recoveries.

'Do the doctors think he'll get better?' she asked.

Sue shrugged.

'Don't suppose they really know, do they? Everyone's different. Some do . . . some don't. Won't be able to go back to his old job, any road. He's a bus driver. Not the sort of thing you can do if there's any risk . . . he could have another attack. Dunno how he'll cope with not racing around . . . he's not very patient.'

Liese, having made sandwiches, sat and ate with her guest, surprised to find she was hungry.

'Can I sleep here? I can't at home as Gran's got my room. She only moved in completely today. She's been coming all day and I stayed with the boys at night. Mum's falling apart. When she is home she mostly sits and cries. Tone and his girlfriend sleep downstairs. I don't want to be alone. I won't be a bother, honestly.'

'The sofa's long enough, but there's no spare bedding,' Liese said. 'The room's warm. The Rayburn's wonderful. On day and night and heats the radiators.'

Sue fetched her duvet from next door. Liese, lying in bed with Helmet tucked against her, watched the moon sail across the sky, and vanish and reappear, looking as it were flying from hunting clouds. She felt as if she had been thrown into deep water.

After years in which nothing much had changed from day to day, she now seemed to be facing one crisis after another. Bill Adams had phoned only that evening to say that he had been unable to find out any more about the woman who alleged she had had Edward's child, but was hoping to find someone who would explore a new lead.

Sam Laycock had also phoned to say that the people who had been going to buy the house had backed out, as they had found something more to their taste at a cheaper price. She felt she could not cope with Sue's problems as well as her own.

There was good news in the morning: Tara, Roger's third queen, had had her kittens. Six little beauties, he reported happily. He had had eight orders for Rani's kittens, but she too had only had six, so he already had several customers waiting.

Liese had to take care not to mix people who wanted cats with those who wished to board their dogs, and those who only wanted to order dog food. She was still worried about making mistakes, although Roger was very tolerant and did not expect miracles, he said.

She loved it when there were kittens for sale, as they had a pen in the office and were tremendous fun. Everyone who came wanted to cuddle them, and they, like Helmet, rapidly learned to like people. Roger agonised every time he sold one, hoping that they were going to good homes. He had a long list of questions and Liese sometimes thought that those wanting his stock had to pass an examination before they were allowed to buy.

Sue had called home briefly, but been sent back by her grandmother and told to do her work as there was nothing else she could do for her parents.

'Gran says I behave as if I don't trust her . . . think she's too old to cope with the boys. In fact she copes with them much better than Mum as she won't stand any nonsense. You should see Ry eat his cabbage! He never will for Mum. Plays her up no end. None of us dare play Gran up.'

Two days before Roger's birthday party Sue was away helping her mother. Liese, deputed to wash all the dog bowls, finished the chore thankfully and went into the office to pour out coffee. Spike and Roger both seemed to be in a frivolous mood.

'Got your party dress ready?' Roger asked her.

'Do we dress up?'

'No. We dress down. It's a pyjama party.'

'In a pub?'

'Ignore him,' Spike said, handing round fancy biscuits that Bill Adams had brought over two days before. 'Between Bill's mum and your aunt and Mrs Hodge in the village, we'll all soon need to diet. They seem to think we starve.'

'It's not a pyjama party?' Liese was not in the mood for jokes. Michael Dutton had not cheered her when she rang him to learn if there was any progress.

'These things can take years,' he told her, which did not help in the least.

It was difficult to concentrate even when she was with the men.

'No pyjamas,' Spike said, aware that Liese had not been listening to him. 'He's being daft. Being sixty has gone to his head. Clean clothes. Casual.' He turned to Roger, who was about to pick up the phone. 'Suppose she thought you meant it? Liese doesn't understand our kinky humour.'

'I wouldn't have come.' Liese often found their jokes tiresome.

'Think Sue'll come? I wonder how her dad is,' Roger said.

Over the past few days Sue had been surprisingly subdued and almost unrecognisable without her mask of make-up and with hair that had reverted to a more attractive blonde colour. Gran, it appeared, had put her foot down, according to her granddaughter.

She returned that evening almost excited, with news of a little progress. Her father had regained his speech and was able, very slowly, using a zimmer frame, to move a few steps. Her Gran was talking of selling her house and moving in permanently, insisting that Sue must get on with her job.

The day before the birthday party Liese slept well, but woke at five, before the alarm, feeling at ease for the first time since Edward had died. She was enjoying the dogs, and Helmet was a constant joy. He was a vocal little cat, mewing in answer when she spoke to him, making her laugh. Kaos no longer visited; there was a very uneasy truce that would, Roger was sure, one day flare into hostility. He was the only cat on the premises that the Tonkinese disliked and no one could work out why as Helmet was totally unaggressive and liable to flee if ever there was an accidental encounter.

Liese stretched and woke Helmet, who greeted her with purrs and rubbed himself against her chin, marching up and down her chest. His tail, erect, tickled her cheek when she sat up.

'You're dotty,' she told him, laughing. He mewed in reply and clung close to her ankle when she put the food in his dish. Once fed, he settled on her bed, curling himself under the duvet where the tiny hump was almost invisible.

There was spring in the air when she walked outside. April had begun gloomily but was now making up for lost time. The misty world was just waking and everything was bathed in heavy dew. The sun was a hint on the horizon. No one was yet about. Shadow's kennel had been repaired several times, but when a bad mood seized him, he resorted to chewing at the wood again. He hated being inside, and even when it was raining slept in the run.

Somewhere in the distance a horse whinnied, followed by the call of an early waking cockerel. There was blossom in the hedges. The world seemed to be full of promise—

rainbows catching the sunshine; summer following spring, with winter long forgotten. One day, all her problems would be over and life would resume a more even course. Harbour after stormy seas.

Shadow heard her footsteps and came to meet her. She had brought a slice of brown bread, and offered it to him. He now greeted her with pleasure, and the day before, when she was quite sure she was alone, she had ventured into his kennel. He had allowed her hands on his back, had licked her finger, and had behaved more like a normal dog than at any time before. One day soon she would start to groom him. His fur looked so shabby.

He had improved. Roger could now take his food bowls out of the kennel and give him more without a scene. There was no longer any need for the horrific treatment with the dog catcher noose and protective clothing. He did not like the men, and he still hated Don, though Liese at times wondered if that had more to do with Venn than with his owner. Sue was afraid of him and he growled at her, not liking the scent on the air and knowing that she did not care for him at all.

Liese was pleased with his progress and was becoming very fond of him. Both of them had to learn to forget a very unhappy past life. She had a feeling that the dog was her passport to the future, and that their fates were linked. Through him she would gain a new impetus in life. Those afternoon sessions were beginning to mean a great deal to her and she had worried all through the weeks until his month of grace was up.

Don said nothing when the deadline passed. There was an improvement, Roger assured him. The policeman, unusually busy due to problems on one of the local housing estates, had little interest in the kennels. They were a dog handler short and he and Venn seemed to be away much of the time.

It was quiet in the yard. A bird broke into song, startling

135

her, but not alarming the dog. He was watching her, and she wondered if she dared open the gate and go inside again. But there was a chance that Gregory would come early, and Spike too was unpredictable. Sometimes he had someone who would spend the night at his home, letting him sleep, and attending to the needs of his mother. When that happened he left home early, glad to be away from an atmosphere that was becoming increasingly difficult. On those occasions Sue or Liese often gave him breakfast.

There was no one to criticise or condemn. Liese had begun to trust people to treat her well, not to carp and comment as Edward had. She had cooked two sausages and cut them into pieces, wondering if she could induce Shadow to learn to sit when told. It would help a great deal when Roger went into his run. She wanted to offer to take the feed in herself, and also to clean the run, but knew that it would not be allowed, and she did not want her sessions discovered until the dog was far more biddable.

He came forward eagerly when she held out a piece of food, and she put her hand through the wire so that he could take it easily. She was concentrating on him, knowing he was relaxing, enjoying the calm expression in his eyes. So often he looked wild. Sometimes he looked desperately anxious, but today he seemed to have made another step in the direction she wanted.

She jumped, startled, when he suddenly leapt at the wire, baying at the top of his voice. She whirled round. Don, walking fast across the yard, his eyes angry, reduced her to a state of abject terror. She began to shake. He was about to report for duty. He sent Venn to the van and came towards her.

The day before had been one of the worst he had ever endured. He had not slept. The anger that had seized him would not dissipate; it had grown during the night. Liese was a ready target.

'What the hell do you think you're doing?' He had to bellow to drown Shadow's barking.

Liese could barely speak, she was so afraid.

'I'm just talking to him. Trying to get his confidence.' It was hard to make herself heard above the barking.

'You got it, didn't you? Making him bark his stupid head off and wake everybody up.'

She had never dared answer Edward back. Maybe that had been a mistake. Perhaps he would have respected her more if she had returned his fire. She summoned her courage and put both hands in her pockets to conceal the tremor. Shadow, sensing the anger directed at the woman he had begun to accept, redoubled his barking.

'He was quiet until you came out with your dog. He hadn't made a sound. I've been here for nearly ten minutes.'

'You aren't employed to work with the dogs. What do you know about them? All you know is a life with a crook who conned people out of their money.'

The accusation was more than she could bear. It was not the first time she had heard it. The policemen she met seemed to think she must have known. Maybe they all had suspicious minds and could not understand that anyone might be innocent.

'I didn't know he was a crook.'

'You're either a liar or a complete fool. Didn't you ever ask what he did for a living?'

Her fragile calm was shattered. The voice was an echo of Edward at his worst, mocking her, despising her, criticising her, condemning her. On those nights he had always been drinking heavily, probably, she now thought, due to some deal that had gone wrong. She had never attempted to argue with him. She was too frightened of his easily roused temper.

She would never be able to stand up to Don. She felt

helpless and the shaking grew worse. She prayed he would not notice.

Neither of them saw Roger approach. Both were trying to make themselves heard above the angry barks of the dog. Shadow was threatening Don, who was upsetting the one person in his life he now cared about. He had reverted to his earlier tactics and was throwing himself against the weldmesh, wanting to attack Liese's tormentor.

'Don. You'll be late for work.' Roger's tone was peremptory. 'Liese. I want to talk to you before the lads get here. Never get the chance. Come over to my place. We can have a talk while it's quiet.'

She was on the verge of hysteria, tears absurdly fighting with laughter. She wondered what Roger thought of as noisy.

Venn, aware of his master's mood, was lying quietly in the van. There was a rip of tyres as Don accelerated away. Shadow continued to bark, but the sound died as they left the yard.

The farmhouse held memories of past owners, each adding a room or two until it sprawled over a remarkable area of ground. The kitchen/living-room was an island of comfort, with deep armchairs, a large wooden table covered in a checked scarlet and green cloth, and a colourful rug in front of the fire where the dogs sprawled.

They came to greet her and sniff her, smelling Helmet on her clothes. Kaos sat on the wooden sill, his tail tucked round him, and stared at her with unwinking eyes so that she felt unwelcome.

'He's busy being a statue,' Roger said, grinning at the cat. 'Actually he's mesmerised by the birds and just praying one will magically fly through the glass so that he can catch it. Coffee? Have you had breakfast?'

'I had some toast.' Was Roger about to tell her to go? Was he as angry with her for talking to Shadow as Don had been? Maybe she should ask him to define her exact duties, so that she did not make more mistakes.

'Have some more. It's all I ever have in the morning.' He put two slices in the toaster. 'Don't take any notice of Don.'

He put instant coffee in two mugs and added water.

'He's not yet got over his wife's death. It was less than a year ago. She had cancer, and took a long time dying. He did much of the nursing. A hell of a thing. I think he came near to a breakdown when Marie went.'

'I was only talking to Shadow. I've been spending time with him every afternoon. He's beginning to trust me. He comes to be stroked when no one else is near. He wasn't barking at me. He was barking at Don and Venn.'

'Is it you taking the liver cake? I thought we had mice.'

'I'll make some. Shadow likes it.' Liese began to worry even more. She needed reassurance. Don had roused feelings she thought had been stifled. Surely Roger wouldn't offer her breakfast if he were about to sack her?

'I didn't think ... have I been running you short of liver cake?'

'Mrs Hodge provides us with an endless supply. Don't worry. I've been watching you with Shadow, it's given me some hope. You're doing fine. Just keep away from Don if you can. He's worse than usual today because Venn found the body of a little girl who's been missing from home. She was only seven. He adores kids but never had any. He's not half as bad as he seems ... Marie used to be able to coax him out of his black moods.'

He sighed as he rinsed the crockery under the running tap.

'Life deals out some lousy hands, but you don't need me to tell you that. Any news about the settlement of your affairs?'

She shook her head.

'It just seems to get worse. I think nothing worse can possibly happen and it does.'

It was time to start work. As she came out of the kitchen Sue walked into the yard, wearing jeans, a neat jersey and a pair of trainers that Liese had given her. Her hair was brushed and had been neatly cut, her grandmother having provided the money and insisted it was done.

'Wow,' Spike said, passing her, towed by an Irish Wolfhound that was possessed of an urgent desire to travel at a racing trot.

Sue made a face at him.

The morning seemed endless but the day brightened at coffee time, when Bill appeared. Although he had no news whatever, he made everyone laugh, and he teased Liese, breaking the feeling of remoteness that had possessed her.

Frankie had sent her a small gift: a ridiculous china owl wearing a gown and mortarboard and carrying a scroll. Bill perched him on top of the filing cabinet.

Evan, who was feeling cheerful after a rare good night's sleep, christened him Mr Chips.

Helmet was now left in front of the Rayburn until lunchtime, when Kaos went indoors and the kitten could come into the office. That day Sue and Liese shared sandwiches in Liese's kitchen.

'I've something to show you tonight,' Sue said. 'And Bill's been asked to the party. Thought you'd like to know. He's always here these days, isn't he? I wonder why.'

'Didn't he come before?' Liese asked. She had always thought he must have some business in the district, as his county boundary was not more than fifteen miles away. He seemed to know many of the men in the area immediately around the kennels.

'I never had any brothers or sisters,' she said, not willing to consider Sue's meaning. 'Bill lived down the lane ... our nearest neighbour. I always thought of him as my brother. I suppose I still do,' she added thoughtfully. 'So don't go looking for any other interpretation. It's going to take me a long time to get over everything that's happened.'

They went back to the office just as a car came up the drive into the yard. Spike was on his way to the lane with a large Irish Terrier on his lead. Paddy was a fighter who had to be watched, and everyone was very careful not to bring out any other dog when he was around.

Before anyone could stop him, the driver of the car opened his door and a big German Shepherd cross leaped out, straight in front of Spike and his charge.

Shadow, although he could see nothing, added his baying to the uproar. Roger raced out as Spike, trying to pull his charge off the other dog, yelled as he was bitten.

Paddy had no intention of letting go of his challenger and the crossbred was as infuriated. After taking one look, Evan fetched the hose and turned it full on, drenching both protagonists as well as Roger and Spike and the intruding dog's owner, who seized his offending animal and pushed him back into the car. Both dogs were bleeding.

Roger for the moment was more concerned with his employee than with the dogs. He inspected Spike's hand.

'Evan! Off to hospital with him. That needs cleaning and stitching. Tetanus up to date?' he asked Spike, who nodded, feeling sick. The teeth had gone deep. The strange dog's owner stood by his car, not knowing what to say.

'Rule number one when bringing your dog in,' Roger said, 'is never let him out of the car until you're quite sure there is no other dog around, anywhere.'

Liese found the first aid kit, cleaned off some of the blood on Spike's hand with antiseptic wipes, and covered it for the journey to the hospital.

Gregory was holding Paddy, who had a bad bite on his

ear and another on his paw. The terrier was growling under his breath. The visiting dog lay with his nose on his paws, apparently aware he had transgressed. There was blood on his muzzle and a torn area on his shoulder.

'This is Bruno, isn't it?' Roger asked. 'Due in today.'

Bruno's owner nodded.

'I'm so sorry . . . he's never done anything like that before.'

'There's always a first time. It had better be the last. Leash him next time before you get him out of the car. He needs treatment.'

'I'm on my way to the airport . . . I've a plane to catch. Look . . . can you get the vet out here for both dogs? I'll pay . . . I'm late as it is . . .'

Liese could see that Roger was not pleased, but there was little he could do. Gregory bathed Paddy's injuries and took him to the kennels, while Roger got Bruno out of the car and into the office.

Liese rang the vet who promised to come out as soon as his two o'clock surgery was over. Nobody had time to go off for the afternoon, as Spike was unlikely to come back that day. Liese and Sue prepared the dogs' feed bowls and then helped with walking the boarders. Once he had been settled, Bruno proved to be an amiable dog. He was sore and uneasy in a strange place, deserted for the first time in his life by his master.

Both dogs needed stitching and injections. Paddy's owners weren't due back for ten days and Roger hoped that by then the injuries would be almost healed. He had never had a dog in his care injured in a fight before and was considerably upset.

He was relieved when Liese reported that both dogs had eaten their evening meal.

'It happened so fast,' she said.

'Bad luck, mainly. I've only just realised that Spike came round the corner of the kennels just as the car door was

142

opened. The yard was empty when they arrived. If he'd only parked a few yards farther up . . .'

Liese's legs ached: she had walked six dogs. She fed Helmet, who wove round her legs complaining that he had been alone all afternoon and not been allowed out and he was hungry because she was late.

She hoped that Sue wouldn't call in. The girl was only ringing home that day and the next, and was not visiting again until after Roger's party. She had more freedom now that her grandmother had moved in with her family.

Liese was too tired to eat. She made herself a coffee, kicked off her shoes, and dropped into the armchair. It was a cool night and the Rayburn gave off welcome heat.

The ringing telephone startled her and made Helmet jump, so that he hissed. She padded across the room, hoping it was Bill. He always cheered her, recounting some funny incident that had happened during the day. Last time he rang he had told her of a meeting he had with a man on the bank of the canal. He had just come off a boat and was wearing immaculate white trousers, a beautifully cut blazer and a yachting cap. He was unable to stand steadily.

' 'S all right, officer,' he said. 'I'm not drunk,' and promptly fell backwards into the water so that Bill had to rescue him.

She did not, at first, recognise the voice on the other end.

'Mrs Grant? Michael Dutton here,' he went on when she answered. 'I'm sorry . . . I have more bad news for you. Your house was broken into last night. Mr Laycock is going through the inventory he made with the police . . . the auction is to take place the week after next. We don't yet know what's missing.'

'The burglar alarm . . .' Liese said. Disaster seemed to pile on disaster—was she never going to be able to relax and enjoy life again?

'The neighbourss were away on both sides. I suspect the intruders had planned carefully, but they were interrupted . . . we think they only got away with some of the smaller items . . . but those are valuable.'

'They're insured,' Liese said.

There was another silence before the solicitor answered.

'It wasn't renewed last time. Do you wish to come over? If so, I'll meet you. They broke in through a window; that has been repaired.'

'Do the police need me?' Liese had no desire whatever to see her old home again.

'Mr Laycock has taken charge. They are quite satisfied with his authority.'

Liese stared at the phone after he rang off. The bleak feeling had returned. She was about to ring Bill, needing sympathy, when Sue bounced in.

'What do you think?'

She was pirouetting on alarmingly high heels, wearing a skin-tight scarlet dress with a remarkably low cleavage. She twirled as if she were on a catwalk. Liese, in spite of her misery, restrained a desire to laugh. Sue was little more than five feet in height and fashionably slim, but instead of resembling a model as she obviously hoped, she looked like a small girl dressed up in one of her mother's more outrageous outfits.

'My Gran gave me some money to buy something to wear for Rog's bash. I hadn't anything. Got this from the Good as New shop. Gran says it looks tarty.'

'It wouldn't go with orange hair,' Liese said, desperately searching for something to say. Today, Sue's hair was almost white.

'I only did that to annoy Mag. It upset Mum and Dad too, but while Mag was there . . . I wore a nose stud too as she thinks they're awful, only Ev thought I had a boil, so I took it out.'

Liese could only think of the break-in. What had they

taken? The loss of even a few of the valuable small pieces would make a huge difference to the final sum raised. She might have known that Edward would let the insurance lapse. She would have to ring Sam Laycock and see if it could be renewed temporarily, just until the auction. The house would have to be insured too; that had probably lapsed as well. Maybe Frankie would lend her the money and she could pay it off in instalments. She didn't want to ask, but it was too important to leave. Suppose an arsonist burned the place down?

Sue snapped her fingers.

'Penny for them.'

'Just a problem with the house sale,' Liese said, not wishing for a long discussion. Sue loved speculating.

'Tough.' She wriggled uneasily. Liese was sure the dress was too tight. She had to restrain herself from comment. She was relieved when the girl left her.

She tried to ring Bill, but he was out and she did not feel like a conversation with Frankie. For some reason she never felt the need to keep cheerful with her old friend, but knowing her aunt worried she did her best to pretend that all was well.

She was not concentrating when she let Helmet out for his last run. Gregory had made him a small enclosure where she put him last thing at night, for a few minutes. Sensing her mood, he eluded her and ran down the steps and across the yard, chasing a length of straw that danced enticingly in the wind. It was not very dark, as a full moon lit the sky and cast playful shadows under the trees.

Liese raced after him, but he had vanished in a dark patch and there was no sign of him in the yard. She searched behind the bins, peered into a cranny between Sue's home and her own and then looked blankly around her.

Maybe he had gone into the kennel yard. She turned the corner of the farmhouse. A small wind ruffled the dying bloom on the lilacs. Beyond the kennels were fields and trees, a parklike country, the cattle hidden now, but she could hear the sound of their breathing. It sounded like a drunken giant, as they kept in unison.

The wind excited the little cat. Kaos had spent the afternoon dismembering a blackbird, to Sue's extreme distress. The feathers lay around the yard and drifted enticingly. One whirled, glistening in the light of the security lamps which had come on as Liese crossed their path.

Helmet pounced and let it go again, practising his own skills against a future to be spent hunting.

Shadow, sitting bolt upright in his compound, watched in amazement as the cat chased his trophy under the gate. He squeezed through the gap, ignoring the dog who, to him, was just another version of Rake.

The feather blew into the water bowl and died, but there was straw on the ground and that came alive in a small gust. Helmet pounced and patted, teasing and letting go, allowing the wind to carry it a few inches and then pouncing again, only a few feet from the big German Shepherd.

Liese was appalled. Suppose Shadow attacked him, or worse, killed him? She had no idea how he behaved with cats. He always barked at Kaos, but the Tonkinese, she was sure, teased him quite deliberately, knowing he was safe outside.

Without stopping to think she opened the gate, offering Shadow a piece of liver cake. He was delighted to see her and bounded up, hoping for a pat. She picked Helmet up, and after a brief greeting, pushed the dog away, laughing at him, and went outside, carefully bolting the door again.

She stroked the nose he had pushed against the mesh, gave him more liver cake, and then, feeling she had made a big breakthrough, carried the kitten back to her own domain.

146

Don was waiting at the bottom of the steps to her front door, almost speechless with rage.

'I couldn't believe that anyone could be so stupid,' he said in an undertone that was angrier than any shout. 'I didn't dare come out. I can see the kennel from my windows. Next time you want to give me a heart attack or commit suicide just warn me and I'll have an ambulance on call. That was insane. I saw him jump at you . . . you were lucky he didn't bite.'

'He knows me,' Liese said. 'Look, I know you think I'm useless, but I could make something of that dog. He's not as bad as he seems. It's mostly men that he dislikes.'

'So how do you get rid of us?' Don asked. Liese had no chance to answer as Roger spoke from halfway across the yard. He had seen Liese carrying Helmet and watched Don follow her, and was sure there was trouble.

'Did you see that?' Don asked.

'The dog didn't even bark,' he said.

'Suppose he'd attacked? That would make headlines, wouldn't it? Do us no end of good to have one of our staff half-killed by a dog we own.' Don had no intention of relaxing his view.

'He didn't attack,' Liese said. 'He wouldn't touch me.'

'Has no one any sense around here? What was he doing when he jumped at you? Playing?'

'He wanted to greet me. He knows me.'

'God give me strength. I'm due on duty. I can't talk now. Tomorrow, we think again as to whether we can risk having you around here. You don't seem to have the sense of a two-year-old. And you're as bad,' he added to Roger.

The older man looked anxiously at Liese after the policeman had gone, knowing she was near to despair. She was shaking again, feeling that nothing would ever go right in her life. Shadow was beginning to love her, and she did not want to desert him. Would Frankie let her take him there?

'Don'll have forgotten by morning,' Roger said, knowing that to be untrue and dreading the scene that would follow. Not the best way to celebrate his birthday. He watched Liese drag herself up the steps and wished he could do more for her. He went back to his own quarters, frowning.

Sue, who had heard the row, slipped into the room, surprising Liese who had given way at last to the tears that had been threatening. She hugged the older woman and then made tea for both of them. She looked like a little girl in the Mickey Mouse T-shirt and knickers that she always wore in bed.

'He didn't mean it,' she said.

Liese was not so sure and lay awake a long time, hugging Helmet. Tomorrow, she was sure, would see the end of her stay here, and the end of her association with the dog.

When she slept at last it was to endure a series of terrible dreams, in which she was in jail with people mocking her and men shouting at her, and Sam Laycock saying over and over, 'You are responsible for Edward's debts.'

She woke heavy-eyed and filled with dread, and had to nerve herself to walk across to the office. She dared not go to Shadow, lest Don came home from his night duty while she was with him.

Life had never seemed more bleak. Not even the brilliant sunshine could cheer her.

Nine

To Roger's relief, Don was on duty all night and had
not come home by morning. Hopefully he might have
forgotten the events of the night before.

The post contained a number of birthday cards which
Roger opened but left lying on his desk. Liese arranged
them on a shelf. Mrs Hodge had provided a cake, ordered
by Gregory, Evan and Spike, for the morning coffee break.
Sue put six candles on it and Gregory, suddenly inspired
by idiocy, blew up six balloons, attached to a huge notice
which said 'ROGER 60 TODAY', and hung it on the gate.

Roger, discovering it an hour later, brought it in, but
did allow Evan to put it up in the office. Presents were to
be given in the evening. Work took precedence.

People were beginning to book for the summer holidays, knowing the kennels were always full at that time
and that advance notice was necessary. Liese, having to
contend with people who were sure she knew them and
their dogs, decided to buy a card index at the first opportunity. Then she could flip through while talking and
discover enough to reassure the caller. Nobody liked to
be forgotten.

It was a Saturday. Four dogs went out that morning,
all triggering Shadow to bark. Yesterday's confrontation
seemed to have unsettled him. She herself felt unsettled,
and desperately worried about the burglary. The thieves
could have taken a major part of the proceeds of the
auction. She had visions of a shortfall of hundreds of
thousands of pounds and unpaid debts hanging over her
for the rest of her life.

She went back to her own rooms to lunch on her own. She was not in the mood for laughter and teasing, and neither, she thought, was Roger. She rang Sam Laycock, but he was out, so she still did not know what had been taken. She fed Helmet and took her sandwiches to eat outside, sitting on the step.

The kitten was tired. He had spent the morning playing with a ping-pong ball that Sue had bought for him. He cuddled beside her on the step, making occasional not very serious attempts to steal her food.

The warmth was wonderful. Liese lifted her face to the sun. She had a sudden longing for blue seas and tropical shores and total peace, with no sound but that of small waves on soft sands. She could not see the kennels from her house, but all morning she had been aware that every time she passed, Shadow came to the wire and stood looking at her with forlorn eyes, as if wondering why she was ignoring him.

Don had returned and was asleep but he rarely slept for long and when up was apt to haunt the kennels, anxious, both Sue and Liese were convinced, to find a way of getting rid of the pair of them.

He scared Sue as much as he did Liese.

It was hard to stay gloomy in the bright sunshine. Perhaps everything would sort itself out and she would be free of worry within a few months. She lifted Helmet and went indoors to select her clothes for the evening's festivities.

She decided on white trousers with a pale yellow silk shirt and a coral necklace that had belonged to her grandmother. An embroidered jacket that she had always treasured would keep her warm.

She had left the door open, and Helmet went out to investigate. She did not see Kaos come to the bottom of the steps. He had slipped through a gap in a window that Roger had thought too small to allow his body through.

Kaos saw Helmet and gave chase, both cats hurtling through the door and across the little sitting-room.

Liese caught Kaos as he leaped, but Helmet, ahead of him, was already in the grate of the little fireplace that she never used, and had vanished up the chimney. Would he come out on the roof? And if so, could he get down? Or would he be marooned there on some ledge, trapped in the dark?

Carrying Kaos, who had no desire whatever to leave the scene, she went down to the office where Roger was talking on the telephone.

'He's chased Helmet up the chimney,' she said as her employer put down the receiver.

'He'll come out. Put food in the grate.' Roger was busy with his accounts, worried by the lack of order that Liese had exposed. Maggie had not listed half the cheques that came in and there was an unaccountable surplus in the bank. A good position to be in, but it would not please his accountants as it was income without an apparent source.

By teatime Helmet was still hidden and there was no sign of him on the roof. He was convinced that if he came down Kaos would kill him. Roger, fetched by an increasingly worried Liese, cursed and thrust an arm up the chimney but could not feel the cat. He added to Liese's worries. There was a wire mesh across the chimney pot to stop nesting birds. The chimney for the Rayburn was several feet away.

Evan shouted to them that the kitten appeared to be trying to push the wire up and escape that way. Roger fetched a ladder and climbed precariously up to the slates. Liese and Sue watched, terrified lest he fall.

He pulled away the wire and grabbed at Helmet who, startled by the appearance of a man beside him, appeared to be trying to climb back down the chimney. He scratched as Roger seized the scruff of his neck and hauled him out. He was black with soot and so, within minutes, was Roger.

Liese was soon in as bad a state as she tried to get the kitten clean in the sink. He scratched both her hands, hating the water, and did his best to escape. He, Liese and the kitchen were soaked.

Don, looking for Roger, knocked at the open door. There was no answer, but hearing voices, he went in and found Roger scrubbing his hands in Liese's bathroom. His clothes were smeared with soot. Liese was drying an animal that resembled a drowned rat, and longing to change her own clothes. Helmet continued to scratch and hiss, hating this rough introduction to an unpleasant world. He had forgotten his days as a tiny kitten and up to now had lived in a cat's heaven. He could not understand why Liese was putting him through such an ordeal.

She set him down by the Rayburn to dry off and offered him food, which he refused. Don, who had been worried when he saw Roger on the ladder, was in no mood to mince words.

'She can't even look after a kitten, let alone cope with a savage dog. Are you completely out of your mind?' he said, continuing the conversation of the previous night. 'That dog goes. I'm getting the vet tomorrow. I don't care what you say. He's not safe. She'll end up badly injured and we'll be liable. And who's going to board dogs with us when that hits the headlines?'

It was not a good start to a festive evening.

Liese did not feel like going with them. She wanted to curl up with her misery. Shadow, she suddenly realised, had been her lifeline. It would be a major achievement to cure him of his aggressiveness, and she was sure that she could do it. He was already showing signs, at least to her, that he had a far nicer nature than anyone suspected. Most of his noisiness and unpleasantness were due to fear, and once he learned to trust his whole personality would change.

She smoothed cream on to her scratches which were

unsightly and smarting. Helmet, considerably subdued, lay in his box, watching her with wary eyes, as if afraid she might pounce on him and subject him to some further form of torture.

It would take some time for him to learn to trust her again, and the situation with Kaos was now worse: she was sure that if the two met there would be major fights and both would be injured.

Sue, surprisingly excited by the prospect of an evening out and a splendid meal, both rare events in her life, had, to Roger's annoyance, already set out on her moped, instead of waiting for a lift from him. He did not consider her outfit suitable for riding. She had added to the glory of the red dress by painting her nails and lips purple, and using far too much mascara and eye shadow.

Liese wondered whether to suggest toning down what Gregory called the war paint, but decided against it.

'It's a wonder she hasn't painted stripes on her face,' Spike said, catching a glimpse of Sue in her finery. They all had a change of clothes with them, though their attire was far more sober than Sue's.

'She'll end in hospital,' Roger said when he discovered Sue had taken her moped. 'That idiotic dress is far too tight. It's chilly now, and she'll be frozen. I don't suppose she had the sense to take it and change when she reached the pub?'

'She did put a jacket over it,' Liese said, with vivid memories of the astounding colour clash. She doubted if the flimsy garment would keep out the wind. There was a stiff breeze tumbling the leaves on the tree branches. The dogs were restless, the cats frisky, and the lambs in the fields beyond the kennels had been skittish and noisy all through the afternoon. Even the solemn cattle on the other side of Liese's yard seemed affected by the weather, and were livelier than usual.

The three men were not in a good mood either, as they

had had to do all the kennel work alone while Roger rescued Helmet. Shadow, disturbed by all the bustle and the men's frequent irritated shouts to one another, added his furious barks.

Don, nursing an incipient headache, lost his temper and decided that he would act without consulting Roger again. He rang the vet and argued with him. Tony hated destroying a healthy animal. Shadow must be put to sleep next morning early, before anyone was about. He was determined that the dog should go. All the same, in spite of his conviction he felt guilty and knew there would be trouble to come.

The evening was salvaged by Sally, the wife of the landlord of the Fox and Grapes, who was renowned for her cooking. Their two dogs, a Labrador named Jade and a Springer Spaniel called Finn, were regular visitors to the kennels, and Roger was one of her favourite people, though a very rare customer.

They were to eat in a room that was part of the landlord's own accommodation, and then adjourn to the bar afterwards. Around the lavish flower centrepiece were tiny china figures of dogs, one at each setting. An iced birthday cake held only one candle, but sported a large 60 and a Happy Birthday message. On it four tiny china pups and six china kittens played among the letters.

The beautifully wrapped parcel which Sally presented to Roger contained a large model of a Golden Retriever.

'I knew you coveted that,' she said.

All the other parcels also contained dog models. Don's offering, of a pointer busily scratching his ear, was made of bronze. Tony the vet, unhappy at the thought of his morning errand, arrived late after an unusually busy and trying surgery. He produced a china collie nursing a litter of pups. Sally arranged the offerings on top of the piano.

Liese wished she had been warned. The book token that Spike had bought on her behalf seemed inappropriate. Did Roger ever have time to read? She handed him the envelope with misgivings.

'Great,' he said when he opened it. 'I can frivol and buy the latest detective story without feeling guilty.' He grinned at Liese. 'I only buy technical books as I can set those off against tax.'

Jade and Finn, escaping from the private sitting-room, raced to greet old friends, tails wagging as they hurled themselves at the men. Finn whimpered with delight, pushing himself against Roger, demanding petting. The Labrador, older and more sedate, went from one man to the other, telling them that she remembered them all.

'Come on, dogs. Out. One day I'll go to training class and amaze you all with my well-behaved dogs.' Ted, the landlord, laughed as he caught their collars and pushed them into the next room, shutting the door on them. Low moaning whines continued for some minutes.

Ted was a big man, topping both Roger and Don who were both over six feet tall. He had little trouble with awkward customers. He sat next to Roger, having taken on bar staff that night so that he and his wife could share the celebration.

'I made you a feast, so enjoy it,' Sally said, bringing in a large tureen and serving out the soup. Even the plates had dogs' heads on them.

The place beside Liese was empty. She had looked forward to seeing Bill. Maybe Sue had misheard and he had not been invited, she thought, but he arrived, out of breath, just as Ted began to carve the large joint of pork.

He handed over a little box that contained a cartoon-like dog with a nodding head.

'Sorry, folks,' he said, taking the plate of soup that Ted handed him. 'I had just started out when I came across an old man in his dressing-gown wandering along. He thought he was going to meet his son and go to Chelsea football ground to watch the match.'

He laughed.

'The poor old boy's a hazard on our patch, but luckily we hadn't far to go. Had to report it, though, and write up a hundred copies in triplicate before I left work.'

'You're lucky,' said Don who had decided to bury his ill-humour, revealing briefly a flash of his former self. 'I always have two hundred to do. The dog has to do seven. All this modern bureaucracy: consult with everybody from the Prime Minister down and keep them all informed.'

Everyone laughed.

'Why does the dog do seven?' Evan asked.

'He has to inform the other dogs on the team, doesn't he?' said Don.

'And I thought I was hard done-by,' Tony said. 'The ministry only want thirty-seven copies of everything.'

'George Spencer was in the bar last night,' Ted said, 'complaining he has to fill in bits of paper for every sheep, cow, chicken, duck and horse on his farm.'

'It won't be pollution that sees us off this planet,' said Roger. 'We'll all disappear under a sea of official reports.'

Liese, listening, thought that the conversation, though silly and light-hearted, was perhaps a little too near the truth.

'Don't look so serious, Scrag,' Bill said, noticing her expression. 'We're just relaxing and moaning in our own way. The paperwork gets us all down, and we spend too much time doing it, instead of doing our proper jobs.'

All the same, Liese changed the subject and asked what kind of soup Sally had made. She had never tasted anything like it.

'Nettles. The woman makes food you'd kill for,' Spike told her, with memories of the fish and chips or chicken in a basket produced as gourmet meals at other pubs.

By the time they had eaten everyone was in a better mood, and soon laughter was ringing out as Spike gave a vivid description of a stint on a farm where he had helped dip the sheep. He had landed in the trough, bowled over by an irate ram who disliked the procedure.

'No wonder you're a bit potty,' Gregory said. 'Sheep dip does strange things to people.'

'I was ten,' Spike said. 'They didn't know so much then. I survived, though I was scared stiff, I can tell you. I was sure the sheep already there would drown me.'

'Talking of troughs,' Bill said, turning to Liese, 'why did your aunt take a bath in one?'

Liese's description of the scene she had found at Frankie's home provoked more laughter, and it was a very happy group that left the dining-room to sit in the bar. Sue was bubbling over with high spirits, sure that everyone was impressed with her appearance and her new dress.

Liese was glad that the girl hadn't seen the amused looks the men exchanged when she first appeared. Three huge hooped earrings in each ear clattered when she moved her head.

Ted put three small tables together and Sally brought coffee. Someone put on a tape. The sound made conversation difficult. Sue sat with tapping feet.

'The Lennard dog is coming in tomorrow,' Roger said. There were groans.

'I wonder what they'll find to complain about this time.' Spike made a face. 'What was it last time? He behaved so oddly when they got him home that she knew he'd been lonely and nobody had taken him to bed with them, as she'd asked.'

'At least he's never done what Finn did and got his head caught in the gap between the kennel door and the wall. I still can't make out how he did it.' Spike looked at Sally, who laughed. 'Or was I supposed to keep that quiet?' he added.

'The firemen told me. They had to remove the hinges. You can't keep secrets here,' she said. 'It would be Finn. When he was a puppy he jumped on to the back of a chair while chasing the cat and then on to the mantelpiece where he marooned himself.'

'And then he panicked,' Ted said as he sliced the cake. 'Yelled the place down as he was too scared to go back the way he had come. I've never seen a puppy on a mantelpiece before. I think he and I were both terrified he'd fall before I reached him.'

Liese's head was beginning to ache in the stuffy atmosphere. She longed for the evening to end, for fresh air, and for her own bed.

Bill was telling an idiotic story about a call-out to investigate a man who had been seen behaving very oddly. In the end they decided that they were looking for a ghost.

'Did you find it?' Spike asked. 'Was it wearing chains and groaning and carrying its head under its arm?'

'You're all idiots,' Sue said. 'There's no such thing as ghosts.'

She began to sing with the tape. Evan scowled at her, as she was out of tune and he was gifted with a wonderful voice and adored classical music. He sang in the local choir. He wished he were at home with his wife and baby, but the party was important to Roger who thought it a treat for his staff.

'Pass the cake round,' Roger said now. 'There's enough for everyone in the room. Share the celebrations. It's not every day you're sixty. Can't say I welcome it, nor the advertisement,' he added, nodding to the poster that Ted had made to announce the fact, flanked by four red balloons. 'Wonder who started this silly craze?'

He was interrupted as he picked up his own slice of cake and Bill signalled.

Everyone joined in singing 'Happy birthday to you'. Liese, listening, thought how long it was since she had been to a birthday party. She suddenly felt that she had spent ten years in hibernation, or maybe in purdah, out of contact with reality.

The music on the tape changed, setting Sue's foot tapping even harder. Liese longed to go home, to crawl into bed and sleep for a week. The pain in her temples was now an insistent throbbing. Somehow, the stress of the recent weeks had caught up with her. She wished someone would turn the sound off, but it continued relentlessly.

'Let's dance,' Sue said, jumping up suddenly and looking at the men. The evening, as far as she was concerned, had turned into a right drag and she wanted to liven it up. It was a party, for goodness sake. She intended to enjoy it.

Nobody moved. Bill was watching Liese, worried by the small frown and the paleness of her face.

'All right?' he asked her.

She nodded, making an effort to smile. Don had sunk back into moroseness. This time last year, his wife had been alive. Sally brought a message to the vet, who made a hasty farewell and went off to help a cow with a difficult calving.

Sue was impatient.

'Oh, come on. Don't be spoilsports. Spike?'

'Sorry. Never could dance. Got two left feet.'

Gregory and Evan began a game of darts. Roger grinned.

'I'm too old. Got a bone in my leg.' He went across to the bar to join Ted. Bill followed and bought Liese a small glass of brandy, insisting she drank it.

'Medicinal,' he said.

Sue eyed him for a moment and then thought better of the impulse. He was Liese's bloke. She looked around. The room was almost empty. An elderly couple sat at a table near the door, talking in low voices. A solitary man was at the other end of the room, staring broodingly into his Scotch. He had eaten too that night, at a table in the bar. No one had ever seen him before.

'I bet he's a sales rep,' Sue said. 'Maybe he'll dance. I'll ask. I'll take him a piece of birthday cake.'

'I wouldn't,' Liese said. Something about the man disturbed her.

'Not wise,' Evan added.

'You're all as stuffy as Mag. I want to dance.'

She waltzed across to the stranger who lifted his head and looked at her out of deep-set brooding dark eyes that dominated a saturnine face. He reminded Liese of the paintings of ascetics in mediaeval pictures. His almost black hair was bisected by a central streak of pure white. Dark eyebrows flared outwards and upwards.

It was an arresting face that would inspire both painters and sculptors. As the thought struck her she looked straight into the dark eyes and was filled with unease. He turned his head away as Sue spoke.

'Will you dance?' she asked. 'My lot are too stuffy.' She was tapping one foot as she spoke, unable to stand still. She pirouetted. 'My boss wants you to share his birthday cake.'

He looked at her and smiled. So might the tiger have smiled before it ate the lamb, Liese thought, and was startled by her own imagination.

'No cake, thanks. Dance? Why not?'

There was a small space always kept clear for those who did wish to dance. He bowed to Sue. Everyone in the room was silent, watching, as he stood up and took her in his arms. The rhythm changed, becoming faster so that their feet flew. The music drowned all other sound, rising to a flood of staccato beats.

The red dress was brilliant against black trousers and a black roll-necked sweater. Black hair and black eyes. They swirled together. Red. Black. Red. Black. Sue's hair was a pale gold drift against his shoulder. It had been piled on top of her head, but now flew out as she spun. The watchers were mesmerised, unable to look away.

The music paused, and Sue kicked off her shoes. Then the beat began again, speeding until the two were a spinning top, whirling faster and faster as the music rose to a crescendo. The red dress was a blur. The two pairs of feet moved swiftly, and then, so suddenly that it was a shock, there was silence.

The man swung Sue into a chair and looked down at her. She reminded Liese of a rabbit she had once seen caught in her car's headlights. He turned to them, a triumphant expression on his face. He towered above every other man in the room. His presence dominated them.

'I wouldn't like to meet him alone on a dark night,' Bill said softly in Liese's ear. She shivered, suddenly cold. The room, though bright, held areas of darkness in which the shadows moved as if possessed by living beings.

She let go of his hand, embarrassed. She had not realised she was clutching it, holding on to it as if it were her only sanity.

'I'm sorry,' she said. 'I can't think . . .'

'Be my guest.' Bill would have liked to say that she could hold it for ever, but they had not yet resumed their old easy friendship. She still treated him as if he were someone she had only recently met, although she did confide in him to some extent as he was involved with the investigation into Edward's affairs, even though peripherally. So far he had found nothing to disprove the claim that the boy was Edward's son. But nothing to prove it, either.

'I know how you felt,' he said, knowing Liese wished she had not held his hand. He was aware that she intended to keep her distance from him. 'I don't like that fellow either.'

The man had brought Sue a drink from the bar and sat down opposite her.

'Do you dance for a living?' she asked, when she had regained her breath. 'I've never danced with anyone like you.'

'Nor ever will again. I dance, but that is not my profession. Those who dance with me never forget me.'

'What do you do?' Sue had drunk enough to make her unwise.

The narrow lips smiled again, but there was no mirth in the cold eyes. Liese looked away, suddenly wishing to be invisible.

'I'm a warlock.'

His voice rang out in the silent room. Ted paused in the middle of polishing a glass. Gregory, about to throw a dart, swivelled to stare at him. Don looked up sharply, hard-eyed, and Bill drew in his breath. Roger stood with his glass halfway to his lips and Evan crossed himself. Spike choked on his drink and Sally, recovering after dropping a glass, thumped him on the back.

'What's a warlock?' Sue asked.

'A male witch.'

Sue laughed.

'You're having me on. There aren't any witches. They're just old women in stories for kids.'

'So you don't believe me?' He glared at her. 'Nobody laughs at me. Ever.'

Sue, though she was half afraid of the man, couldn't resist replying.

'Sue,' Liese said, a warning in her voice.

'Of course I don't believe you.'

He leaned over her and very gently stroked her forehead with one finger. Up from the tip of her nose to the root of her hair and then across.

'You will believe,' he said. His voice rang out, growing in authority. 'You will believe in a Power greater than you have ever known. You will believe that lightning can strike from a clear sky. You will believe in ghosts and demons and devils and all the sins of mankind. You will believe in curses that condemn men and women to crawl in misery for all of their lives.'

162

There was a smile on his lips as he surveyed the silent room.

'You will fall into the pit of Hell and remember it for ever. You will never forget this night. None of you.'

Nobody moved. Nobody spoke. The fervent voice continued. He was a priest preaching to an unbelieving congregation, a man trying to convert them to his ways.

'Before tomorrow dawns, you will all believe. None of you will walk easily again. The earth beneath you will quake and shiver and open to reveal a world you never imagined in your worst nightmares. A world where no one is safe and nothing is sacred, and where my Power reigns supreme.'

He looked at Sue.

'Tonight will change your life. Remember, no one can beat me. I am invincible.'

They watched him walk out of the room. Liese drew a deep breath as the shadows vanished and the room resumed its normal appearance. Ted's beloved horse brasses glittered, polished till they reflected the light.

The elderly couple, looking bewildered, left. Sally parcelled up the presents and put them into a wicker basket for Roger to take home.

Only Sue, who had been drinking steadily all evening, seemed unconcerned.

She giggled.

'What a weirdo. I thought he'd vanish in a puff of smoke.'

Suddenly the whole episode seemed absurd. The room was too warm. Liese removed her jacket. How could she have felt so cold?

'Time to get back.' Roger had asked Mrs Hodge to sit in at the kennels, as he never left the dogs on their own. She was always glad of extra money. He wanted to relieve her, and there were still jobs to be done.

The three men departed, to save him some of the

last-minute chores and check all their charges. The place was full. Three dogs needed medication before they were shut in for the night, and an Australian terrier with diabetes needed his insulin.

Bill hesitated at the door, and then returned to Liese. He handed her a tiny gift-wrapped parcel.

'I've been carrying this for days,' he said. 'I haven't known whether to give it to you or not. I hope it might help . . . to know . . .' He seemed to have run out of words, and stood back as Don pushed past them, wanting to get home. He felt even more at odds with himself than usual and the last episode had upset him. The evening had been spoiled for all of them.

Liese took the little gift and tucked it into her handbag. Roger and Sue were arguing. Roger wanted to put the moped in the back of his Discovery, Sue wanted to ride. She gave in sulkily, but went to the ladies' room, while Roger settled the bill. They heard her engine as she roared off.

'Damn the girl,' he said furiously. 'She'll kill herself.'

'I'll follow her.'

Bill ran out to his car and a moment later accelerated out of the little car park, not at all sure what he could do. He had not realised that Sue had come on her moped. Everyone else had been very careful to keep well within the drink-drive limits.

'It's only a mile home. She can't come to grief in that distance,' Roger said. Then, just before reaching a sharp bend, he braked as he saw Bill's car, parked halfway across the road.

Bill himself was farther on, talking on his mobile phone. He finished and shone his torch on the moped, which was smashed against a tree right on the bend. Sue lay beside it, in the road, and Liese ran to her. Roger took off his coat and covered her. She opened her eyes and looked up at him.

'Sorry,' she whispered. 'Should have listened . . . he did it. Cursed us . . . said life would change . . .'

'Multiple injuries,' Bill said. 'Can't shift her. Liese, stay with her and I'll stop traffic on this side. Roger, you take the other. Police and ambulance will be here soon.'

Roger parked the Discovery across the road behind Bill's car. Luckily no one came down the lane except for a local farmer who produced a rug from his car and added it to Roger's coat. Liese was shivering. Clouds hid the stars and the moon had vanished.

Sue's fair hair was matted with blood. The make-up was grotesque, standing out starkly against her white face.

What kind of injuries? Was Sue dying? The man's voice echoed in her ears: 'Tonight will change your life.' Would she be crippled? Liese could not imagine all that energy and joy destroyed.

Her helmet had protected her head, but Bill was sure that both legs were broken and there might be internal injuries. The girl seemed to be drifting in and out of consciousness.

The ambulance siren was a welcome sound and even more welcome were the professionals who took charge. Sue woke briefly and looked at Liese.

'Don't . . . leave . . . me . . . please . . .'

'May I come with her?'

'Sure. You a friend?'

'We work together and she lives next door to me.'

'I'll follow and bring you back,' Roger said.

'I'll talk to the police,' Bill said as a patrol car arrived on the scene and a uniformed man climbed out. 'You didn't see anything . . . I did. I'll go and tell the lads and help at the kennels, and make sure someone tells Sue's folk.'

Liese felt as if life had become unreal. Sue had slipped into unconsciousness again and the men were working on her. She dared not speak lest she break their concentration. She prayed to a childhood God who she hoped existed and shivered again, remembering the cold eyes and the sombre voice prophesying all that was evil in the world.

They sped through the night, the siren sounding, and arrived at the hospital, where Liese felt as if she had slipped into a television series. She was able to tell the receptionist Sue's name and the kennels address, but she had no idea of her home address, or her religion.

Roger, arriving, to her relief, a few minutes later, could not remember Sue's parents' address either.

'Her father's here, in the stroke unit,' Liese said, remembering suddenly.

'That's a different hospital.'

The receptionist sighed. It had been a busy night.

The nurse who came to speak to them told them Sue had internal bleeding and would be going at once for surgery. There was nothing they could do. Roger brought two cups of coffee from the machine, sugared both heavily and sat with Liese in the waiting-room to drink them.

'Do you believe in curses?' Liese asked.

'I believe in foregone conclusions. Sue had too much to drink and lost control on the way home. Bill said she went as if she were racing at Monaco. I ought to have made sure she didn't leave the pub. I never thought she'd go out the back way.'

'I should have gone with her.'

'It's easy to be wise afterwards.' Roger stood up. 'You need sleep. There's nothing we can do now except pray for her. She's in good hands. They'll do all they can.'

By the time they reached the Discovery the rain was sheeting from leaden clouds and lightning lanced the horizon. Thunder rolled, drowning the engine noise, and sheets of colour dazzled the sky.

A stretcher was being unloaded from an ambulance. A taxi drove away in front of them, and two women came out of the entrance and stood by the car parked beside them, both crying.

Liese felt bleak as Roger drove out into the main road. 'You will fall into the pit of Hell' . . . had the man really said that? She listened to the din, wishing they were safely home. Twice they had to stop as hailstones covered the windscreen and beat against the metal. All the demons of Hell were abroad.

'All we need,' Roger said after one particularly loud crash. 'I wonder if any of the men have stayed at the kennels. Mrs Hodge would have gone home as soon as they arrived. Some of the dogs are terrified of thunder. God knows what shape this lot will be in when it's time to go home. Would insurance cover them from being frightened out of their wits? I've never known a storm like this.'

A fireball danced across a distant field and shattered a tree with a deafening crack. Liese prayed that lightning would not hit them. She closed her eyes as yet another flash split the sky. She was beginning to believe in curses and witchcraft.

They stopped for petrol at an all-night garage.

Roger filled up and went into the kiosk to pay. He came out with a packet of cigarettes. He lit one and handed the pack to Liese.

'I didn't know you smoked.'

'I don't,' he said.

After a moment's thought she took one herself, but after two puffs decided it offered no comfort and stubbed it out in the ashtray. She watched the windscreen wipers racing. Thunder echoed and re-echoed above her and forked lightning flamed.

Suppose the kennels were struck? The thought of fire and all those dogs made her feel sick. Was Helmet scared of thunder? She had a vision of the little cat crouched and terrified, in a dark corner, or worse, taking refuge in the chimney again. She would have to block it.

They turned into the long lane that led to home. The rain was easing and the thunder was dying away, a mutter in the distance. The headlights picked up Sue's shattered moped, lying on the grass verge. Roger loaded it into the back of his vehicle in silence. Liese could not bear to look at it.

Spike met them.

'I rang home. Mrs Cox said she'd stay with Ma tonight. I can doss down in Sue's pad. She won't mind. How is she?'

'Bad,' Roger said, taking the little Highland White that Spike was carrying. 'This the only one that was scared? What the hell's that noise?' he asked, suddenly becoming aware of the pounding beat of rock music.

'I put the portable radio in the kennel block; thought the noise might drown the storm.'

Liese left them and was thankful when the sound ceased. The storm was circling and a sudden flash and crash was succeeded by sheeting rain. She ducked her head and ran across the yard. As she did so, all the lights went out.

There was a torch in the office. She fetched it and, passing Shadow's kennel, saw the dog crouching in the rain. The light caught his eyes.

'Shadow. You poor fellow.' He was soaked and shivering. As another peal of thunder echoed, he ran at the wire, whimpering. She raced back to the office, where a spare collar and lead always hung on a hook.

Shadow had spent hours in terror. He had never known a storm before and the lights that flashed time and again blinded him, so that he lay with his eyes hidden by his paws. The shelter of the hut seemed to add to the noise as rain drummed on the roof. The hailstones flailed him. The thunder rolls were those of a giant animal venting its displeasure. He was beyond all protest.

Don had said that he was to die in the morning. Liese

was suddenly filled with anger. The dog trusted her and she was betraying him. She leashed him and led him out of his run. He was thankful for company and to be taken away from a place that had become associated with events more frightening than any he had ever known. As lightning flared again they reached the steps to Liese's rooms and the dog pulled her up them, desperate to reach sanctuary.

Roger would be angry and Don would probably see that she was sacked at once, but she didn't care. Shadow was only too thankful to reach a warm room out of the rain. She piled logs on the Rayburn and fetched a towel to rub him dry, using the torch to give her light.

The house brought back memories to the dog. Memories of a rug by a small girl's bed; memories of warmth and comfort; memories of little hands stroking him. When he was as dry as Liese could get him, she flopped into the big chair. He lay against her legs, desperate for contact.

She slept for about an hour and then woke as the lights came on outside. Helmet was curled up against the big dog, who lay exhausted, but watched her anxiously as she moved. Was he going to be returned to his cold outside place again?

Liese did not feel like going to bed. She changed into her daytime clothes and made herself a cup of coffee, Shadow living up to his name and following her everywhere. She remembered Bill's little parcel and, curious, took it out and undid the wrapping.

There was a letter inside and a small box, wrapped in silver paper covered with minute blue flowers. Two tiny pressed flowers held the ribbon wrapped around it. It was a very pretty little object. She read the letter and was reduced almost to tears.

Hi, Scrag.
    You know I'm not a man for words, but I can't

sleep and I want to talk to you. Tell you I'm here. You look at me as if you never knew me. I used to dream about you; and then you married that scheming bastard, who only wanted your money. We all knew that . . . I couldn't believe it when I saw you in the kitchen again at Bryn Mawr . . . a ghost of the Scrag I knew.

Do you remember winning the poetry reciting competition at school? Why did you choose 'Cynara', I wonder? That has haunted me . . . 'I was desolate and sick of an old passion, I have been faithful to thee, Cynara! in my fashion.' And you behave as if I were just another person in your life, of no real importance; maybe the brother you used to think me.

You told me that the day I tried to kiss you. I can still feel the slap on my face. Worse, I can still feel the hurt of rejection. I even wrote a poem . . . well, sort of. Please don't laugh:

The world became bright when again I found you
I dream of you with flowers around you.
I wish I could with love surround you
And keep you free from fear.
There's not a lot I can do for you.

I saw the little box in a tourist trap and fell for it. I hope you'll keep it and value it . . . and maybe one day, when everything is sorted in your life, you'll stop thinking of me as a brother . . . I'm not. I'm the bloke next door. I've tried to replace you and never managed it.

I've been carrying this for weeks and never had the courage to give it to you. I hope you won't decide never to see me again.

The box had a tiny decorative card pasted on it on which was a rhyme.

This is a very special gift that you can never see.
The reason it's so special is it's just to you from me.
Whenever you are lonely or ever feeling blue
You only have to hold my gift and know I think of you.
You never can unwrap it. Please leave the ribbon tied.
Just hold the box close to your heart. It's filled with
    love inside.

She went back to the letter.

> OK, Scrag. It's corny . . . probably pretty awful, but
> flowers die and I can't equal the jewellery that you
> must have owned . . . Edward liked to dress up his
> prizes. He left you a lousy legacy. I don't have much
> to offer . . . but you can trust me. I'm here anyway.
> I wish . . . oh, what's the use?
> The box says it for me.
>
> Bill

She stared at the little box and then took it and the
letter into her bedroom. She had a tiny casket on the
dressing-table that had belonged to her mother. It contained her mother's engagement and wedding rings and
a few brooches, as well as the coral necklace that she had
worn the night before.

Her only treasures now. She held the box for a moment
against her face. She was still too numb to think of Bill
in any other way. Besides, suppose she was never free of
debt? Why did everything take so long to settle?

It was good to know that somebody cared, other than
Frankie. She had been so lonely, all those years.

Shadow was watching her, his head on one side. There
were more urgent matters to consider. Right now she had
to think of him. She had Don to face. He was not going
to put the dog down.

Even if she prevailed, it would mean the end of her job. Don would never agree to her staying on. Maybe Roger or Evan would drive her to Frankie's, and she could stay there with the German Shepherd. She was going to need all her courage. She knelt down and put her arms around the dog and he leaned against her, revelling in her presence. He, too, had been lonely.

She glanced at the clock. It was already seven. She heard the vet's car drive into the yard. Don's bellow of rage brought Roger running. Together the three men stared at the empty kennel.

Ten

Don's yell triggered Shadow. He exploded, racing to the window, looking out with his paws on the sill, barking. Helmet, who had never been so close to such a din before, leaped to the top of the refrigerator where he sat, eyes wide, trying to get as far away from the dog as possible.

Liese stared at the dog, wondering if she was about to find out how much disaster she had courted. Would he respond to her at all when he was infuriated by something that was going on outside? Worse, was Don right and was she crazy to imagine she could even begin to cope with Shadow?

If she touched him, or tried to stop him verbally, would he turn on her? Her night in the chair had done no good at all. She was stiff and aching, and remembering the events of the night before, felt frightened. She had a conviction that Sue had died of her injuries. Roger had left the smashed bike in the yard outside. It was a mute reminder. Perhaps Gregory would put it in one of the sheds, out of sight. She couldn't bear to look at it.

Her scratched hands hurt. She lifted Helmet from his sanctuary, intending to put him in the bedroom, but he had not forgiven her and scratched again, upset by the dog she had introduced into her household. Now she had a disturbed cat to add to her worries. Worse, he too would have to come to Frankie's if Roger sacked her. She did not intend to part with him.

It was cold, after a late frost. The Rayburn had gone out and it was a pig to start again. It was not going to be a good day. She shut Helmet in the bedroom. The angry voice had stopped. Shadow quieted and came to her to look up with anxious eyes, as if pleading with her to keep him there and not return him to his uncomfortable and lonely quarters.

He needed to go outside, but it was early and maybe he could wait. She dared not take him now. She knew the cause of the uproar. She was not yet ready to face the three men, although she knew they would be searching for the dog. They were would-be murderers and could wait.

She had no food for him.

She took a half-loaf from the bin and gave it to him. He settled to devour it, looking at her as if surprised by her offering, but eager to eat it. He held it between his paws and then looked at her again, as if telling her this was the most wonderful food he had tasted in all his life. She felt a small lift in spirits. When he was with her he was the most endearing animal. If only he would learn to trust other people.

She had to go out and confess. She dragged a comb through her hair and wiped a tissue with cleansing cream over her face as she had not removed her make-up the night before. The rouge stood out like an angry patch on each cheek. Exhausted eyes stared back at her from the mirror. No time for a shower now. She snatched a padded anorak, zipping it as she ran down the steps, slipping halfway, as they were icy. She grabbed the rail and stood still, her heart thumping. All they needed was another person with a broken leg.

She hesitated at the corner of the kennel yard. Don and Roger had been searching and met again by the empty kennel. Neither man had slept well and tempers were fraying. Tony stood waiting, annoyed because he had wasted his time. He had not finished with the calving until just after three. He had arrived home tired and irritable an hour later and, since he had to be up at five, had not gone to bed at all.

Don, turning his head, saw Liese. He had not wanted her around. The dog was to be dead and removed before she was up.

She was aware of the atmosphere before she spoke. Roger had been amazed to find Tony there and was convinced Don had discovered that one of the boarders was ill. When he heard the reason for the vet's presence he exploded.

'How dare you decide without consulting me. This is my business, remember, until you retire and become a full partner. Since when did I abdicate?'

Liese had never seen Roger lose his temper, and did not know that he could. He was one of the most placid men she had ever met. Unlike Don, he never shouted, but the quiet voice left no one in doubt of its owner's fury.

'Where is the dog? Nobody would steal him. Did he undo the bolt and open the gate by himself?'

Liese summoned all her courage, and walked forward to face them.

'He's in my cottage. He was soaked and cold and terrified by the storm and I couldn't possibly leave him there. And nobody's putting him to sleep. He isn't a vicious dog . . . he's miserable and terrified and you never give him a chance.'

The knowledge that she would soon be leaving emboldened her.

'You never give anyone a chance.'

Don stared at her, looking as if he could not believe what he had heard.

'I told you she was insane. You wouldn't believe me. Suppose the brute had killed her?'

Liese was suddenly so angry that she could have choked the man.

'If you want to criticise me, do so to me. I exist. I'm adult. I'm not deaf, and I'm far from insane. The dog's terrified of you. He came here, torn from everything he had known, was put by himself in an outside kennel when he's obviously been house-kept. You dressed up like a space man, grabbed him by the throat with a noose, dragged him out of the kennel and fought with him while it was cleaned up. You did that for a couple of weeks. And you expect him to like you?'

The three men looked at her in amazement. None of them had thought her capable of so much passion.

'He doesn't trust you . . . any of you. Tony sticks needles in him. Nobody takes much notice of him, except to yell at him to shut up, which only makes him worse. He's miserable and lonely and scared and you expect him to greet you like a pet dog that everyone loves. You're the ones who are out of your minds.'

The spurt of anger died. I'd better go and pack, she thought drearily. But how do I transport Shadow? Maybe Bill would help; if he borrowed a van and she sat in the back with the dog and the cat . . . and came home to Frankie like a beaten dog with her tail between her legs, having failed miserably to hold down her first job.

She fought tears, not wanting to break down in front of the three men. She turned away from them, only to face Evan and Gregory and Spike, who were staring at her in amazement. Evan looked as if he feared that she would spontaneously combust.

She turned to Roger.

'I realise I can't stay. I'll go to Frankie. I'm taking Shadow and Helmet. The cat's mine, and since none of you want the dog I don't see why I shouldn't have him. You can keep my wages to pay for him. I'll buy him, so I'll say what happens. He's no longer your responsibility.'

'You haven't paid for him yet, so he still is our responsibility. Roger may not accept that but someone has to be realistic around here. Tony can put him down in your house as easily as in the kennels. I say he's unreliable, and likely to do someone a major injury. You have no experience at all. He's not safe. You've had the devil's own luck, but it won't last.'

The hectoring voice had taken her back to Edward, who had always won. She had never been able to stand up to him for long. Don too thought her stupid and useless and maybe he was right. She hadn't thought her actions through. Her idea was crazy. Bill would be on duty; nobody here would dare transport her; they all needed their jobs. She could never travel with the dog on public transport.

'Just hold on.' Tony was also angry. Liese was obviously unharmed, so the dog was by no means as dangerous as they had imagined, and what she said made sense. It was the first he had heard of the episodes with the protective clothing and the dog catcher. 'I'm not destroying him. I had no idea that Roger didn't know I was coming. I'll be sending you a bill for wasting my time.'

He strode towards the gate, but then paused and turned to Liese.

'Don't give up on him. With that amount of belief you can do something with him. He's less than a year old and he's healthy. I loathe putting a young dog down. If you want to travel with him let me know. I'll give you a sedative for him for the journey.'

Don turned away from them and strode back to his cottage. The slammed door reverberated like a shot. Venn crawled back into his bed, wishing to remain unseen, which was always wiser when his master was angry.

Liese turned to go.

'Liese!' Roger put a hand on her shoulder and spun her round. 'There's no need to leave. Don'll get over it, given time. I have seen you with that dog. I've been too busy . . . not thought hard enough . . .' He turned to the men, 'Time to begin work. Get on with it. You can put my dogs in their runs and the Westie back in her kennel.

The Setter's owners are due at nine-thirty to collect him. Give him a run and a good brushing. I've things to sort out . . . and I want to ring the hospital.'

'Shadow needs his food, and exercise.' Liese had not worked out how to cope with the dog during the day. She knew she now had to think hard to work out a successful management technique for him. 'I don't want him back in the kennel. He's obviously been house-kept. He behaved last night as if he'd suddenly gone to heaven. Helmet slept between his legs, and only flipped when he started barking when Don shouted.'

They turned the corner of the farmhouse into Liese's yard.

'I can exercise him here and in the lane. We hardly ever see anyone in this part of the place. He won't see the other dogs. He needs to get used to people slowly, one at a time. I don't think women are a problem. It's men.'

'I'd like to see how he behaves. But I need somewhere to hide.' Roger did not want a disaster on his hands. He had to be sure that Liese could cope.

'Go into Sue's sitting-room and look through the window from behind the curtains. I'll bring him down. He needs to go out.'

Shadow greeted Liese with delight, leaping at her, putting his paws on her shoulders, whimpering frantically in excitement. Her return signified an end to loneliness. She had comforted him, and during the last few weeks had also brought him his favourite titbits.

She had collected more liver cake from the office before she went in to her own home. It was her passport to success and his reward for good behaviour. From now on it would be a training tool. She had read through Frankie's books on the new methods of training developed since her first efforts with Mac, and had been impressed by the differences and the more relaxed way of dealing with dogs.

178

So much had changed in ten years. Far more was known about dogs' mentality and the way they learned. No more choke collars which she had always hated. Roger stocked half-checks, made of webbing with a small chain linking the two ends, that worked in the same way but far more kindly.

Gentle voices; praise and reward when the dog got it right, and no sort of correction at all if it made a mistake. That was due to confusion and the handler's inability to communicate what was wanted to the dog. As she put the collar on the dog, Liese felt a sudden rush of excitement. He was hers. Maybe she could prove to herself that she had lost none of her old skills, and that she was worthwhile, not a total failure as Edward had always said, and as now Don was beginning to convince her.

She could find time for Shadow before work, during the lunch hour and in the evening. Her duties ended at six. He would be company, and during the long light evenings she could walk him, and enjoy the exercise.

Meanwhile she had to get the dog out. She coaxed him down the steps. He came reluctantly, afraid he was about to be put back in his kennel. She turned fast, not towards the other yard, but towards the lane, and he was suddenly eager. This was different. She checked to make sure that no one was about.

He pulled. That would have to be cured, but he had to learn to trust her first and work with her. There were enticing scents on the grass. He had known nothing but concrete for weeks, and he savoured the ground, his nose pressed down, his expression blissful.

When she was sure he was comfortable she turned to walk him home. At the entrance to the yard he dived towards the steps, anxious to get up them before she could take him back to his old quarters. Liese was afraid he would pull her over. She dropped the lead when he was two steps up and watched him leap in front of her, turning at the door to wait for her to open it.

There was a bag of dried dog food on the steps, which Evan had put there while she was out, taking great care not to be seen. Once he was inside, Shadow bounded round the room, then stood at the closed bedroom door, looking at her.

She suddenly realised he was waiting for the cat. Helmet, released, raced happily up to the dog and greeted him, nose to nose, Shadow bending his big head. They licked one another. It was time for food and the little cat led the way into the kitchen.

She had forgotten a dog bowl. She put the food in the washing-up bowl and watched the dog wolf it. Helmet, making sure he would not be interrupted, started on his own ridiculously small meal.

After a minute Liese decided they were safe together. Shadow seemed to have no intention whatever of harming the cat. In any case, he could jump high out of harm's way and there were plenty of refuges for him around the room. She locked the door behind her, lest Shadow could open the latch. Roger was standing at the foot of the steps.

'Well?' she asked.

'I wouldn't have believed it.'

She had forgotten to make herself breakfast. Spike had plugged in the percolator. Roger poured out two cups for them and she raided the cake tin, suddenly hungry. There was a note on the desk.

'Rang the hospital. Sue is very poorly and has been unconscious since the operation. They don't know how she'll progress or if she'll have permanent damage. Evan.'

She handed it to Roger.

He read it and said nothing, but the sigh he gave told Liese more than words would have done.

'Go into the shop,' he said. 'Find yourself a bed for the dog and two rugs. Grooming tools and collar and lead. A water bowl and another for his food. I paid nothing for him and I'll not charge you that. The things you buy for him and his keep and vet bills are now down to you. You can add up the total and pay me week by week. Ask Evan for a big bag of food for him. I'll donate that, with my best wishes.'

He walked over to the window and looked out at the yard. Gregory was passing with a Samoyed that was more interested in the smells on the ground than in walking properly. Put in the paddock he came to life as his handler took a ball out of his pocket and threw it.

Roger inspected the cake tin and selected a currant bun.

'You've saved me a lot of agony. I thought Don would succeed in having him put down. He did that once before, when I was away. He doesn't believe a dog can be cured of difficult habits.'

Liese wondered if Roger would let her borrow the van and drive in to see Sue. The girl's mother would probably have brought her the things she needed. Hopefully her grandmother was as capable as Sue made out and would be able to keep the family together, as there were now two invalids to visit, in different hospitals.

It was difficult to concentrate, but thoughts of Sue had driven out her own worries, which now seemed insignificant compared with the possibility that the girl might either be paralysed for life or brain damaged, or even die; maybe that would be better than either of the other alternatives.

Bill rang during the morning, asking for news.

'I've got a new dog,' she said, before he rang off. 'I've adopted Shadow. Otherwise he would have been put down.'

She hesitated.

'Thank you for your letter. And your gift ... I value them.'

'No problem, Scrag. I just wanted you to know. I know

the scene. Good luck with the dog. I'll expect wonders when I next come over. Take care. I'll be seeing you.'

Evan had wandered in while she was speaking. He helped himself to coffee and cake and flopped into the chair.

'Baby's teething, poor mite,' he said. 'Gums like fire. Screamed for nearly three hours.'

'Poor little soul,' Liese said. 'It must be hard for all of you.'

'I warned Sue,' he said. 'She didn't know what she was meddling with. It isn't over. It's only just beginning. She was the first.'

Liese stared at him in dismay, but he did not explain his remark.

*   *   *

Sue was in a nightmare. She could hear, but not see. She was awake, but no one knew it. She was on her moped, riding through the night, faster and faster, spinning suddenly into nowhere, hitting a wall. She was dancing, faster and faster, so dizzy she could not stand upright. The world was whirling round her.

She was diving down a long tunnel, into darkness; more darkness and then a sudden blinding light and people calling her. She was going away, into another world, another place, where no one could reach her or hurt her any more. Peace. And no more pain.

Pain. There were hands on her, there was a voice speaking to her, calling her back, urgently.

'You don't do it, damn you. I didn't work on you all night to have you escape now. Come back. Come back. Damn you, you stupid girl. Come back.'

The voice was disembodied. She was disembodied, but then she was suddenly trapped and waves of pain engulfed her so that she cried out.

'She's back with us, thank God. I thought we'd lost

her then. I couldn't face telling another family that we'd failed.'

She wondered what the words meant. There was a sudden prick and the world slid away, and the dreams vanished. She slept.

She came back to a half world, drifting in and out of it, not sure if she were awake or dreaming. She remembered laughter, laughter that pealed from the skies, laughter that echoed like thunder, sounding in her ears as the speeding bike betrayed her and she soared into the air. Laughter that mocked and derided, reducing her to nobody. A giant face loomed over her, repeating the words, 'Nobody, ever, laughs at *me*. You will believe.'

Hands that touched her. Liese had been there; or had she dreamed that? Liese, with tears pouring down her cheeks, sitting beside her while they rocked through the night, a siren blaring. She knew, vaguely, that she had been in an ambulance, but it did not make sense.

People drifted in and out of her mind, but she did not know where they belonged. Men . . . and dogs . . . Liese, who lived next door. Next door where? The boys . . . Tone, who was small and naughty and always laughing; and suddenly was grown up and the merriment had gone. Her mother? Where was her mother? She wanted her and cried out for her. She was a little girl again, a little girl lost in some terrible place, all alone.

She went down into the darkness, and then began to surface, as if rising through water. She was dancing, spinning, whirling, faster and faster, faster and faster, until she fell down and down into a pit that yawned, bottomless, beneath her.

She woke and saw a face that was older than time looking down at her, a toothless mouth that grinned insanely, grey hair that lay in spikes on rounded shoulders, and a voice that said, insistently,

'You've taken my dog. What have you done with him?'

183

Sue screamed.

There were running footsteps and a gentle, reproachful voice.

'Emmie. Emmie. How in the world did you get here?'

A nurse. She was in a hospital. Her arms and legs seemed unable to move, but she could see and she could hear. There were white walls and a white cover on the bed. She could see flowers out of the corner of her eye but her head would not turn. It seemed to be held rigid. There were tubes.

Dogs. They were part of her life. Perhaps she owned one, but no single animal came to mind; instead a sequence of many breeds. A face bent over her, but this was young and pretty and framed by a white cap and did not rouse fear.

'Don't mind Emmie,' she said. 'It was a horrid wakening for you, but the poor old thing doesn't know the time of day. She's quite senile.'

'Tammie,' said another voice. 'I don't think she's well enough to understand ... she's been unconscious for three days.'

'Do under ... stand.' It wasn't her own voice; it was a whisper that took enormous effort. It hurt to speak, to think, to try to move. Every inch of her felt tortured with pain.

'What happened? What's wrong with me?' She had forgotten again. The dreams were just dreams.

'You crashed your moped,' the second nurse said. 'Rest now. You'll soon be feeling better.'

The injection sent her back into a sleep that was dreamless and free from pain. She woke with a clearer head, although that still ached. There was a corridor which she could now see in a mirror, and a woman in a white coat was pushing a trolley loaded with cups of tea and plates of cakes.

Someone came in through the door. Sue's mind wavered for a moment, panicking, and then a voice spoke, and she was back again, whole again, the world around her explicable.

'Hi, Mum,' she said, trying to make light of an unbearable situation.

'Oh, lovey, lovey. I thought you'd never wake. I've been here as often as I could. Only I have to see Dad, too. He's much better. Sends his love.'

There were arms around her, comforting her, although it hurt to be held. There were tears on her face that weren't her own. It was too much effort to speak.

Her mother let go of her and sat down in the chair, leaning forward so that Sue could see her. Something was restraining her neck. A man in a white coat came into the room and, when he saw she was awake, smiled at her.

'Welcome back. You've been leading us a merry dance. Good to know we were successful.'

'A brand snatched from burning,' Sue said, in the faraway voice that seemed to come from deep inside her and to be incapable of any strength. She amazed herself as much as her listeners. 'Why can't I move?'

'Mainly because you're in plaster. You managed to break more bones than anyone thought possible. You had quite a spill, young lady. You're very lucky to be alive. You should begin to make progress now. It's nearly a week since you came in.'

A nurse came to recharge the drip.

'Sleep,' she said, after making Sue as comfortable as possible. 'No one will interrupt you for some hours.'

Within minutes she was drowning in darkness that was even more frightening than before. No one could reach her. She was isolated in a strange cold realm, neither in the world nor out of it. She would never be part of it again. She was struggling to cut an immense birthday cake. She put a slice on a plate and carried it over to a man

185

who had come through a huge door that opened into further darkness.

'I control the thunder. I control the world. I control you. You will never be free of me again, never be free from fear. Fear of the curse I have put on you . . . fear . . . fear . . . fear. Believe in me . . . in my powers. Believe.'

She remembered when she woke. Remembered the party and the dancing and the unbelievable words he had spoken. Tonight will change your life. She couldn't move, not even a finger. Was she doomed to live the rest of her life crippled, perhaps in a wheelchair, able only to turn her eyes and perhaps her head?

Time passed. She drifted in and out of sleep and in and out of nightmare. Some of it seemed worse when she was awake. Her mother came every afternoon, for over a week, and then others began to visit. Tony brought his precious Walkman and her favourite cassettes. Gran brought more flowers.

The doctor who visited her most often came in after eight days and sat by her bed.

'Nurse says you have nightmares and wake screaming. Tell me your dreams.'

'I don't remember them when I'm awake,' Sue said, crossing her fingers because it was wicked to lie. She did not want to remember the birthday party. Her dancing partner loomed large in all her dreams, more terrifying than she had found him in life, and she knew he had cursed her and she would never be free of him.

'I think you need my friend, not me,' the doctor said, and left the room, mystifying her.

She knew now that she had broken both legs, one arm and several ribs. Her unbroken arm was bandaged across her chest so that movement did not pull on the ribs. Her helmet had protected her head, though the bang had given her mild concussion. She was wearing a neck collar, to prevent her turning her head.

There was progress, though it seemed so slow. She felt as if she were indeed in limbo, belonging nowhere. The hospital seemed so remote from the real world. One day merged into another and she lost all sense of time. The drip was removed and she had her first cup of tea, hot and sweet, given to her in a feeding cup so that she felt like a baby.

She was drifting in a half sleep when a man she had never seen before came into the room. For a moment she looked at him in terror and he saw the fear in her eyes.

'I've come to help,' he said. 'Trust me. Your doctor tells me your body's healing but that there's a shadow on your mind that's preventing you from getting really well. You don't want to talk about it?'

The mere thought of talking about it brought the panic back. That would make it real. So long as it was only a memory she could pretend that it hadn't really happened. To give it body and substance would give it more power. Common sense told her that the accident was due to her going too fast and having had too much to drink. But common sense did not always triumph.

The man leaned over her, his hands crossed over one another. He held them just above her head. They were warm, they were hot, they were comforting, bringing a feeling of peace and relaxation such as she had never known before. He moved them over her body, not touching her, and wherever he paused, she felt a flow of energy returning.

'Can you tell me now?' he asked, after half an hour's work on her. He sat in the chair beside her, positioning it so that she could see his face. His bright blue eyes seemed to search into her mind, but did not bring fear.

He leaned over her and took both her hands in his and held them.

'Challenge the memory,' he said. 'Bring it out and talk about it and it will wither and go away.'

187

She shivered, sure she could not find words, but suddenly they were spilling out of her as she told him about the birthday party and the man who danced with her.

'I never believed in such things,' she said. 'I don't understand. How can anyone exert such power over other people? I know now he meant what he said.'

'God cast Lucifer out of heaven and with him went some of the angels: fallen angels. Their power only comes when people believe in them and cease to believe in God Himself.'

'Who are you?' Sue asked.

He laughed.

'A messenger, carrying words of faith to those caught in a mesh of evil. My power is greater than theirs because I believe passionately that there are more good people than bad in the world, and that there is a Being somewhere that watches over us. He can't interfere any more than a parent can interfere when a grown-up child is in trouble. We all have to choose our own paths. I believe He watches and suffers all the troubles of the world. As His Son did when He came to earth.'

Religion had not played a major part in Sue's life. She listened, frowning, trying to understand a concept that was alien to her. The soft voice was still speaking.

'Often He allows us to learn a lesson we will never forget. How we react to it depends on us; it may be a disaster. It should be a challenge.'

'I'm scared silly. Will I ever not be frightened? Will the curse last for ever? He did curse me.'

'Trust me. I can help you, but my power is not mine alone. I need the angels behind me. Maybe one day I'll be an angel myself, though a pretty ugly one.'

Sue grinned at his choice of words.

'I'm still cursed. It might affect the others . . . they were all there . . . the people I work with . . . and my family . . .'

'That I don't know. I have intervened for you. Believe

in my power, not his. He's lost his hold over you. You'll never meet him again. He's a wanderer, a mischief-maker. He was passing through and he saw his chance and took it. It's his idea of fun.'

Sue thought of her Gran whose favourite saying was 'It takes all sorts'.

'What is he? Is he a man?' She had a vague vision of some supernatural alien empowered with immortality like the beings in so many television series about space and other worlds.

'He's human, but has no redeeming human traits. Pure evil. The police and the lawyers will tell you that they meet them now and then. Most of us are lucky enough to avoid them all our lives and never know they exist. There is no kindness. No charity. No tolerance. Only a supreme belief in himself and his wants. Luckily you are young. The young are resilient.'

He took two roses from the vase on the bedside-table.

'Look at these. Perfect beauty created from love; from wonder; from awe. No man could have made them. Copies maybe, but not the living growing flowers, the softness of the petals, the supple stem, the delicate fabric of the leaves. They live. They breathe. They draw up water. They open to the sun. No artificial flower can do that. Believe in all that's good and protect yourself.'

'Will I walk again?'

'If you choose. It will take time and courage. No one promised us an easy journey through life. I'll be back tomorrow. I'll come every day while you need me. This evening you'll be hungry and will eat.' He put his hands on her forehead and she felt warmth flood through her. 'Tonight you'll sleep and your dreams will be dreams to cherish. You have many friends; so many people asking after you. Welcome back to life.'

He stood up, exuding an immense confidence that gave Sue hope. She watched him walk through the door; a small man, a dapper man, neatly dressed, with grey hair and grey moustache and those amazing blue eyes. In spite of his sombre clothes there was an aura of light all round him.

The nurse returned to help her eat her meal and then washed her. Sue, who had insisted even as a toddler, that she dress herself and do things for herself, felt irritated by her own helplessness. She might not do well at the kennels, but at home she took responsibility and looked after the others. She had not been so dependent since she was a baby.

She spent the evening listening to her favourite group on the Walkman, and daydreaming that she won the lottery and bought houses for Tone and her parents and wonderful presents for Gran and all the boys.

Next morning there were cards from all her friends, from the kennels, and a tiny parcel which a nurse opened for her. It contained a small box lined with velvet in which lay a silver emblem on a silver chain.

'It's pretty,' the nurse said. 'Would you like to wear it?' She fastened it round Sue's neck, underneath the collar. 'That can come off soon. Shall I read the note to you?'

'Please.' Sue was feeling better. The tubes had gone, and she was able to eat proper food. Although she could not use her arms and legs, she did at least feel human again.

'Dear Sue,' Evan had written. 'My Mam sent you this. It's a silver bullet and will keep you safe against witches as they are terrified of them. Wear it always. My Mam can see the future. She says leave the kennels and start to paint and work with your talent. She saw the picture you drew for us when the baby was born. She reads the stars and cast your horoscope last night. Believe her. Get well. Evan.'

Roger had sent an absurd card picturing a hippopotamus in bandages, lying in a hammock, with a balloon coming out of his mouth saying, 'I didn't ought to have done it.'

Spike had sent a picture of a dog with its paws over its eyes, and a cat in front of it. The caption read, 'What I can't see won't hurt me.'

Gregory had sent a card in which a shepherd and the dog were inside a pen and the sheep were circling them. It was blank inside except for his scrawled words, 'Get well soon. Oddly, we miss you! Never realised it, but you made us laugh.'

Liese's card was floral: brilliant pansies, tied with ribbon, in a posy, attached to a box of Sue's favourite chocolates. So far she had not been allowed any but family visitors. Maybe they would all come and see her. There was no card from Don but she had not expected one.

She was still in a private room but they might move her to a ward soon, they told her. There were treetops outside the window so she had to be high in the building. A small brown bird sat briefly on the sill and stared in at her, as if amazed by humans and their trappings.

She slept and dreamed that she was drawing on a great canvas, putting in the people she knew, with their dogs round them. They seemed to form a pattern: Don and Venn; Roger and his dogs; she painted Liese into the picture with Shadow beside her.

She woke to sunshine streaming in through the window, the leaves casting dappled shadows that swayed and moved as if they were dancing. The dream was vivid in her mind and her sanity was restored. Nothing would ever be the same again but the fear had subsided. Lee and Shad. How daft could you get. As if anyone would ever tame that monster. She was still laughing when the consultant came in with his retinue.

They stared at her in amazement. She was suddenly and vividly alive, giving them a glimpse of her real self before the accident.

'How are you?'

The shadows had gone from her eyes, and though she was in pain, she was no longer haunted. The pills they gave her kept the worst of it at bay.

'Fine,' she said.

Outside the door, the specialist looked at his team.

'The Healer again. Don't ask me how he does it. It's happened over and over, so when all else fails, don't give up. Find Dr McDowd or someone like him . . . it can't do any harm and, as you see, it may do a power of good.'

The younger men looked at one another. McDowd had been retired for some years, but he was a legend still. His methods had often been unorthodox. It was a legend none of them had believed. Now they began to wonder. Sue had changed overnight, and it appeared that miracles still happened.

The specialist's official notes merely said that the patient had begun to recover, although there was still a long way to go.

Eleven

The weeks sped past. Liese was busier than she had been since she came to the kennels. She did much of Sue's work, and Shadow took up a great deal of her spare time. Everyone meant to visit Sue in hospital, but only Evan managed it. The others consoled themselves with the knowledge that, with such a big family, she would not lack company.

'I wish someone would invent a thirty-six-hour day,' Spike said. 'And a three-day weekend with dogs that don't need food and water and exercise.'

Weekends had been easier for them as Liese helped Roger with the feeding and watering. Two of the men came in to exercise. They stored their weekends to take odd days off, or add them to their holidays, when Roger could sometimes get temporary help.

Although they all felt easier once they knew that Sue was recovering, there was more tension in the kennels than before.

Don refused to have anything to do with any of them, and had not spoken to Roger since the morning that Liese had taken Shadow. He had written one note which he left on Roger's desk, saying that he was thinking of dissolving the partnership.

'Can't you manage without him? He doesn't do much around the place,' Liese said, wondering if Roger would not be better on his own.

'Trouble is, if he does go I have to buy the cottage back from him. That was written into our contract. It would be very difficult to find the money at present. It would mean a swingeing great loan, and that's the last thing I want. I had to borrow from the bank to pay for sound-proofing the kennels, as the people who moved in to the old farm down the lane complained about the barking.'

His worries reflected on the men so that everyone was short-tempered, and, to add to their woes, they had in several of the most difficult dogs that had ever been boarded. Roger allowed no one but himself to feed, water and exercise them, adding to his own burdens.

'All six come from the same place,' Liese said. 'What do they do to them?'

'They're all rescues from St Bridie's Centre,' Roger said. 'The owner is a friend of mine, and has had to go into hospital for an operation. The dogs are farmed out to anyone with space. I took those that had been abused. Pete'll be able to take them back in a few weeks' time, but meanwhile, we cope.'

'Do they come in free?' Liese asked, her mind on the huge bills that always needed paying. Money now seemed to dominate her life.

'No. They have an insurance that covers things like that. We won't lose out.'

Each day seemed to make a difference to Shadow. He had never had anyone to care for him in his early weeks, and his spell with his small mistress had been very brief. He slept in his basket beside Liese's bed, and, when the alarm went, he was sitting beside her, nosing her neck, asking for petting.

When she sat down he was beside her, and if her hands were free he pushed against her, making her feel as if he were trying to melt into her, revelling in the close contact he had lacked for so long.

Their first walks were exhausting as he not only pulled, but dashed excitedly from side to side of the lane, eager to savour the smells on the verges. They were well into May and every creature had youngsters who explored busily, leaving tantalising memories behind.

Liese decided it was time to teach him manners. Every time he pulled, she stopped dead, holding on to him with all her strength. He began to learn that they went nowhere unless he was more decorous.

Helmet was happy now to stay in the house since the dog was also there, but there was a problem with the litter tray, which Shadow raided. Evan solved that for her. Liese took the dog into Sue's house and sat there for two hours, reading, while a cat flap was fitted into the bathroom door. It was too small for the dog, but it ensured that the cat had no problems either.

Roger tried two temporary staff, but the first was appalled when she discovered she was expected to clean out kennels, and left without starting work. The second thought she was going to a boarding house for human occupants and not a boarding kennels, and she too left immediately. He gave up.

Four weeks after the birthday party, Liese, emboldened by Shadow's behaviour with her, took him into the kennel yard one morning before anyone else was about, intending to give him a free run in the paddock. He could never be off lead. It was a mistake, as Don came out of his cottage to go on an early shift. He kept his van in the yard. The dog lunged and barked furiously, almost pulling her over, but luckily the policeman was late and confined his comment to a glare as he opened the rear door for Venn, and then drove off.

It took time to settle Shadow. She soothed him and fed him, and went across to the office. The telephone was ringing as she opened the door: Gregory was going to be late. His clutch had gone. He'd had to be towed to a garage and would come by bus but that was slow and meant a mile walk down the lane.

'I could meet you.' Liese drew a rather sick-looking rabbit on the notepad and scribbled it out. 'Roger said I could borrow the van at any time.'

'Don't bother. They'll need you to help, and in any case I've no idea what time I'll arrive.'

She had just put down the phone when Spike rang.

'Liese ... tell Roger I'll be late. The woman who was to spend the day with my mother is ill. She may be off for a few days and I've got to find a substitute. I can't leave Ma alone.'

One of those days, Liese thought. They had had too many of them since Sue's accident. The girl had done far more work around the place than anyone had realised. They only noticed it when she was no longer there.

Where was Evan? He should be in by now. Roger was preoccupied as he had a queen due to kitten and she was not well. Liese did not want to interrupt him. Tony had spent a long time there the evening before, and when she met her employer briefly as she now helped with the evening inspection, he had been brusque, always a sign that he was worried.

She took up the appointments book. Sandy the Welsh Terrier had been with them for a month and had been due out yesterday evening. His owners had asked, when they left him, if they could call in late, but nobody had arrived.

Maybe they had been delayed or had had an accident, but she had better check as another dog was coming in and they needed the kennel. She noted the entry in the book and rang.

'The number you dialled has been discontinued.'

Surely she hadn't made a mistake. She tried again with the same result and then rang the operator.

'I'm sorry. That number is no longer listed,' he said. She looked up with a worried expression as Roger came in.

'Nothing but bad news,' she said. 'Gregory's clutch has gone. Spike's sitter is ill. Evan hasn't arrived yet. Sandy should have gone last night. I rang his home and the number's disconnected.'

'That's all I needed,' Roger said. 'Maya kittened yesterday. It was a dodgy labour and I had to have Tony to help as the kittens are big and kept getting jammed. Luckily he didn't need to do a caesarian as I don't think she'd have come through. As it is she's pretty ill. One of the kittens was dead when I got up this morning. I tried to revive it . . . no luck.'

Liese poured him coffee and offered him the cake tin. He shook his head.

'Can you ring Tony? Also you'd better ring the Luston police and find out if that address actually exists. Then can you help with the kennel work? I can't manage alone. We only need Evan to have a mishap too . . .'

The feeds were already late as Gregory and Spike should have started them half an hour ago. By the time Liese joined Roger in the kennel block, where all the dogs were complaining loudly that they were starving, she had more bad news.

'There is such an address, but the couple who lived there have emigrated to Australia. They went three weeks ago. They are the people who left the dog here. I suppose they couldn't afford the fare out for him.'

'So dumped him on us.' Roger measured dog food into a bowl. 'Is Tony coming soon?'

'He's had an accident. He skidded on an oily patch this morning and hit a tree. He's not badly hurt but they're keeping him in till tomorrow for observation. Dick's out with a calving cow but will come as soon as he can.'

Roger stared at her.

'I'm half beginning to believe in Sue's curse. Nothing's gone right since that damned party.'

Liese, measuring dog food into an endless series of bowls, felt slightly sick. She didn't want to remember that night's events, but it was impossible to ignore them. She prayed the phone wouldn't ring again, as they were only halfway through the feeding. Big bowls for big dogs and little bowls for little dogs. She had put too much in the one destined for the Chihuahua. She removed half hastily. He'd be bloated all day, as he'd eat it. He was a greedy mite.

She had to concentrate.

At last all the dogs were fed, the bowls collected and washed ready for evening when the whole sequence would begin again. Roger always fed all his boarders as well as his own animals twice a day as he was afraid that a large meal might cause a torsion.

'Blast,' he said, looking at the diary. 'Ludo is due to go out at ten and we were asked not to feed him as he's always car-sick. Too late now. We won't be popular. Let's have coffee. I'm shattered. I need to look at Maya first and I wish Dick would hurry up.'

Evan arrived in a hurry and a flurry of apologies, together with Gregory whom he had picked up in the lane.

'Been up all night with little Gwenno.' He helped himself to coffee and a bun, and handed a steaming mug to Gregory. 'I overslept and Einir's none too grand either so I had to ring to ask her Mam to come over, and wait till she arrived. Was just about to leave when the baby was sick and I had to clean her up.'

He paused to eat and took a second bun.

'No time for breakfast. Where is everyone?' It was already eleven and usually they came into the office for a break.

'Spike's sitter is ill.' She began to wash the coffee mugs in the little sink in the corner of the office. 'Roger started the work on his own, but he's very unhappy as Maya's ill too and one of her kittens died in the night.'

'Told you there'd be trouble,' Evan said, his voice more singsong than usual. 'Ma said the curse would affect us all . . . maybe not at once, she said. But you'll see. Can't get away from it. There's worse to come.'

'Rubbish. It's just coincidence. There's always bad luck. Swings and roundabouts,' Roger said as he erupted into the room, and Kaos, who had been curled in the chair, leaped up with a small hiss, then settled when he saw his owner. Liese poured a mug of coffee and handed it over.

Rake pawed indignantly at her knee. She had forgotten his tea. She laughed as she poured it out, and put it down for him. She always added cold water as he never waited for it to cool down.

'Nothing to do with Sue's dancing partner. The man was a nutter.' Roger was determined to do his best to scotch any suggestion of a curse, in spite of his own doubts. He drank and then swore because he had burnt his mouth. 'Another kitten's dead. I just checked on her. Where the dickens is that damned vet?'

He was unable to be still. He sat, and then paced to the window, opened the door and looked out into the yard, and came back to sit on the corner of the desk and swing one leg.

'Fading litter?' It was a known phenomenon. Gregory meant to be reassuring, and then realised that he perhaps painted an even worse picture in Roger's mind, as his employer glared at him. Whole litters of puppies and kittens could die for no reason, and often they appeared very healthy. They just failed, one by one, over a period of days.

The words triggered memory. Frankie had lost two litters during Liese's stay with her, both going the same way. One pup survived from the first litter, none from the second. The first time there had been ten pups, and the second eight. It had been traumatic, finding another gone almost every time one of them visited the whelping kennel. Time to change the subject, Liese thought.

'Sandy's owners have gone to Australia and dumped him on us,' she said, turning to Evan.

Roger gave a great sigh.

'You can bring him in here and then get his kennel ready,' he told Evan. 'We've a dog coming in at two, and we need it. Just as well Ludo's owners are late, as he hasn't been groomed. My dogs'll have to stay in the house all day and Sandy can go in their shed. Can't put them together till they're used to one another. Can't do with a fight. Sandy's sparky. Snaps and shouts whenever he sees another dog close to.'

Kaos stretched himself and sauntered out into the yard. Two minutes later there was a squeal of brakes and a screech of pain and then the sound of a man swearing comprehensively. They raced out to find Dick Hunter standing, white-faced, cradling Kaos in his arms, which were covered in blood.

'Roger. I don't know what the hell to say. He ran in front of me, came from nowhere. I couldn't avoid him.' The vet was almost in tears. 'Can you find me a large cardboard box? Line it well with padded newspaper. Not too big. I'll have to take him back with me. A blanket to cover him. He'll be badly shocked.'

Evan, returning with Sandy, took one horrified look and went back to the kennel with the little terrier. He had to evict Rake, and no one was going to remember to keep the office door shut for the next half hour or so.

'He's alive at least. What are his chances?' Roger was stroking the cat's head.

'Can't tell.' Dick was desolated. 'He's a broken leg. If nothing else is broken there'll be tremendous bruising. Pray God there aren't any internal injuries. The gash is on his side; a lot of blood, but it's not gone deep. I wasn't going fast as I'd just come into the yard. Was about to pull up.'

Kaos began to cry, a miserable mewling sound that brought tears to Liese's eyes. Watching the two men walk towards the farmhouse, she felt life couldn't possibly get worse. Gregory and Spike returned to the kennels. The dogs at least were fed, but none of the boarders had been exercised.

Liese had not even looked at the morning's post and there had been three calls on the answering service, all waiting for her to ring them and confirm bookings. Without Sue, the day began at seven for her as well as all the men and they were rarely finished before seven in the evening.

By lunchtime she felt as if she had lived through three days, having been busier than ever before as Roger, after Dick's inspection of Maya and her kittens, had decided to go back to the surgery holding Kaos in his arms. It would comfort the cat and also prevent any movement. Evan had had to drive over and bring him back. She was about to go across to Shadow. She sighed as a car turned into the yard.

'We've come for Ludo,' the woman said, pleasure in her face. 'I'm sorry we're late, but my husband had a sudden call from his business. Can we come with you to fetch him?'

Liese had forgotten they were due. At least Ludo should now be groomed. His dense coat needed daily attention or he looked terrible. Maybe his meal would have been digested and he wouldn't be sick, so that she was quite sincere when she assured them that it didn't matter in the least.

She smiled.

'Not to worry. He's all ready.'

She called to Evan who had just started out with a chocolate Labrador. Ludo couldn't come out until that was safely back in its kennel. The poor dog was dismayed to find his promised walk consisted of a few yards before being returned to his quarters. He howled in disappointment when Evan passed him with Ludo.

The owners paid but were in no hurry to leave. They hugged and petted their dog, and wanted to know all about his stay. Had he been good? Had he eaten well? Had they had any problems medically?

Ludo was bounding with joy. Liese always felt relieved when the dogs greeted the families happily. A dejected look and no tailwag sometimes meant problems and not a happy home.

She wanted her lunch. The hour was shrinking by half and she had Shadow to take out. By the time they went she had only twenty minutes. Shadow greeted her as if she had been away for a year.

Fortunately he was happy to curtail his usual walk, so long as she stayed with him. She checked on Helmet who was curled tightly on her duvet, sleeping in an errant ray of sunshine that appeared briefly out of a mottled sky.

She had taken a large rawhide chew from the shop to occupy the dog during the afternoon, knowing his time with her would be brief.

Chews were new to him, and she was relieved to see him happily occupied before she left, taking a hastily cut sandwich back to the office with her.

She had forgotten about Sandy, who was leashed and tied to the office table leg. He was an attractive little dog with a merry face. When she sat down to eat her sandwich he came to her and put a paw on her knee, his black and tan face close to her hand, his eyes pleading for a taste of her food.

Evan came in at four, having been home to check on his wife and baby.

'My neighbour lost his little dog a week ago,' he said. 'Midget was sixteen, a good age, but that doesn't prevent his owner from being devastated. I called in on him. He jumped at the chance of having Sandy. Says the house is so empty.'

He patted the little dog.

'The old boy's over seventy and couldn't face the hassle

of a pup to house-train and teach manners. I didn't say anything this morning in case he said no. I'll drop him off on the way this evening. Poor little fellow. I wonder why they couldn't ask us to find him a home instead of just dumping him. Not that he's the first.'

'And they haven't paid for a month's board,' Liese said. 'That's over a hundred pounds. Does that happen often?'

'Five times in the last six years. Roger can probably stand it now as we're always nearly full if not quite full, but in the early days it was a disaster.'

Roger, coming in for a short rest, was told the good news but he was distracted.

'Kaos is still in surgery. The leg has needed some rebuilding. Dick's pretty sure Maya's kittens are suffering from fading litter syndrome. Another one died after lunch. One minute they look fine, the next ... I can't believe it. It's touch and go whether she'll survive and her milk's almost dried up, so it's two-hourly feeds.'

'We can all help,' Evan said. 'Einir's Mam is going to stay with us, so I can spare the time. Gregory always can ... Spike will if he can sort out his Mam. And there's Liese. She did it with Helmet, so she knows how.'

'I doubt it will be for many days,' Roger said. 'I dread going back to them. What's worse, they were all sold in advance. I'll have to return the deposits and tell the owners. There isn't another litter due for nearly eight months.'

Liese stared at him, wondering how much the financial loss mattered. The kittens sold for £400 each; over two thousand pounds. Previously she would never have thought about financial difficulties. Now they seemed to haunt not only her, but almost everyone else she knew.

She had spent ten years living in a dream world that bore no relation whatever to reality. Reality was the letter she had had that morning from Sam Laycock, saying that another deal had fallen through and the house price was still unrealistic.

Evan untied Sandy and went out to his car. Roger restrained himself from saying 'Drive carefully.' He had become only too aware of accidents since Sue's disaster. It surprised the men as their employer never fussed.

The Welshman had also offered to give Gregory lifts to and from work until his own car was back on the road. It meant a considerable detour and Roger had suggested they come in half an hour later, but neither would hear of it.

The day ended at last. Roger had refused help with the kittens, at least for that night. Liese offered to do the final kennel check on all the boarders, and was surprised to have her offer gratefully accepted.

She gave Shadow his last short walk and flopped into her chair, cutting herself a slice of pizza and settling with a cup of coffee.

The ringing phone annoyed her. She did not feel like talking. It had been a terrible day.

'Bill?'

She was surprised. He rarely rang so late. It was almost eleven.

'Hoped you wouldn't be in bed.' He sounded jubilant. 'I felt it couldn't wait. One of my CID pals went to a car boot sale today. Would you recognise your property if you saw it?'

'Of course. You've got it back? All of it?'

'Every item. How's that for service, Scrag? It was utterly ridiculous. They weren't professionals. Just three joyriding kids of about sixteen out for a lark. They collected everything very small and portable and were selling those miniatures and jades at a fiver each!'

He laughed.

'They'd no idea what they'd got. Luckily they'd only

sold one and Neil was able to get it back from the buyer who was only at the next stall. He apparently thought he'd just landed a piece of heaven and was due to make his fortune.'

Liese's mind was racing. Would they allow the stolen stuff to go back in time for the auction? It had already been delayed twice. Were they damaged? If they didn't go into the auction was a private sale possible? How long did the police keep evidence?

'Liese? Are you still there?'

'Yes, but I'm gobsmacked. They're all there and not damaged?'

'Yes and no. The little idiots did realise that if they weren't perfect they'd get less for them. There were forty of them. £200 to them was a lot of money. They'd no idea they were worth thousands, especially those jade animals.'

'I did love those. The only things Edward ever bought that I really liked. I'd love to keep the tiger. He's marvellous.'

She sighed.

'Neil says there's no need for you to identify them. Sam Laycock has everything listed and we have copies of what was stolen. Thank God for idiots. One bloke we arrested recently had stolen from a house and then tried to flog everything he took in the pub down the street an hour later! The owner was there having a drink and didn't even know he'd been burgled till he saw his property!'

Liese laughed. At least that was one load off her mind. Bill was still talking.

'Think that monster of yours would accept me yet? And what about an evening off and coming out for a drink?'

Shadow was watching her. His eyes now followed her wherever she moved and if she went out of sight he was up in an instant, looking anxiously to see where she had gone. Jealous of her distraction, he brought his grooming brush from the box and laid it at her feet.

'I think it's too soon yet,' she said. 'Going out is a better idea. I'd love a change of scene, but please, not the birthday party pub.'

It brought back memories that she wanted to discard. Maybe in time. None of them had yet been back to the Fox and Grapes.

'I'd like you to meet Shadow when we've both plenty of time and it can be done outside, with you at a distance at first. He's OK now with the kennelmen so long as they don't come near the house ... that's very much his territory.'

'Like every other dog,' Bill said.

But he wasn't, as he would not allow any of the men within yards of him. They had to keep their distance. She dreaded meeting Don, and avoided him as much as possible.

No one looking at the dog now would imagine he could be so difficult. He was lying on his back with his paws in the air, his mouth open, his tongue lolling out, his eyes laughing at Liese.

Helmet, sitting behind him, was idly tapping at the waving tail.

She felt happier when Bill rang off. Shadow was waiting for her to finish, and as she picked up his brush he stood up, eager for grooming, enjoying the feel of her hand holding him and her vigorous attack on his coat. The warm weather had brought all the animals into moult and the dense fur was coming out in clumps.

As she tidied it into a polythene bag she suddenly remembered Spike roaring with laughter at the end of a telephone call.

'It's not really funny,' he said, when he had control of himself again. 'That caller has a young German Shepherd and rang to say she doesn't know what's wrong with him

. . . all his fur's coming out and she thinks he'll end up bald. She'd never heard of moulting! It's her first dog.'

Liese knew how she felt: she herself was on new territory with Shadow. He was just beginning to appreciate praise. He was willing to co-operate when it suited him, but outside, the smells on the grass verge, the sight of flying birds, or even a helicopter at a distance in the sky were enough to take his mind off her and focus it on his own interests.

Only now did she realise how easy Mac had been to train. Frankie, watching her once when she had been teaching him, had said, 'You don't know you're born,' and Liese had never understood why.

She had had an idiotic idea that her aunt was jealous because she did so well with Mac. Frankie's own competition dog, Sousa, remained an also-ran all his life. Liese was sure that was because Frankie, though she was a very good judge, was unable to train. Now she realised she was wrong.

In the months she had been at the kennels, Liese had met more dogs than she had ever met before in her life. Easy dogs, teachable dogs, forlorn dogs, slow dogs, fast dogs, lethargic dogs that rarely responded even to games.

'Mac was a dog in a million and I never even knew it,' she told Shadow, who waved his tail, sure she was telling him how great he was. Nobody had ever taught him to sit or lie down or walk sensibly when leashed, or even come when he was called, and he found Liese's insistence on such matters very difficult to understand.

He was learning in the house that when she wanted him he was always rewarded when he reached her, either by a tugging game on a multicoloured rope, or with tiny bits of exciting food, often saved over from her supper.

Roger had given her a rather revolting red plastic rat.

'Maggie stocked up with the things, but nobody wants them,' he said. 'Most unattractive toys.'

Shadow fell in love with his rat. He carried it around when Liese gave it to him on coming home at night. She hid it for him to find behind chairs, under the edges of rugs, under cushions, and both enjoyed the game.

He became so attached to it that he insisted on carrying it when they went out. This, she discovered with delight, gave her a major asset: rat was too precious to drop in order to bark, and he had begun to raise his head and just look at anyone who came near, instead of barking at them.

Roger, before going off with the dog food, now came daily to the gate of her yard while she had the dog on his lead, playing with him. At first he barked but then, as soon as Liese produced his rat and threw it, he forgot everything else, and became obsessed with finding his toy and carrying it to her to be thrown again.

Nightmares were rare now, but she still had them, especially after a letter from either Sam Laycock or Michael Dutton, whose occasional reports bore little news that was good. On such occasions she woke to find Shadow beside her, pushing at her with his nose, as if aware of her unhappiness. Each day seemed to produce more endearing habits.

Yet outside he was a different dog. He was now walking fairly well on the lead, but any training other than in the house produced all kinds of absurd and irritating reactions.

He grabbed the leash and shook it. He jumped on Liese instead of sitting, and if she turned away he grabbed her sleeve, occasionally too hard so that he nipped her. Both arms were covered in tiny bruises, a fact that she hid from the men.

There was no vice in the act. He was playing, but had never learnt to moderate his bites, because he had been taken away from his littermates, and nobody else had taught him. She began to spend time offering him a dog biscuit and refusing it if he grabbed.

He understood the word 'gently' when there were no distractions, but not when he was outside and something happened to stress him. She wished she had more time and also her own car. He needed to be taken out and about and to get used to travelling; one day, she hoped, life might settle so that she could live normally again, instead of counting every penny and having to put money away in case it was needed to top up that raised by the various sales.

The day after Kaos' accident started badly. It was a bright morning after very heavy rain in the night and the yard was slippery. It was also windy, which always made Shadow frisky and almost unmanageable out of doors.

Told to sit, he put his paws on Liese's shoulders and licked her face. When she tried again, he put his paw over the lead and held it down firmly, looking at her as if to say, 'And now what are you going to do?'

'I'd like to shoot you at times,' she told him, not meaning it, and he waved his tail and looked at her, his eyes alight with amusement.

'I suppose you think you're funny,' she said, and turned to walk him back to her rooms.

He caught a new and enticing scent on the wind and lunged towards a patch of grass that was protruding through the cobbles, where a stray tom cat had sprayed.

The stones were slippery and Liese, caught off balance, fell heavily, but held on. She limped indoors, cursing. Shadow followed meekly. It was breakfast time and he was quite unaware of his sin.

She put down his food and cuddled Helmet, who felt neglected. She examined herself for damage. A few bruises, but the pain in her ankle was easing and with luck she would be able to walk in a few minutes. Her arm was very sore, but it was her left and would not affect her writing.

If Don heard what had happened . . . even Roger would be dismayed and might have second thoughts and insist she gave up her attempt to civilise a dog everyone else regarded as a villain.

She glanced at the clock. She was going to be late if she didn't hurry. Her heart seemed to be beating at too rapid a speed and she felt shivery. She hoped to heaven that her arm wasn't broken.

She held on to the rail of the steps, aware that her ankle was swollen and very painful indeed.

Gregory passed her, walking a Saluki. It was a long time since she had seen such a dog. Racing hounds, prized by the desert sheikhs, as were their Arab horses.

Khan had been with them for over two weeks and Evan had told her that in earlier times they were considered a gift from God and could never be sold. They were only given as a token of great friendship or as an act of homage to a more powerful ruler. The breed had been part of Muslim culture.

She poured herself coffee and added several spoonfuls of sugar, marvelling at the odd scraps of information the Welshman had stored in his brain.

Sitting at her desk, she began to feel better and her injuries less painful. There were aspirins in the first aid box and she helped herself to two.

She looked through the window, watching the sleek beauty and superb movement as the dog walked up the lane.

Gregory drew his charge into the hedge as the vet's Land-Rover passed him and turned in to the approach to the kennels. Dick was much older than Tony, grey-haired with a small moustache. He brought in a box and very gently lifted Kaos out. The cat's fur was shaved on his side where there was a long, neatly stitched wound. His front leg stuck out stiffly, encased in plaster.

'He's not eating yet,' Dick said. 'I think he needs home and TLC.'

'What were you feeding him?' Roger asked.

'Fishy or meaty morsels, and I tried Brunchy biscuits.'

'He hates those.'

He took his cat from the vet. Kaos snuggled against him and gave a plaintive mew, holding his leg out as if for inspection. It was a travesty of sound compared with his usual robust cries. Liese swallowed a lump in her throat. It was such a shame to see his beauty marred, and know he was in pain.

'Oh, feller, feller,' Roger said softly.

Liese nerved herself to walk across the room without flinching, and poured coffee for both men. Dick took his and cradled it with his hands, frowning as he looked at the cat.

'I am so mad at myself,' he said. 'To think it's my fault . . .'

'It might have been anyone. Maybe I'd better confine him like the queens, as he does tend to dash out of all kinds of weird places. It's as much my fault as yours. I should have realised the hazards.'

He sighed.

'Maya's worse, and there's another dead kitten. Only two left now. I really do feel as if we're jinxed. This fellow *is* going to recover?'

'I don't think he'll curl up and die on us. He's suffered extreme shock, but he's a fighter. He needs lots of attention. I'd give him drops of glucose solution . . . make it with a tablespoonful in a pint of water, in a cow syringe every hour.' He laid the big syringe on the desk. 'And of course Rescue Remedy. I know you use that.'

'I've been giving it to Maya, and the kittens. It hasn't done them much good.'

'I've never known anything stop fading once it starts. She's a very sick little cat. Perhaps Liese would nurse Kaos while we go and look at her. I think he'll be better for company and cuddling.'

Liese took the small body in her arms. It was difficult to get him comfortable. The plastered leg was remarkably awkward and also very hard. She was afraid of manipulating it, lest she hurt him more. He seemed to feel it did not belong to him.

She stroked him gently, and he rewarded her with a very tiny purr and lick of his rough little tongue across the back of her hand. Evan, coming in for coffee, tightened his lips.

'I don't care much for his chances,' he said. 'There's a pattern in all this. We need a healer.'

He looked at Liese.

'You don't look too good yourself. Don't fret. There's a way out.'

Liese looked at him blankly. He sometimes said the oddest things. She watched the small chest rise and fall, and felt the warmth of the little cat against her. He was leaning against her sore arm and as she tried to ease his weight she felt a sudden stabbing pain. Dear God, don't let it be broken. I can't hide that.

Evan, to her relief, had turned his back and was staring out of the window. Gregory was coming down the drive.

He lurched into the room, his face white except for a swollen, bloodied nose and a rapidly purpling eye. He collapsed on to one of the benches.

'A van came up behind me. Three men. Two got out and one thumped me, so that I fell over. The other cut Khan's lead, which I was hanging on to for dear life, and snatched him and bundled him in the van and they drove off. It happened so fast. The dog didn't even bark. I couldn't stop them.'

He sat, staring at them. Evan opened the first aid box

and produced antiseptic wipes which he used to bathe Gregory's face.

'He's due out the week after next. He's a champion and at stud. What do we tell his owners and how the hell do I tell Roger?'

Twelve

Roger, coming into the office a moment later, stared at Gregory and then looked at the shocked faces of the other two.

He listened in silence as Liese explained.

It was some moments before he rallied sufficiently to speak at all. It was a disaster to lose any dog, but Khan was exceptional. Insurance would pay the £5,000 he was worth, but it would not replace the dog, or the potential of his pups. He was four years old and his stock was already winning high awards. It took time to replace quality, and very few dogs proved to be as outstanding as the Saluki.

Cotter's reputation would be lost as the theft could not fail to make news in all the dog papers, and might even be picked up by some of the nationals. They would need to advertise in the papers and on radio and put out posters in the hope that someone, somewhere, would recognise the dog and report him. The kennels' insurers would help with that.

'I've never known anything like this before,' Roger said. He walked over to Gregory who was leaning against the wall, looking extremely ill. Liese felt that if anything else went wrong she would scream. She wanted to comfort both men, but all she could think of was Khan, driven off to heaven knew what unpleasant fate, maybe never to be seen again. His captors were unlikely to treat him with the care and affection that had always been his. It didn't bear thinking about.

Dick, having checked Maya, put his head round the office door, saw Gregory and came inside.

'What in the world?'

Gregory wearily repeated his story.

'I ought to have stood up to them or at least tried. They came so fast. I never saw the man who came behind me and cut the leash. He thumped my arm on the elbow with a tyre lever . . . you know how that feels . . . I yelled and started to run after him, but another came round the corner of the van and laid into me . . . I felt like a punchball . . . I reckon he was a professional boxer. He knocked me down. By the time I'd got up they were off.'

'Pity Don's on duty,' Evan said.

Roger phoned to report the theft and the injuries to Gregory. They would need a statement and Dick, diagnosing a cracked jaw and possibly a broken cheekbone, as well as a cut that needed stitching, suggested it should be taken at the hospital, since both that and the police station were in Luston. He would take Gregory, as the hospital was only a small detour off the road to a farm he had to visit.

'Did they knife you?' he asked.

'No. I fell on a very sharp piece of rock at the side of the road. Khan was frisky and I thought he could do with a longer walk than usual, so I jogged up to the bridle path on the edge of the moors. They must have been following me, they blocked the entrance.'

'Do you think we'll get Khan back? Is there any chance?' Liese wanted to ring Bill, but he would be on duty.

'They are sometimes found. If people can make enough fuss. We'd better get cracking. He isn't tattooed but if we're lucky he might be micro-chipped. That might put them off.'

'His owners are in Florida and we don't have a contact address. We can't really send an SOS, can we?' Liese asked. 'We've another ten days before they come home.'

Dick helped Gregory out to the Land-Rover.

'Have any of you noticed a van around here?' Roger

asked, frowning. 'They must have been watching and known the routine; and they also knew the dog: Khan isn't the only one that's worth a lot of money, but he's the most valuable. We've two others in just now that would be worth stealing; both won their groups at Cruft's. Suppose they come back?'

'There's been a white van around for several days,' Evan said. 'It's passed me twice and once it was in the layby with the bonnet up. I didn't take much notice. Thought it was someone local with business around here. It looked like a small builder's van.'

'Maybe they'll find him before his owners come home.' Roger did not sound as if he believed his own words.

And all Edward's debts will vanish and I'll never have to worry again and swans will migrate to the moon and cats have wolfcubs instead of kittens, Liese thought but did not say, as the men went off to their kennel work.

She would wash the bowls and see to all the feeds. They needed more dog feed. Roger would have to fetch it and be out for part of the day. Sue's brought disaster to all of us. I'm beginning to believe all sorts of nonsense. I'll probably even see Allie next time I go to Frankie's, she thought, and surprised herself.

A few minutes later, jumping up to answer the phone, she realised that her ankle was causing her real problems. The pain knifed through her. After she rang off she soaked a bandage in cold water and bound the ankle up. Luckily the leg of her jeans hid the swelling.

She washed the bowls, standing with her knee on a stool, and hastily put her foot on the ground if any of the men came in. They were all too preoccupied to notice her. How in the world was she going to exercise Shadow?

Don's voice startled her when he came into the office, just before lunch, another man with him. She had thought he was on duty.

'This is Detective Sergeant Maine. I'll fetch the others.

There are questions they might be able to answer.'

He went out, leaving Liese marvelling at his unusual calm. Maybe the presence of a colleague made him more careful.

She collected her wandering thoughts as the visitor spoke.

'You haven't seen a white van outside your yard, or when you've been out with your dog? I understand you have a German Shepherd in your house.'

He smiled at her expression, which asked how in the world he knew that.

'I told Don you were pretty isolated there, with everyone else in the main block, and your own yard as well. He reckons no one is going to argue with your dog ... I gather he's got a bit of a reputation.'

Liese wondered what Don had actually said.

She shook her head.

'That little by-lane is really a cul-de-sac. People only seem to drive down it by mistake. I haven't yet taken Shadow into the main lane, in case I meet any of the men with kennel dogs. I can't see them from my yard. We've been so out of routine for the past few weeks that I never know when they are walking them. They grab any spare moment.'

'That would give you problems,' Bob Maine agreed. 'I had a good look round with Don before I came in. This place really has two frontages.' He accepted the mug of coffee that Liese poured out. I'll offer people food in my sleep, she thought, as she brought out the tin of cakes. 'Your part is very secluded. They'd need to be somewhere with a better view of the main blocks. There's no view at all of the main block on your side.'

Don came back with the three men, who could add very little to the facts they already knew.

'We're going to have to change the routine,' he said, having apparently completely forgotten his differences

217

with Roger and Liese. 'None of the dogs are to be walked up the lane. They're restricted to the yard and the paddocks. Two of you at all times, one keeping watch. That hundred-yard drive is useful; I'd be surprised if they'd come down it.'

He picked up a package he had put on Liese's desk and unwrapped it.

'Walkie-talkies for everyone. Liese, make sure yours is handy. If you hear strange noises at night, yell. Roger'll be over at once.'

Fat lot of good that'll do if there are several of them, Liese thought, suddenly worried about her isolation. And suppose the noise was a vixen screaming or a hedgehog grumbling? Both had startled her before now, and Spike had explained them in the morning. The loneliness had not bothered her before. Shadow would most certainly warn her of any strangers around.

Her back door, which was the one leading on to the yard, was anything but secure: there was a flimsy lock and no bolts. The front door, which opened on to a tiny garden and then the lane, had a mortice lock and inset bolts, though up to now no one had ever considered the two little annexes as likely targets of crime.

Evan had other problems.

'How many dogs are still unexercised? Did Gregory say? If we're to work in pairs we need to work out a rota.'

They were in more trouble than ever, Liese realised, as normally all four men walked dogs; now only one would in fact be doing so, while the other watched. Until Gregory came back, the third would have to do the kennel work and take turns at exercise with one of the other two.

'Liese, you'd better not exercise any dogs except your own,' Roger said. 'And close that gate. Don't go outside it. I'll get Hanson over to erect a large run round the bottom of your steps, with a gate on it. That will give you some added protection. You can bolt the gate from the inside and then I needn't worry about you out in the yard late at night. It will also let Shadow run out of the door and down the steps and you'll know he can't escape, instead of always having him on the lead.'

Nothing felt right. When the men had gone Liese took two more aspirins which did alleviate the pain in both her ankle and her sore arm. That now was bruised down one side, but she could move it freely, and decided it was certainly not broken. She found arnica lotion in the first aid kit, which seemed to contain a remarkable number of remedies, and put soaked pads on her arm and ankle.

Maybe miracles did happen on occasion, she thought, when Hanson the builder came into the office at just after four to say her barricade was now completed.

He was a young man, with a mass of long curly hair and eyes that seemed never to stop laughing.

'Looks a bit like a zoo pen,' he said. 'Dangerous lady to be locked in your house at night. Or are they keeping all the lads away from you? I can see you need to make sure that monster of yours doesn't escape,' he added, realising Liese did not appreciate his levity. 'Barked his head off. What is it you've got there? A wolf?'

'You've been quick,' Roger said, coming into the office after inspecting the new pen.

Cliff Hanson grinned, a man at ease with himself and other people, and happier than anyone Liese had met for a long time.

'I aim to please. I've done you an extra, a freebie ... fixed the corner of the cat pen. I noticed the wire was beginning to come away. Don't want you losing your queens or getting the wrong toms to them. You can pay me by taking Kaiser for a weekend. Moll and I will have been married six months at the end of September. Having another honeymoon. See yer.'

He went off, whistling jauntily, leaving Liese wishing she could meet the world with such an attitude.

The pen solved her problem with exercising Shadow. She need not worry about being pulled over again and hopefully there was a big enough area for her to use for training. She had no time to check.

There were two Westies running in the paddock outside the window. They lived together. She watched them romping riotously, delighted to be free. They raced and rolled, small legs kicking in the air, and then were off again in a game of tag that ended in a joyous encounter, both dogs play-fighting and play-biting with pretend growls and little squeaks.

It was a rare day with the sun shining from a clear sky, marred only by a very few tiny fluffy clouds. The summer leaves were still bright and fresh, with blossom on many trees. The distant woods were a myriad shades of green and a skylark was singing, a bird now so rare that Liese could not remember the last time she had heard one. She watched it spiral into the air and wished she were as free.

The cattle in the next field were basking contentedly, soaking up the sun, so welcome after days of rain.

'They put my pen up fast,' she observed to Evan who had come in for his own break, and was opening a pack of sandwiches. He had not had time to eat before. Mealtimes were very odd today, she thought. The kennel work came first.

'Cliff brings six men. They go into action like a drilled team and never waste time. I've never seen any workmen so efficient. They're always very busy and get through an enormous amount of work ... and it pays,' he added, looking thoughtfully at a tomato as if he had never seen such a thing before.

The phone rang and Liese made a face as she listened. She sighed as she rang off.

'That was Dick. He's just called the hospital. He was going to take Gregory back to his place so that his wife could look after him for a few days, but they're keeping him in overnight. His cheekbone's cracked and so is his jawbone, but not broken. Is there anyone we ought to tell? Mother? Girlfriend? He's not married, is he?'

'His parents are divorced. Both remarried. Mother's in Canada. I don't think he has any contact with his father and I wouldn't know about a girlfriend. He plays his cards close to his chest.'

Liese wondered how it was that she knew so much about Evan and Spike and Sue and nothing at all about Gregory. He talked about dogs and football and motor bikes, and maybe something he had seen on television. Never a word about himself.

She had a sudden memory.

'He borrowed his brother's motor bike a few months ago but I don't know where he lives. Perhaps if he doesn't hear from Gregory, he'll get in touch with us . . . we can't do more, can we?'

She looked up, feeling dismay as Don came through the door. She felt even more uneasy when Evan left the office. Don poured coffee and foraged in the cake tin, selecting a scone which he buttered.

Liese went on drafting the replies to three letters which Roger would need to sign, afraid to say anything, and aware of a long, thoughtful scrutiny.

'I met Sam Laycock last week,' he said at last. She stared at him in astonishment. Was he checking up on her?

'We have mutual friends, and I was at a small dinner party to celebrate a colleague's engagement. I've known him some years. His wife and mine belonged to the same WI group.'

Liese suddenly realised he was embarrassed.

'Seems I misjudged you. Trouble with my job is that you tend to think the worst of everyone. Had no idea that things were so bad. One thing, you're well rid of him. Look, I don't want you walking dogs even just to the paddocks. If those jokers are around they'll pick on you as the easiest target. I won't be happy till they're caught.'

'Any chance of that?' Liese asked.

'They'll come a cropper, sooner or later. If they come back here, we're prepared. I've a team coming to put up video cameras, and warning lights at the gate and sirens. They'd have to come at night now no one is walking dogs up the lane. I don't think they'd come right down here in broad daylight.'

He helped himself to more coffee and another scone.

'Not had time to eat today. I only hope they intend to use Khan at stud and not as dog-fighting bait.'

'Used at stud?'

'It's a cunning wheeze. Pick a good dog and line up about ten bitches for him. Since he's a known champion they can charge around £250 a time. Easy money. His stock is known to be winning, so the pups are registered with false pedigrees . . . you can buy those if you know the right source. When they start to win, the owners are in the money, even if they don't have Khan down as the sire.'

He started eating his third scone.

'Alternatively they have his stud card . . . anyone can get those by writing and asking if they want to mate a bitch to him. They register the pups as his . . . who's to check? And sell them abroad to people unaware he's been stolen. His owner may never find out that there are pups around from bitches they've never seen.'

He was eating with relish.

'Once he's done his job they usually dump him somewhere as it's not safe to keep him too long; someone might recognise him.'

Liese looked at him, appalled, and then turned her head as a small determined paw pulled the door open and Kaos limped in. He was on three legs, still holding his paw up in the air, as if not sure whether it was part of him or not.

'Determined little beast,' Don said, as the cat came and looked at him, asking to be lifted. Don was in the chair which, Liese suspected, Kaos regarded as his property. 'Last I saw of him he was on Roger's bed.'

He frowned when Liese moved suddenly and caught her breath. 'You look worn out. Go and exercise that dog of yours. Don't bother to come back. I'll mind the shop. I'm taking four days' leave, which I hope'll give us time to catch our villains. Everyone's overstretched and I can help. Also, Venn is a major asset. They may think us an easy target, and both Merlin the Staffie, and that Gordon Setter, are top winners and command high stud fees. I suspect we're up against people who are part of the dog scene elsewhere.'

Liese hobbled over to her own quarters, glad there was no one to see her. She had never seen Don in such a good mood. It was engendered by a very successful foray with Venn, the two of them arresting one of the most dangerous men on their patch. He would be safely locked up for a long time and there was no way any clever lawyer could wriggle him out of his dilemma.

He had been arrested on premises while in the act of doing considerable damage, and had injured two policemen before the dog attacked. Both Don and Venn were due for a commendation.

He was beginning to get over his wife's death and feel part of the world again. Aware that he had made everyone suffer in the past few months, he was trying to make amends without quite knowing how to do so. He still hated returning to his empty home. He and Marie had been married for sixteen years and it had been a very good partnership.

Liese, walking back to her own domain, was suddenly wary, afraid that someone might be lurking there, lying in wait.

The pen was bigger than she had expected, covering

half the yard, with a door that could be bolted and pad-locked on the inside.

It took her several minutes to climb the steps, having to pause on every one to rest her ankle. She needed more pain-killers. She had not been back to the house all day and Shadow greeted her riotously, so that she had to walk past him into the kitchen and pretend he was not there to avoid being knocked over. When he was so excited he would not listen at all.

He stared at her when she opened the door as if unable to believe that she was not going to leash him. He hurtled down the steps into his yard and for a few minutes raced headlong, round and round in circles, overcome with freedom.

She sat on the top step, watching him, and wished he could have the run of the paddocks. He needed to stretch his legs and work off some of his pent energy.

The phone rang and she went inside, suddenly aware that she did not need to be with the dog every second of the time. He could not escape. To her surprise, when she vanished from his sight he ran up the steps and came to look for her.

'Hi, Scrag,' said Bill's voice. 'I think it's time for that drink, don't you? Sounds as if life has been even more traumatic over there. I met Don. I'll be there by seven. Since Don's got a few days off Roger doesn't need you to help last thing. He's given us his blessing. I'll be at the gate. Don't want to risk upsetting your fellow.'

'Suppose I said no?' Liese asked, feeling absurdly elated.

'I'd come and carry you off. The brutal sheikh and the gentle maiden. We can make that long-overdue visit to Sue first, and then a pub meal. Or maybe fish and chips . . . end of the month and funds are low.'

She grinned as she rang off, and looked at Shadow who was sitting watching her, as close to her as he could get, in spite of the open door behind him inviting him outside.

He now loved to lean on her, pressing against her legs, hoping for acknowledgement.

He had come of his own free will to find her. The bond was growing. She heard a mew from outside and suddenly realised that Helmet too would benefit from the pen, as the top was covered with wire mesh. Roger had thought of that. She was late with feeding them both and he was up the steps and into the kitchen as soon as she opened the refrigerator door.

They always slept when they had been fed. She secured the pen from inside and went out of the front door to greet Bill, who frowned when he noticed that she was limping.

He knew one of the doctors at the hospital and went to find him while Liese visited Sue who, though surrounded by family, was delighted to see her, and was well on the way to recovery.

She greeted Liese with an enormous grin.

'Hi. This is my Mum and this is Tone and this little monster's Ry.'

'She's making the most of it. Queen holding court,' Tony said.

Liese laughed.

'Maybe she deserves it,' she said. 'The court, not the accident,' she added hastily.

'Ev's been telling me what's going on,' Sue said, when her mother and brothers had left, and she and Liese were alone. 'He usually drops by, as he passes the end of the road on his way home.' She tried to wriggle. 'This damned plaster don't half itch.' She laughed again. 'Never thought I'd be plastered for weeks on end. Anyway, there's this bloke here who comes to see me . . . he's a wizard . . . oh hell, I don't mean that.' She looked dismayed. 'He's done wonders. I'm going to ask him to drop by Cotter's. Don't tell Rog. He'd say no, but once he's met the doc . . . he can put the whole world right, I reckon.'

The bell that signalled the end of visiting time sounded, and Bill reappeared.

'You're going to be looked at now,' he said, after she had kissed Sue goodbye and joined him at the ward door. 'Aren't policemen wonderful? I can always call in a favour.'

He led the way to a small room where his friend was waiting.

'This is Dane Harper. Genius at meeting the wrong people in the dead of night, but I'm told he's quite a good medic.'

Dane gave Bill a playful punch.

'We were in the Scouts together. I could tell you stories . . .'

'Don't,' Bill said. 'Or next time someone tries to beat you up I'll stand and watch.'

He examined her ankle and her arm. Bill whistled when he saw the bruising.

'What did you do?' Dane asked. 'Argue with a brick wall?'

'My dog pulled me over. I went down with a crash on the cobbles, but only because they were slippery,' she said. 'And don't you dare tell that to Roger,' she added to Bill.

'Bad bruising and a slight sprain. No real damage,' Dane said, prescribing strong pain-killers since she could not take time off work. 'No alcohol,' he added, 'or you'll be in real trouble.'

'Good,' Bill said. 'I needn't be jealous when she has a bottle of wine and I drink mineral water because I'm driving.'

Dane made out a prescription which they collected from the hospital dispensary. Bill bought them both coffee from a dispenser and she took two tablets before they left.

'This isn't a pub,' she said some minutes later as they drew into the car park of a small restaurant. 'The Lucky Dip. What is it? A transport café?'

Though it looked ramshackle outside, the inside was a surprise, with small tables beautifully set, orchids on each, and an atmosphere that enchanted her.

'No. It's run by a friend of mine. Always promised I'd come and eat. Never did. Got him out of a nasty spot one night when three muggers attacked him. So I get favours here, too.'

Bill proved a good companion, making her laugh with silly stories and reminding her of long-ago days when she had never even heard of Edward. One night they had been called out to a house where there were the most extraordinary noises. After a great deal of investigation they found a mouse had got into the back of the electric fire and was desperately trying to free himself.

'Once we'd traced the noise we took the back off . . . you should have seen it run,' he said. 'The poor woman was most embarrassed, but we pointed out it's better to have a false alarm than none at all when it's necessary, and she couldn't know what was causing the din. Mice are anything but quiet!'

Liese, revelling in a meal she hadn't had to cook, felt more relaxed that she had for years. Callum, the res-taurant owner, joined them for coffee, and heard Bill's last story, about a trapped cat.

'Funniest cat I ever met belongs to the two old ladies who teach my small son in nursery school,' he said. 'He's the biggest and tommiest tom cat I have ever seen in my life. His name's Mollie.'

'I don't believe it,' Liese said.

'True as I sit here. I asked why and was told, "So the children don't ask questions!" Myself, I'd have thought it would provoke more questions.'

He filled up their coffee cups again and left them. Liese, looking up at Bill, saw him frown.

'You've something to tell me,' she said, suddenly sure that the evening had more purpose than just a night out. 'Not about Khan? You haven't found him dead?'

'No. There's no news of him yet. I don't think they'll kill him, at least not unless their plans go wrong. They want him for stud. It's about that wretched woman and her son.'

Liese felt a sudden wave of misery. She could never get away from the legacy that Edward had left her.

'My friend Tom, who's been doing a bit of digging, found out quite a bit about her. Her name's Anita Lester, which he thinks is an alias, but she's used it for at least fifteen years. When she first surfaced she was one of those raving beauties that drives even sensible men a bit crazy. She's still very good-looking but there's a difference between twenty and thirty-five.'

Liese sipped her coffee, and absentmindedly accepted the two mint chocolates that the waiter put on her side plate. Bill handed her his.

'At the time the first boy was born she had at least four men in tow, one of them being Edward. She also had a close woman friend, in whom she confided. Till Elizabeth was due to be married, and Anita and her friend's fiancé took off for Paris for a week. Elizabeth is very bitter and only too willing to talk, although she has since married someone else.'

'Was that Edward?'

'No. But Tom traced the man. He too is married. Anita told her friend that this man was the father of her son. He too has been paying £1,000 a month for the boy's upkeep. He remembered Edward and several other men and women in the group at the time; they went out together, partied together and I suspect probably took drugs together, though maybe not to a disastrous extent . . . toying with the scene. Though one at least did die of a drugs overdose.'

'Edward tried to introduce me to them all, when we were first married,' Liese said. 'I hated it, and in the end he got fed up with me, because I wasn't able to be as

228

extrovert as they all were. I just didn't fit. I wouldn't even try cannabis.'

'I should hope not,' Bill said, horrified, contemplating a society with very different standards from his own. 'Anita has done the same with a second boy. He too has about four "fathers"; it's very profitable, but now the other men know I doubt if it will go on.'

Liese stared at him, wondering that any woman could behave in such a way.

'It can't get worse,' she said, contemplating an even bigger abyss opening in front of her.

'It doesn't get better. Two of the men are in positions that could be affected by the story if it came out. If she loses her source of income, she could well turn nasty and go to the tabloids. They'd pay her a fortune. The story of the year. The public would lap it up.'

'It doesn't prove anything,' Liese said. 'All that could disprove it would be to find out if Edward was actually somewhere else at the right time . . . and I doubt if anyone can do that.'

'He was seen with her quite often even after you were married,' Bill said. 'She has dates of hotel holidays she spent with him. And photographs to prove it.'

All those years, Liese thought, suddenly furious. She had wasted all that time on a man not worth a single penny, and had let him spend her fortune. Why didn't I wake up?

Bill was still talking. She wished he would stop, but she could not go on in total ignorance.

'The boys are at prep school now. When they were small she had a housekeeper and a nannie. Lives in style, does our Anita.'

He leaned across the table and took her hand.

'I'm sorry, Scrag. I don't think she's going to give up. A dead man can't disprove paternity whereas live men can if they take DNA tests. It might hit the headlines some time, and I thought it better if you knew. I wish . . .'

I wish you'd married me and never met the bastard, he thought suddenly and savagely, dismayed by her stillness and the loss of colour in her face.

I should have known that there were breakers ahead, Liese thought as they drove home. The moon shone on the tiny patch of garden in front of her little house. Bill dropped her at the gate. He put an arm round her and held her close, and she leaned against his shoulder. He resisted the temptation to bury his lips in her hair.

'We must do that again,' he said. 'When I don't have bad news. Maybe it wasn't the way to do it, but I wanted to have some time with you before adding to your woes.'

'I'm beginning to believe in that wretched man and his curse,' she said, her voice forlorn. 'You seem the only one it hasn't affected.'

If only you knew, Bill thought. I want to be with you, to look after you, and you barely notice me. That's curse enough.

'May it stay that way,' he said, as she opened the gate to go inside, triggering a warning bark from Shadow who had heard Bill's voice but not hers. She called out to him and he quieted.

'Maybe when I have some free time we could try introducing me to that monster of yours. Think if I come armed with a pound of cooked garlic sausage he might think I'm worth knowing?'

'We can try,' Liese said. She had half expected a kiss and was not ready for it. Bill was fun, and a good friend still, but that was all. A shoulder to lean against, a man who knew almost as much about her childhood as any brother. She knew what he wanted and sighed. Life was so unfair.

Shadow was waiting for her, but this time his greeting was less effusive. Maybe he was learning at last, she thought, as he followed her into the bedroom where

Helmet was already ensconced on her duvet. He greeted her with a mew and went back to sleep again. Bedtime, so far as he was concerned, was at ten each night and if nobody else was ready he went off by himself.

She lay in the dark listening to both animals breathing and to owl calls in the woods. It was very peaceful. A new moon hung outside her window, a star beyond it, and a small wind rustled the curtains. She put down her hand to stroke Shadow's ears and was rewarded with a lick.

That night she dreamed of Edward again, telling her she would never be free of him. She woke feeling heavy eyed and unrefreshed, and took two of her pain-killers as both her ankle and her arm protested when she got out of bed. Rain fell from a dismal sky.

Shadow, racing round his new territory, refused to come in, and she had to entice him with a slice of meat cut from the little joint she had cooked two days before, for sandwiches.

She limped across to the office. The next seven days were to be some of the worst she had yet experienced at the kennels.

Thirteen

Roger was already in the office when she walked in. Maya lay, unmoving, barely breathing, in a box beside him. She had no interest in life and did not even open her eyes when Liese came over to look at her, tears pricking her eyes.

'Her last kitten died at midnight,' Roger said. 'I tried.' He put out a hand to stroke the little cat. There was not the slightest response. 'Dick says, if we can get her through today . . .' He did not sound as if he believed his own words.

'If we don't find Khan I think I'll sell up. I can't take this. I'm getting old.'

Liese could think only of practicalities. It prevented her dwelling on other more unpleasant possibilities.

'Have you eaten at all since yesterday?'

'I don't want food.'

'Then you'll have coffee.' She poured it out, sweetened it, and while Roger was looking at his cat she added a few drops of the Rescue Remedy that stood on the desk beside the jug of glucose mixture.

'She needs about twenty drops of that every half-hour,' Roger said. 'She won't even lift her head. She hasn't moved since lunchtime yesterday. I'll have to help with the dogs. Can you look after her?'

'Of course I can. I'll make out a chart of times, and tick each one off as I feed her. Then you can see that it's been done when you come in. Has she any medicine to take?'

'She's had her first dose. I had to crush the tablets and

feed them to her with the glucose solution. The next are due at two; every eight hours.'

He finished his coffee and walked to the window. Outside rain fell steadily, and the grey skies promised more to come.

'So long as she keeps breathing. If only she fights as hard as Kaos . . . he refuses to stay in. I put him with the other queens. I'm scared he'll limp out of the office and walk under a visitor's car.'

Dick had promised to come daily, refusing to take any fees for treating either Maya or Kaos. Tony, his wrist bandaged, called in at ten, and looked at the Tonkinese.

'I wonder . . .' He did not finish the sentence.

We're all walking wounded, Liese thought as Gregory came in, looking as if he too had spent the last week without eating or sleeping. He had discharged himself from the hospital and rung Evan, asking him to collect him. The Welshman had gone straight off to the kennels when they arrived, knowing they would be overstretched.

'Ought you to be here?' she asked.

'Can't sit at home by myself, brooding,' he said. 'Thinking about it, I found I was scared just at the thought of bringing a dog out of its kennel.' He took the mug that Liese offered him. 'I decided I'd better get stuck in . . . like getting straight back on a horse after a toss.'

He looked at Maya.

'What have we done to deserve this? I begin to think we really are cursed. Daft. I don't believe in them, but that fellow was very convincing. Shook me, just listening to him. Do you think . . . ?' He broke off, having looked through the window and seen Roger approaching. He had reached the kennels and discovered he needed to look at Maya again, just to make sure she was still alive. He couldn't bear to leave her, or think of her dying without him there to comfort her last moments.

Although it crucified him, every animal he had ever

owned had died in his arms. He bent over the box.

'You won't forget? Do you think her breathing is stronger? I couldn't bear her to die on me. She's only four. One of the best I ever had, and so affectionate.' He looked at Gregory, as if he had only just noticed him. 'You look as if a puff of wind will blow you over. Better stick to feeding and watering today, and only the very tiny dogs; the Papillon, the two Yorkies, and the collie pup and the Chihuahua. Anything bigger might pull you over.'

'Honey Carter's due in today,' Liese said checking the book. 'She has diabetes and needs insulin injections. I'll write out the instructions to tape on her kennel door. She has a special diet too.'

'She's been in before. Spike's good with her, and she doesn't seem afraid of him when he does the injections.'

Gregory sat down to drink his coffee. Liese was sure he should not be back to work so soon. The stitches on his forehead gave him a raffish look, and his black eye, though fading, was still coloured. Spike, coming in briefly, looked at Maya and went out again with a set mouth. He found Don standing by Khan's empty kennel.

'We can't let it. It's been booked for a month, and hopefully we'll have the dog back in a couple of days,' he said, but did not sound as if he meant it. He contemplated it as if looking might produce the dog, or turn the clock back. He spun round as Roger spoke.

'When they come back ... do we send a letter to be waiting for them, or phone them? How in God's name do we tell them we've lost their champion? It's bad enough when it's anyone's dog ... but they brought Khan here because they trusted us to keep him safe and in tip-top condition.'

'No one could foresee what happened.' Don was part of the kennels again and fiercely protective of their reputation.

The dogs were happy enough to cut short their exercise,

most of them disliking the rain. Roger would have worked through the break, but he wanted to see Maya. When he appeared in the office Liese insisted he sit down and have coffee. She had brought her toaster across and made him eat, not happy until he had eaten four slices.

The food restored him enough to make him realise he was hungry and he attacked the cake tin, eating four scones and two buns. Don, making toast for himself, watched his partner but said nothing.

Roger looked at the chart. Maya had had four lots of the solution he had made. There was no change.

'I looked up Kahn's owners' address in the diary,' Liese said. 'I'd think they'd come to pick him up without going home first as we're halfway from the airport. So it's no use sending them a letter.'

'We'll be ruined.' Roger had lost all his energy, and seemed suddenly a very old man. 'Cotter's . . . the kennels that allowed a very valuable dog to be stolen. Great advertisement. They say a bad press is as good as a good one, but not in this case. Owners meet at shows . . . at dog clubs . . . at the vet. They talk. Dear God, how they talk.'

Don was in charge, never relaxing for a second. He organised the kennel work, did more than his share of dog-walking, collected all the bowls for Liese to wash, made sure that Gregory had frequent rests and kept Spike and Evan working harder than they had ever done before.

He used Roger's computer to design a poster. Bob Maine called in briefly to report a total lack of progress and took it to photocopy, as well as photographs of the dog which Liese had found in one of the back numbers of *Dog World*.

By lunchtime vets and kennel owners and those running rescue organisations in the area had all been informed. Liese suddenly realised how useful it was to have a policeman on the premises.

No use trying to keep the theft quiet when they needed

the dog back. Every policeman in the county was looking out for a white van, and for rumours of the arrival of a new dog. The Saluki was very conspicuous. Liese rang the local radio station, and they also had a message put on the Internet where dog owners corresponded regularly.

So far there was not even a sighting, but a colleague rang Don to say that two more dogs had been stolen from gardens where their owners were sure they were safe, and another had been taken from a car at a service station in the short time that it took the owner to pay for her petrol.

Bill, ringing for news, told Liese that they had reports of thefts of dogs over a wide area.

'It's so easy with the motorways. They can be in Wales at eight and in Manchester or Liverpool by ten. The dealers there would have no idea the dogs had been stolen. Or else they've a hide-out somewhere. Chin up, Scrag. It's a great life if you don't weaken.'

Liese's thoughts seemed to go round in circles. Khan was such a lovely, happy dog. Was he being well treated, or was he in a squalid kennel, dirty and uncared for, beaten if he wouldn't co-operate?

Would the thieves spoil his wonderful temperament, making him wary and perhaps vicious, having learned that people could be cruel? Or would he be anxious and clinging, needing reassurance, terrified to be out of his owners' sight—if he did come back. He had to come back. She couldn't bear to think of the family's distress if they had to be told their dog had vanished. The two small boys had so obviously adored him.

Champion he might be, but he was obviously a much treasured family pet.

Roger haunted the kennels, inspecting every dog, afraid it might have vanished or developed some sinister illness that would spread like wildfire, affecting all his boarders. He wanted reports on all of them. Were they eating well?

Were their functions normal? Was any dog coughing? Or worse, had any diarrhoea?

The next two days were as bad. Several times Liese, going to find Roger and give him a message, saw him standing by Khan's empty kennel, staring at it. She slipped out and warned the men, knowing he would not want to be discovered.

Don made large meals, and forced his partner to share them, pretending that he was distracted and had overestimated the amounts he needed. Roger ate without even tasting the food and did not seem to realise that Don's efforts were unusual. Maya was alive, and that was all that anyone could say for her.

The evenings were a relief, when Liese could relax, with Shadow lying as close to her as he could get, watching her every move. She did not feel like training sessions, but he seemed calmer daily, at least with her, and she valued his company and that of the little cat, who curled on her lap, his now noisy purr drowning the ticking clock.

The birthday party . . . that was the start of the bad luck, the three men said, talking it over at coffee time when Roger and Don were absent. Mine began weeks before, Liese thought. Did Edward curse me before he died, wanting my money and hating me? Am I doubly cursed now? Do I believe in curses? Will our troubles never end?

There was no news of Khan. Bill was away, seconded briefly to an area where there were major problems due to a strike at a very big factory. She missed his phone calls, which were now several times a week.

Roger came into the office the next morning and put the cat in her box. She lay inert. He stroked her fur, which had lost all its gloss.

'Six more days, and then we have to tell Khan's owners he's gone. And Dick says if Maya is no better when he calls today he thinks he ought to release her, as she won't recover.'

237

Liese, dripping glucose solution into the cat's mouth, holding her head tenderly, looked up at him in horror.

'Frankie revived one of her dying cats with a dose of brandy,' she said. 'Can't we try? Nothing will make a lot of difference now.'

'It's a thought,' Roger said. He returned a few minutes later with a small bottle of brandy and poured some into a cup, drawing it up into the syringe. He stroked her throat to force her to swallow.

She spluttered, but it went down. She licked her lips, and settled again.

'At least she's still breathing,' Liese said. 'And that's the first time she's licked her lips.'

It was a small consolation. Roger went out to join the working team. The time dragged. Liese answered letters, booked in two dogs, and assured another client that they could cope with her two while she and her husband went to a wedding and would be away overnight.

She kept looking at Maya, as if that would give the little cat strength. The brandy had done some good, and she did seem to be just holding on, but the improvement was so slight. Dick, when he called in, was horrified by the amount they had used and they dared not try it again. He gave her another injection which she accepted without any protest, a bad sign in itself. She was alive . . . please God she would survive, and they would find Khan and life could settle again.

Time crawled on.

The man who appeared at coffee time came in and smiled at them. Roger looked at him, raising one eyebrow.

'You want us to take your dog?'

'Sue sent me. She tells me you're all in great trouble, and feels it was due to her. I've been able to help her and she thinks I could help you.'

'You're Doctor McDowd,' Evan said.

'Help how?' The past few days had frayed Roger's temper, and he was not inclined to be patient. He could not imagine how anyone could help.

'I've come to lift the curse that Sue brought down on you.'

'That's rubbish. No such thing.' Roger was suddenly unreasonably angry. Life had ceased to make sense, and he hated an upset routine. Curse or not, nothing would go right if Khan weren't found. What could this absurd little man possibly do? 'It's just coincidence. Happens all the time. Sue's just a kid . . . believes in all sorts of nonsense.'

'Perhaps I can show you,' he said, and walked over to Maya's box, lifting out the little cat. She opened her eyes and looked at him.

'Poor little lady. She's lost all her kittens, hasn't she? She's a very sick little animal.'

Roger glowered at him, wondering if everyone knew all their business.

'The milk's not quite gone . . . she wouldn't be here alone if they were still alive.'

The visitor held his hands above the small body. The hands mesmerised Liese. They stroked and caressed, yet never quite touched Maya. He spoke to her softly, his voice coaxing. He had a beautiful voice, deep and soothing, a voice that comforted and consoled, a voice that Liese could have listened to for ever.

He took a small phial from his pocket, and put five drops from it on her forehead. He handed it to Roger.

'It's similar to Rescue Remedy but more potent. Put five drops on her head every two hours today; then three times a day till it's finished. She'll be hungry tonight, and want something solid. Try her with a little steamed fish.'

He handed her to Roger, who took her. He was temporarily speechless. Maya put up a paw and patted his face, and then snuggled against him, purring. She was far from full strength but she was vastly better than she had been even minutes before. When he put her in her box she sat, somewhat unsteadily, so that he had to prop her, and washed behind both ears before curling herself up and settling.

'I can help you all. Let me try. It does no harm, and I promise you, I am on the side of the angels.'

'He helped Sue,' Evan said. 'It was the hospital doctors who brought him to her.'

The doctor turned to Liese. He walked over to her and put his hands on either side of her head, about two inches away from her hair. She felt a flooding warmth that spread over her whole body and a sudden conviction that things would now change and they would all be restored to their normal lives again.

Colour came into her face and her eyes brightened and the men stared at her. This was a Liese they had never seen before, recapturing her former enthusiasm, and feeling that she had a future. The fog of misery that had engulfed her lifted. She felt reborn.

'Who are you?' Gregory asked, meaning what are you, but not liking to say it.

He had left Liese and walked over to Roger, who was too astonished to resist. The hands were now above his head and he felt as if he were basking in a summer sun.

'I trained as a doctor. I couldn't cope with the things that happen . . . the people I couldn't help . . . the pain I could never alleviate . . . the deaths I couldn't prevent. Then one day a little girl came into the hospital, with a brain tumour, in unbearable pain. I couldn't cope with the anguish of her relatives. She had no chance and she was so small. Only four years old.'

He left Roger and walked over to Gregory, concentrating on his badly damaged face.

'Poor mite. She was so afraid. Without thinking I began to stroke her head. I was suddenly aware that I had a power I had not recognised before, in my own hands.'

Gregory felt the pain ease and the feelings of guilt vanish. He could have done nothing more to prevent Khan's abduction. The knowledge brought immense relief. The hypnotic voice continued.

'The wee girl slept and they decided to risk an operation. It was successful, and I helped, every day, to heal her. She is now a married woman with a young family and no recurrence of the cancer. I was worried at first in case what I was doing was wrong, but how could it be? Such a gift has to be God-given, coming from the angels, not from devils.'

The Scottish accent was as soothing as the deep voice.

David McDowd looked down at Liese.

'Have I helped?'

'Yes, indeed.' She felt relaxed, and able to cope with anything that cropped up.

'I can't change events. I can give you courage, and counteract evil,' the doctor said.

Roger watched the change in his staff with disbelief. They all looked more alive, with brighter eyes, and moved with confidence. The strange atmosphere that had depressed all of them had lifted. Maya was watching him, her eyes once more focused, instead of staring into a remote distance as if she saw a future that none of them could share. He offered her a tiny piece of scone, and she nibbled at it daintily.

'Can you lift the curse?' Evan asked, with a sideways glance at Roger, who was too bemused to interrupt. He was afraid to take his eyes off Maya, lest he wake and find he had been dreaming and she was still dying. He lifted her out of the box and held her against him, and she snuggled close. He could just hear the faint purr. 'If there really is a curse.'

'You met a strange man. Whether he had the power to curse you no one will ever know. But if you believe he did, then he has conquered you. He certainly has some power; Sue was very aware of it when he danced with her. She said she felt like a rabbit caught in a car's headlights, with no will of her own to move away from him. Some talk of possession. Some of hypnotism. Nobody will ever know.'

'So you cast out demons,' Roger said, stroking Maya who was now asleep. 'And how do you do it?' There was scepticism in his voice.

David McDowd laughed.

'I don't bang drums or beat with sticks and rush around screaming spells and incantations,' he said. Liese, looking at him, had the absurd thought that angels came in unlikely disguises. 'Nor do I use eye of newt, or frogs' legs or other weird objects.'

He was so matter-of-fact, laughing at himself, not making a mystery of what he did, yet unable to explain it. Liese was not sure what she had expected when he came in. He was such a small man, no taller than she. He reminded her of her grandfather whom she could just remember as he had died when she was four years old. His hand, when she touched it accidentally as he took the proffered mug of coffee, was colder than hers. Where did all that heat come from?

She looked at the clock. There would be no free time today, but that did not matter.

Only Don was missing, and she was sure that he would never have allowed the doctor to try his healing hands. He had stayed in the kennels, as he rarely took a coffee break.

'Can't stop for a breather when you're busy tracking a crook,' he said, when Roger suggested it during their early days together.

Rake had come into the office that morning and was lying under the desk. He was always so unobtrusive that Liese often forgot he was there, and was startled when he suddenly decided he needed attention and thrust his cold nose into her hand. Now he came and cleared up the dropped crumbs from the floor, and went over to the visitor, who rewarded him with a pat.

'What a lovely fellow. May he have some of my scone?' the doctor asked. Rake took the offering gently and then dropped to the floor, his head on the black shoes.

'Never done that to anyone before,' Evan said. 'How do you lift curses?'

'You need to believe in faith, in prayer, in God himself.' He looked as unlikely a preacher as a healer, Liese thought. If anything, she would have guessed him to be in insurance or banking, a sober occupation indicated by the dark suit and white shirt and tie, which looked so out of place among the men in their jeans and anoraks.

'There is no curse on you. It has been lifted. You need to believe that and trust in God with all your hearts. Not the all-seeing deity of the legends, or the wrathful Old Testament God, but the wise parent, who grieves when his adult children suffer, but leaves them to work out their own salvation . . . or not, if they take the wrong path.'

'Will the disasters stop now?' Spike asked.

'Afflictions are sent for purposes beyond our under-standing. We suffer, we endure and become stronger as a result. We may find that as a result of some accident we take a different path . . . start out in a new direction.'

As I have, Liese thought and wondered where her own road was likely to lead her.

'There is an old Chinese proverb that says: "Life is like an intricate piece of embroidery. From the back it is a meaningless mass of tangled threads with no apparent design. But on the other side there's the perfect pattern of the embroidery with not a stitch out of place." When I feel life has played me a dirty trick, I try to remember that.'

He took another little phial out of his pocket, dripped the contents on to his finger, and made the sign of the cross on each forehead. They watched him, mesmerised, only Evan entirely believing.

He walked over to Maya and stroked her and put three drops on her furry head.

'I didn't think I could come today, but I was impelled here by something outside myself. I changed another appointment, sure I was needed. Tomorrow would have been too late for your little cat. She brought me here. I'll leave my card. If you need me, call me.'

He put the little white card on the desk, smiled at them and went out of the door. Liese, rallying herself, went after him. She was not at all sure she believed in him but she did feel much happier and anything was worth a try.

'Dr McDowd!'

He had his key in his car door, but he turned to her.

'Could you help my dog?' she asked, though she wondered how that could be done. Shadow would never let him near, or would this man be an exception?

'Tell me about him.'

He listened, his eyes watching her all the time, so that Liese felt as if he could see into her mind. She found it odd that that did not worry her.

'He dislikes men, so we won't even try to see if he'll accept me. Bring me some of his fur. I may be able to help at a distance. He's suffering from fear. He needs you to give him courage.' He smiled at her expression, a wonderful smile that lit his face and made her feel as if she had received a blessing.

'Don't be disappointed. I can't work big miracles. Only tiny ones, and even then I need help from those I set out to benefit. Turn your mind against me, and I can do no good at all.'

Liese was aware of the eyes that seemed to probe deep into her soul.

'We all have a purpose in life. We all influence others, some for good and some for harm. Every act is like a stone thrown into a pond, with widening ripples that reach out and may touch people we don't even know. Sometimes we meet strange companions. Everyone here is altered by your presence and you by theirs. You may never know how.'

Liese brought him the fur from Shadow's last grooming. After he had gone she let the dog into the pen, wondering if she could leave the back door open and let him have total freedom, as he could not escape. But someone might come into the yard and that would set him off. Better to be safe, and not risk it.

She sat on the bottom step. Even her sprained ankle and bruised arm were less painful. The dog came to her and leaned against her and she hugged him. Helmet, at the far side of the pen, was sitting, frustrated, watching a bird walk beyond the wire, pecking at insects that ran between the cobbles. He clicked his teeth, irritated beyond measure, and the dog turned his head to look in amazement at such strange behaviour.

Liese laughed, and called both animals to put them indoors again. Suddenly and for the first time, she realised that this was home. She missed Sue, who was now out of hospital and making good progress.

Roger had put down a saucer of mashed fish for Maya, who was out of her box and on the floor, tucked neatly over her meal, eating with obvious pleasure.

'She's definitely on the mend,' Roger said. 'Dick rang. He has some motherless kittens—only a day old. The mother died having a caesarian. She's not lost all her milk and he thinks they'll bring it back. He's coming later today.'

It was well after eight o'clock before the kennel work was finished. It had been an extraordinary day. Liese tried to ring Bill, but there was no reply. She heated a quiche in the microwave, and sat down in the armchair to eat it.

She wondered how much she believed in the healer. In

spite of her scepticism, she felt so much better, and for the first time began to consider her present life. She cared passionately about the kennels, feeling responsible for much of its smooth running, and was beginning to be fond of all the men. Even Don seemed to have changed his attitude.

So much had happened, most of it involving her. She had suffered with Roger while Maya was so ill. She stroked Shadow, who lay against her leg, and was comforted by Helmet's soft warmth. She could never understand how he could feel as if he hadn't a bone in his body when he chose to lie on her lap, yet if she picked him up he was a coiled steel spring, struggling for freedom. He only came to her when he chose.

Would the healer help Shadow? she wondered. Would her own affairs ever be sorted? They seemed to worsen almost daily. She heard Don's van drive out, and saw Roger walk into her yard as if checking to make sure she was safe. He looked up at her window as if wondering whether to call, and then turned away.

If only they could find Khan. There were so few days now before his owners returned. She sighed, knowing that there was very little possibility of the dog coming back to them safe and well.

Fourteen

Four more days before his owners came home and there was still no sign of Khan. Don received information about one dog, but it proved to be of a totally different breed, and was straying, not stolen.

Maya, though still far from recovered, found a new interest and satisfaction in nursing her ready-made family. Roger was relieved to hear her frequent purr as she cuddled them close. She no longer came into the office. She needed privacy for her nursing duties. Tony brought tins of convalescent diet to coax her appetite back and ensure she ate well enough to produce milk.

Helmet killed his first mouse, the smallest that Liese had ever seen. It was unwary enough to venture into the new enclosure. The little cat was delighted with himself and carried it proudly, refusing either to eat it or let go of his trophy till evening, when Liese found it and gave it its last rites in one of Roger's flower beds.

Liese could not stop thinking about Khan. Roger was dreading the return of his owner. She was far from pleased to find a letter in the morning post from Michael Dutton. He never sent good news. She already knew that the auction of the household contents had raised much less than they expected. Another possible sale for the house had also fallen through, at the last moment.

Some of the debts had been paid. The sum that remained outstanding made her feel sick when she thought about it. She read the solicitor's letter. She was still staring at it, her face white, when Roger came in.

'Liese?'

'They're almost certain that child is Edward's . . . and the mother says that she has a major claim on the estate. Edward was leaving me and going to her, and told her he had made a will in her favour which disinherited me. He left it with a solicitor friend who drew it up for him, but the friend is working for a year in the States and he doesn't have an address. He's due back next month.'

'Do you think he was leaving you?'

'Some of his clothes were missing, but that was usual when he went away on business. Except, if he intended to go and live with her, why did he spend the weekend with someone else? I can't bear any more . . . every time I settle down something else hits me. It just gets worse and worse . . . I can't believe it. I keep thinking I'll wake up and find it's all a nightmare . . . and then realising I am awake.'

'That's life,' Roger said with a sigh. 'He probably couldn't stay faithful to anyone. A tom cat of a man. There's nothing much you can do yet. There may be no will. The whole thing may be trumped up . . . a try-on. She obviously knew Edward at one time, and thinks she's on to a good thing, with a story no one can now disprove.' He stared out of the window, as if hoping that Khan would suddenly materialise. 'The trouble is, legal affairs take so long . . . it was nearly three years before we were granted probate on my father's will. He drew it up himself and it didn't mean what he thought it meant.

'You've missed this,' he added, handing her a second letter which she had put in with his. It was from Sam Laycock.

He wrote:

In answer to your last letter . . . I am shattered to realise that I did not make the position sufficiently clear. It has been proved beyond doubt that all those signatures supposedly yours are forgeries. You won't have anything left after Edward's estate has been

248

sold, as there won't be enough to pay the debts, but I cannot stress enough that you are not liable for any of the debts left over . . .

However, I do hope that at least you now feel better about not inheriting a vast millstone of debt left by your late husband.

She handed the letter to Roger.

'It's good news in one way,' he said.

She turned her head as the office door opened.

'Bill! What are you doing here?'

'Sounds as if I'm not welcome.'

'She's not herself,' Roger said, dispensing coffee, and adding extra sugar to Liese's cup. 'She's had news that's knocked her sideways.'

'What this time?' Bill seated himself on the edge of her desk, and foraged in the cake tin. She handed him the letters. He read them, frowning.

'She probably hasn't a leg to stand on.' He hesitated. 'I've brought bad news, too. Frankie's in trouble.'

Every other thought was driven from Liese's head.

'What kind of trouble? Has she had a heart attack? Is she ill? Do I need to go to her?'

'Whoa, whoa. Your jokers with the white van targeted her. They were probably after dogs the night you heard intruders, not horses. They came while Frankie was out, broke into the house and took every dog. Bonus and her pup, and a bitch and pups your aunt was looking after for a friend who's in hospital.'

'Mac?' Liese asked. They surely wouldn't have taken the old dog.

'We think he tried to attack them. He was kicked and his jaw was broken. He had a heart attack that evening and died, which was perhaps just as well. He only had a few weeks left as he had kidney failure. It saved Frankie a decision she didn't want to make.'

'How is Frankie?' Liese felt desolate. Poor old Mac.

'Unluckily she came home early that day. She shops for my parents, and usually has coffee with them on her way back. But Dad wasn't feeling too good so she didn't stay. She saw the van as she turned into her yard. She ran across to them, yelling, as they were loading the pups. They knocked her over. She's badly bruised and very shocked and distressed, but nothing's broken.'

He grinned.

'It's not really funny, but you know Frankie. She kept her gun by the door and threatened anyone who came until she'd identified them. She fired it at one man. He wanted to interview her for the local paper. He reported her. We've had to take it away.'

'She'll be terrified, all on her own. Are you taking me back with you?'

'She's not alone. She says don't come. She's OK. Colin's Mum is a widow. His father died recently and she's been feeling down. Colin collected her and she's staying with Frankie. They get on like a house on fire. She's not been able to cope with the farm they own, and they're talking about her selling up and then using the money to do up the old flat over the stable. Remember it? It would be ideal for both of them.'

He sipped his coffee, and then looked across at Liese.

'She's vowing to get the villains cursed from here to the end of time. Or alternatively to hunt them down and strangle them with her bare hands, and a moment later she's crying about Mac and the stolen dogs, and the fact that the pups are at a critical age and anything bad happening to them now could ruin them for life. It's a mess.'

Roger put his mug down with a bang that made Rake bark.

'I wish we could catch them,' he said. 'I only hope they don't turn up here again. I'd like to make them wish they'd never been born.'

'Leave it to us,' Bill said. 'We're the experts. You'd get yourself into trouble. Khan's the real reason I'm here.' Bill straddled the bench, and stroked Rake who had come to investigate him and was sniffing delicately at his trousers, scenting Venn who had greeted the newcomer a few minutes before. 'I've been seconded to work with the local police.' He hesitated, wondering whether to tell them he'd put in for a transfer, but it might not come off. Better to say nothing yet. 'Don's putting me up, so I'll be around quite a bit. There've been more thefts from this area.'

More distraught owners, Liese thought. It was bad enough losing a boarder; to lose Shadow ... she swallowed, mourning Mac, her first dog.

'We think they're based somewhere close to you. Frankie's the only victim from our patch, but we're pretty sure from her description that it's the same gang. We've had an idea. It needs your co-operation.'

Bill sounded as if he had his doubts.

'I hope you'll agree. We want to spread it around that you have another very valuable animal here.' He was not in uniform. He looked even bigger dressed in corduroy trousers and a dark blue jersey with leather patches on the shoulders and elbows. 'We'll be waiting. There are a dozen places to hide, and with so many men and dogs coming and going, a few more or less won't be noticeable. Two will be extra staff.'

Roger frowned. Life was difficult enough and he was not at all sure that anything would bring Khan back now. He pulled gently at Rake's ears. The dog was leaning against him, looking up at his master as if trying to work out just why he was so distressed.

'We think our ploy will bring them. We'll catch them red-handed, and if we know who they are, then we know where to look. We suspect they're stealing to order, maybe to sell the dogs and bitches abroad. There has to be a holding kennels. They can't move them on immediately.'

'They'd have to come by night,' Roger said. 'Unless they stage a hold-up down here. If they come back to keep watch, they'll realise that we aren't walking dogs in the lanes at all. It would be better if Liese went over to Frankie, out of harm's way. They're violent men, judging by their attack on Gregory, and Frankie wasn't handled gently.'

'I belong here,' Liese said, and realised she meant it. 'Besides, it would upset Shadow to be moved and I don't think Frankie's place is suitable for him. He'd have to stay in kennels; she has too many visitors and there's Frankie herself and Colin's Mum. He's stopped barking at you and Evan and Gregory and Spike. He still can't take strangers.'

'You didn't see me early today,' Bill said. 'I came to the edge of your yard when you were playing with him and watched for a few minutes. He ignored me. I thought it better not to speak, or draw attention to myself, so I left you to it.'

'He can't take another change yet.' Liese was determined.

'So, what's your plan?' Roger asked.

'There'll be a piece in tomorrow's local papers and on local radio about you and Don branching out and starting to breed German Shepherds. You've spent £4,000 on one of the top bitches in the British Isles. She's just come out of quarantine, which is why she isn't well known over here, and is already in whelp to this year's German Champion of Champions. Pups are due in five weeks' time. They won't be able to resist it.'

'That should make *The Guinness Book of Records* for the longest whelping time in history,' Roger said.

'You bought her six months ago and used AI as you didn't want the pups born in quarantine. It's quite common: often people abroad want to use one of our stud dogs, but nobody wants them to land in quarantine afterwards.'

'Where will she be? Not among the boarders.'

'No. Don suggested we do up that spare kennel in Liese's yard, and turn it into a whelping block. It could actually be useful afterwards, if anyone wanted you to deliver and look after pups. Hanson and his team are coming in today to add an annexe and an enclosed run that can't be seen from the road. We went into this very thoroughly. It backs on to your walled garden, and the gate there.'

'That's not been used for years,' Roger said.

'Hanson can re-hang it. Men can slip through into the back of the annexe without being seen. I'll be in Sue's place with Don and Venn.'

'Done your homework.' Roger sounded grudging. 'All the same, it's sod's law that if anything can go wrong, it will. They may not rise to the bait; they may try and take other dogs from the kennels.'

'We'll have the kennels wired so that if the dogs there bark, it'll sound all over the yard. Believe me, it'll be pandemonium if they do try to be silent. If they leave without trying for our bait, there will be men waiting to follow them.'

'And if they don't come at all?' It was Gregory's voice. Liese had been aware of the three men coming into the office, but had been concentrating on Bill. Gregory waited for an answer.

'We're no worse off. If we can find their hide-out we ought to get Khan back, and other dogs they've taken, and also Frankie's. It'll be worth it if we do.'

The write-up for the paper, together with the photograph of a long dead German bitch, impressed everyone. Breeders knew other people's stock well, especially if they judged them. It was hoped that by going so far back nobody would be aware of the true identity of the animal in the photograph.

'Obviously she's never been shown in this country, so

no one will think twice about that,' Bill said. 'She's been renamed. So far as we know there never has been a Leda von Munich. If you look you'll see she was bred in a small new establishment just beginning to make its name, run by a man called Hans Weber. Both are as common as John and Smith here. If you look in the paper you'll see she's not been shown, but a leading German judge has tipped her as star quality. It would take someone very knowledgeable to challenge us. If anyone does pick it up it won't happen immediately. If it does, by then it will all be over and we can print the full story.'

Hanson brought his team who worked fast and efficiently. He came into the office to report progress, but looked at Roger with a puzzled expression on his face.

'We knocked out the security lights when we rewired the kennel,' he aid. 'Are you sure you don't want them repaired till Monday?'

'Quite sure,' Bill said. Liese looked at him in astonishment, and he made a small signal. The builder went out, shaking his head as if he thought the rest of the world was daft.

'We're assuming we're under surveillance,' Bill said, seeing Liese's bewildered expression. 'Colin's pretty certain he saw the sun flash on binoculars in the wood. They're likely to have night glasses too. It's a well-equipped gang. Roger and I are going to discover the loss of the lights this evening when you go out, and are going to try and fix them . . . only we won't manage it. It ought to bring them . . . an extra bonus.'

Liese was not at all happy. Bill went on explaining.

'If they did work and you were out in the enclosure you'd be a target . . . easily seen. I wish I could be with you, but you know that's not possible. Take Shadow out early for his last run. They won't come before bedtime. You're always up at the crack of dawn and an extra hour won't hurt him.'

Liese felt as if she had been living on her nerves for months. Khan had to be found. Please God, she said, over and over. Did God ever listen? Or was this, as the healer had said, yet another test for all of them and for Khan's owners too?

For some reason the words of the priest at Edward's funeral came into her mind. Life is a perilous journey. Hers was a long voyage in a leaking boat, with the seas battering her. Soon, she was sure, it would sink.

Bill was looking at her, his expression concerned.

'Liese? Are you all right?'

No, she thought, I'm not all right. I'm tired. I'm so fed up with Edward's affairs. I'm finding Shadow has changed my life. I can't ask friends round to share a meal. I can't take him anywhere. I seem to take two steps forward and five back. I wouldn't be without him, only . . . I wish I was a little girl again with a mother to cuddle me and tell me it will be all right in the morning. Only it won't. Ever.

'I'm OK,' she said aloud as Colin came into the room, sure they were sharing his enthusiasm for all the preparations.

'Kennel work is a doddle after police work,' he said, laughing. 'I've walked dogs, fed dogs, played with dogs. It's years since we had a dog . . . they're so full of life and fun and so rewarding.'

Unless they're like Shadow, Liese thought, suddenly wishing she had never started on her campaign to civilise him. He would never be an easy companion. She must have been mad.

Colin was talking eagerly. He almost bounced on his heels as he spoke, and he gesticulated, so that Rake came out to watch him, fascinated by this noisy man who moved about all the time.

Don had been busy. He had arranged for a van to come to Cotter's, with the logo of a well-known quarantine kennels painted on the side. A placid four-year-old bitch had been found in the German Shepherd Rescue kennels. She had been mated, and pups were due in four weeks' time. Her owner, an elderly widower trying to keep on his wife's breeding, had died of a heart attack a week earlier, and had made no provision for the future of his dogs.

Roger had agreed to keep her and find homes for her puppies, so the new whelping kennel would not be a waste of time and money.

As soon as she arrived she was installed. Liese worked out a rota, so that nobody went in to attend to her when Shadow was outside. At first he was suspicious, sniffing the air, aware of a newcomer, but as he could not see her he soon ignored her existence.

Nan's quarters had been carefully planned so that her run backed on to the walled garden and was not visible from Liese's yard. She could then be taken through the gate to run free in the garden itself without Shadow seeing her. No one was sure how he would react to a newcomer and nobody wanted Nan frightened by his aggressiveness. Spike walked through Liese's yard with her food and water bowls, and went in through the obvious entrance.

'Hopefully, they're watching,' Bill said. As a stranger to the district he was one of the new 'kennel staff'. The watchers might recognise a local man. Colin was the second 'new man'.

Liese took in one of Nan's meals, her mind on Khan and the shortness of time left. The bitch was already showing signs of producing a big litter, and was mildly uncomfortable, so Dick had prescribed five small meals a day, as well as vitamins to boost her. Evan's Mam had sent raspberry leaf tablets to make the birth easier.

Dick laughed but agreed they could do no harm and might even make a difference, though he doubted it. She was, he said, in splendid condition, a very well cared-for animal.

Nan looked up eagerly as Liese entered her quarters.

There was a big roomy annexe now, with a whelping box already installed so that Nan could get used to her new quarters well before they were really needed. She had been a much loved pet, and had lived with her master in the house. She missed him, and the company of the other two bitches he had kept after his wife died. She was lonely and came to greet Liese with small moaning noises of pleasure, her hind legs bent in an odd movement of greeting.

Liese knelt and put her arms round the bitch's neck.

'Poor old girl,' she said. 'Two new changes in as many weeks, but you'll be fine now.'

Dick's voice behind her made her jump.

'It's a good job she's not like your monster, or we would have trouble. She's a poppet, aren't you, girl?' He patted the wise-eyed head. 'Luckily we did have some information with her as well as her papers. She had one litter two years ago, when she was two herself. No problems. Her owner kept detailed notes, of mating time and whelping time, and when her seasons are due. She was two days early last time. Good time for pups to sell . . . nice long evenings to house-train them in. It's no fun in gales and snow.'

Nan was to be taken through the walled garden into Roger's house at night. She would have company. Kaos had already discovered her and visited when Roger took her her first meal. He followed his master like a dog. He was hobbling around, taking some weight on his leg, and appeared to be doing exercises. One step and then lift the plastered leg and hop; two steps and then lift it again. He was now taking five steps before he began to hold it high.

Roger, seeing Nan greet the cat with pleasure, left the two together. She was fretting for her owner and maybe the cat would help her and she would be less lonely. So long as he had a warm furry body to curl up against, Kaos did not mind which dog's bed he shared.

'I sometimes think he imagines he's a dog,' Dick said, pushing an inquisitive small feline nose out of the way as he ran his hands over Nan's body.

'She knows what it's all about. The pups'll help her forget her master. She had nine last time. I hope it's a full house . . . it'll keep her busy.'

And I hope they don't fade, Liese thought, as she went back to her own quarters.

It was Thursday and Khan's family were due on the Saturday.

Nobody slept that night.

Nobody came.

Liese took Shadow out as soon as it was light. Both her arm and her ankle still hurt, and it was, as yet, impossible to try him on the lead. If he pulled her she would be in real trouble.

It was a bright, sunny morning and the dog decided to live up to his name. He had never been aware of his shadow before, but now he suddenly saw it. He tried to back away from it, growling. He ran round in circles trying to escape it; it was thrown against a wall and he backed away, puzzled when it vanished as a cloud hid the sun.

For a few minutes Liese forgot her worries and was entertained by his antics. He played the fool, racing round the enclosure, rolling on the small patch of grass in the far corner, kicking up his legs, and then picked up his kong and threw it at her, inviting her to play.

He was ecstatic, enjoying a freedom he had never known, even if it was in an enclosed space. There was room for him to run, to stretch his legs, and when he was outside Liese was with him, throwing his toy for him to fetch, playing training games with him that he did not know were training.

She had not realised that they had made progress. As he was racing back with his kong, she suddenly called,

'Down!' and he dropped to the ground, so suddenly and with such fervour that she limped over to him and hugged him.

'You're terrific,' she told him. Though she knew very well he was unlikely to obey that particular command if he were intent on chasing somebody or something. It was a start.

Time for breakfast, she thought. Shadow had different ideas. He came happily to her when called, with the kong in his mouth. He adored the heavy rubber cone, which had an intriguing habit of bouncing off in unexpected directions, so that he never could tell where it would land. He knew if he released it the game would end this time, so he gripped it tightly, his eyes laughing at her. His rat had succumbed to too much attention.

She gave up and went indoors. He followed her. Helmet was already sitting hopefully by the refrigerator door, complaining that it was long past breakfast time. Liese picked him up to hug him but he struggled free.

'You're the biggest liar I've ever met,' she told him. He responded with a tiny bite at her leg.

Liese wished she had not woken so early. There was too much time to think before she opened the office. She made her bed and cleaned the rooms. She washed the bathroom floor, a chore which she had performed the evening before. She washed her own clothes. There was a drier in the kennel block for the dogs' beds, and she went across to finish them off. She put them away.

None of her occupations needed much thought. Worries flared in her mind, reaching astronomical proportions. She wished it was time for the men to come in, for company and voices around her, for conversation to distract her, for Bill and Colin and Don to reassure her.

Roger was threatening to sell up if Khan didn't come back. She could never have another job where she could

259

keep Shadow. He needed much more time before he behaved normally, if he ever did, and Cotter's was ideal for both of them. If Roger did give up there would be only one thing she could do, and that was agree that the dog was put to sleep; nobody else could possibly cope with him.

Their plan wasn't going to work. The men had scented a trap, and wouldn't come. She was sure they knew Bill and Colin were policemen; they had recognised them. Suppose the dogs were for re-sale to a vivisection laboratory? There were illegal ones about. They might have been taken straight there. It would be instant money and no need to look after them or spend anything on food for them.

Suppose they had already been sent abroad? But that surely required papers, and special injections, and permits from the Ministry concerned, whichever that was. Agriculture and Fisheries? Or could they be sedated and smuggled somehow through the Channel Tunnel into Europe, where ready buyers were waiting? People were smuggled, so why not dogs?

They might not even be alive. Would the thieves fall for the bait or would they be suspicious? Suppose a bigger gang came and targeted the kennels as well, and took other dogs, and maybe also took Shadow? They could use anaesthetic darts. Suppose Bill and Colin and Don and the other men weren't quick enough? Or were injured?

She let Shadow out again but had no desire to play, in spite of his demands. He jumped at her, trying to distract her, but she had reduced herself to a state of abject misery, and played with him half-heartedly. This time she saw Bill standing quietly at the corner of the yard, not moving at all. Shadow looked at him and then fetched his kong. He butted Liese with it, but she was lost in a world of her own.

She did not see Colin come to the door of Sue's little

house. He stood still as soon as he realised the dog was in the enclosure. Again Shadow paused to look at him, but continued happily with his game. He had given up trying to involve Liese, and was throwing the kong in the air and running after it, trying to catch it as it bounced.

Both men only moved after Liese had gone indoors again. When they reached the office they found Roger there, checking the diary. He had already opened the post.

'So far, all our press campaign has done is earn us cancellations. Three today. I had one by phone yesterday. They were very sorry, but they weren't going away after all. I only hope that Khan's owners don't take British newspapers while they're abroad, or they'll learn that way . . . and I'd rather tell them face to face.'

He suddenly banged his fist down on the table.

'It's so damnably unfair. It's not our fault. What more could we have done?'

Rake, at the sound of the angry voice, leaped out from underneath the desk and barked.

Roger looked at the clock as Liese came in.

'We've twenty-four hours left and not a whisper from them. It's not going to work. Tomorrow we have to face reality and tell the dog's owner that Khan is lost for ever. I just don't see any other choice.'

Nobody had any reassurance. Colin glanced at Bill, who for once had nothing to say. Liese sat in the empty office after they had left, but she could not concentrate. With two extra men she was not needed to help with the boarders. She tidied the room, washed the already clean mugs, sorted two files of letters, and logged the morning's mail.

She jumped when the phone rang.

'This is Mrs Howell,' said a voice. 'Our pointer, Mayhem, is boarding with you. We came home early, as my husband had an unexpected business appointment. We'll be over for him later this morning. We do so miss him. We'll pay the balance of his stay, of course.'

Liese looked blankly at the silent phone before she put it back on the rest. How many more? Would they have any boarders left?

Fifteen

The day seemed endless. Several owners collected their dogs, coming for them early. Two more rang to cancel. By evening they had only half the number that had been in the previous day, all of them with owners abroad who had not heard the news of the theft.

'We're ruined,' Roger said. 'No one will feel their dog is safe here.'

Liese was angry.

'It's so stupid. Why should we be a constant target for them? You'd think people would realise that Khan is . . . was–' she swallowed . . . 'exceptional.'

'They won't come back. It sounded a good idea, but . . .'

Roger seemed incapable of finishing any sentence or settling to anything. Both Don and Liese tried to persuade him to eat, but he refused all food, existing on cup after cup of black coffee.

The men came in one at a time, instead of all together, spent as little time as possible over their snacks, and went out again. Bill came in twice as if intending to speak to Liese, but departed again without saying anything.

The ringing phone became an instrument of dread. Liese picked it up during the afternoon, expecting yet another cancellation. Instead she heard Michael Dutton's voice.

'I had a visitor this afternoon,' he said. 'She does have a will. Your husband had it drawn up by a friend . . . Brent Harding. He's a solicitor. Have you heard of him?'

'I rarely met Edward's friends, after the first two years of our marriage.' Liese felt remote, divorced from reality.

'My secretary tracked down his mother and managed to get in touch. He returned yesterday, earlier than expected, and rang me. Edward asked him to keep the will in his office safe. I don't suppose he expected to die so young. My suspicion is that the woman was blackmailing him and maybe he was let off the hook with this as a safeguard for her future.'

'What does it say?'

'That he leaves everything of which he dies possessed to her and her son ... only he does say "our son". It could be a forgery. And you could contest it. I'll send you a copy. There's no hurry, but maybe in a few days' time you could let me know what you intend to do.' He hesitated. 'Mrs Grant ... I'm so sorry ...'

'It's not your fault,' Liese said.

She didn't want to spend the evening alone. She had no choice. Everyone seemed to have a part to play in whatever might happen that night. She had none. If only Sue was next door. Bill was there, the other side of the wall, but he was on duty.

She fed Shadow and Helmet and made herself a sandwich, which she could not eat. It was early June and there were hours before dark. Her garden would be ablaze with roses. She missed it; missed the peace, and the hours of work that she had spent there. Missed the joy of planning for the next year. Maybe Roger would let her take over his garden. It was all he could do to find time to keep it tidy.

Only they might all be elsewhere soon. There was no way he could keep going if his business began to suffer as it had this week. Shadow, bothered by her mood, was restless. He dropped his kong in her lap, inviting her to play. She threw it a few inches across the floor, and he looked at her, baffled. That was no fun. Usually when he invited her to a game she hid it for him, and he had a great time finding it.

She switched on the television set. She was exhausted and the programmes lulled her to sleep. She woke with a start and realised it was late and Shadow had not been outside, and she would have to take him. There was no way he could last until morning. She was horrified to see it was two o'clock. She had promised she would exercise him early.

There was no light in the room, only the flicker of the television screen, but outside a misshapen half-moon hung low and would help her. 'Whatever you do, don't switch on a light after dark,' Bill had said. 'It might put them off if they are about to break in.' She switched off the set. She always kept the sound low, so that would not have been heard outside, but would anyone watching have seen the screen?

How could she have been so stupid? Shadow nudged her leg, his way of saying that he must go outside, now. It was urgent.

The thieves wouldn't come. The men were boys, playing a game, and no one would fall for their ploy. In any case, if they did come, why should they arrive at this second? Shadow had to go out. She had no choice.

She opened the door that led down the steps to the run in the yard.

*　　*　　*

Jim Smith prided himself on his organisational skills. Success had made him bold, and the well-planned lightning attacks were bringing in rich dividends. There was a slight problem, because Spud Murphy, the youngest of his recruits, was liable to take more than a dog if he had the chance. Though that too, with care, had proved rewarding. Spud's father, at the moment in jail, was a silver expert and had passed his knowledge on to his son.

The white van had been exchanged for a dark blue vehicle which, though shabby and battered, had a fast engine under the bonnet, and a turn of speed that would surprise any pursuers. They had had a successful evening.

Their first captive was one of the fastest greyhounds in the county, left with his owner's son while he took his wife out to celebrate their wedding anniversary. The dog was a one-off, belonging to a family who were not normally involved in racing, but had been persuaded by a friend to run Grey Ghost. The dog had proved an improbable winner.

The seventeen-year-old son was likely to need hospital treatment, but wouldn't be found till his parents came home. Spud had added a number of trophies and a small collection of snuffboxes to his haul; they were safely tucked under the driver's seat. They would be recognised in this country, but the third member of the gang, an older man who often posed as a clergyman, made frequent sorties through the Channel Tunnel and there were car boot sales as well as fences for stolen property in France.

The other dogs would also bring some profit as all were pedigrees. Jim never took crossbreeds. He knew who let their dogs out alone last thing at night for fifteen minutes and it was wonderful what a bitch in season could do to make a valued pet forget he had a home.

The next stop was Cotter's. They might think their precautions clever, but they were not clever enough. The bitch, he was sure, was not actually in the very obvious kennel block after dark. They would take some precautions. They surely did not imagine she would be safe. It was stupid to broadcast their plans, but fools made easier targets and thank God for them.

'They take the bitch up into the house in the same yard at night,' Jim said. 'Otherwise why all those precautions with the enclosed run, and the padlocked gate? All the same, there is a dog in that kennel . . . so it's up to you, Spud. Doug, have the van open when we come back . . . and both cages open, too. The injections ready?'

'Do you need to ask?' Doug hated being questioned as it made him feel mistrusted. Jim might be fat but he was far from jolly, a man nobody crossed.

Once in the little lane that led off the main approach to the kennels, Jim stopped the engine. They pushed it to the gate, which opened soundlessly. Spud leaped out, ran over to the kennel and cut the padlock. The lump of meat that he threw inside landed at Colin's feet. He moved around, trying to sound as much like a dog as possible. What was in the meat? How long would it take to act? Presumably it wasn't meant to kill. After a few minutes he kept still. Jack Davies, one of the local men, was beside him. As Spud came into the kennel, both men pounced, Colin with his hand over the man's mouth. The handcuffs were on him before he even had time to think, but the restraining hand did not move. There was to be no yell to alert his companions.

Don and a colleague had already caught the driver, who was standing by the van, convinced that no one was about. He too was handcuffed, and Don had a hand over his mouth. The silent dogs in the cages were evidence enough.

The gang members were all dressed in black, wearing soft shoes so that they could move noiselessly. Jim, in spite of his size, could be almost invisible in the dark. He cut through the wire, making an opening big enough to allow his massive body through. The woman would be no problem. A little thing, and she'd be too terrified to stand up to him.

Moonlight betrayed him. Bill, at Sue's window, was ready to race outside but afraid to interrupt at that moment. He was not sure whether the other two men were yet in custody. Roger and two of the local men had decided to take up their stations inside the main kennel block, in case the thieves proved overambitious.

As Jim started up the steps Bill slipped out of the door,

ready to follow him. Liese, unaware of any outside activity, was knocked out of the way by an infuriated dog, a one hundred-pound missile, that launched himself down the steps, hitting Jim with a force that sent the fat man backwards. Teeth sank into his arm.

The man's rank smell triggered memory . . . memory of a helpless pup that was kicked and shaken and beaten and shouted at. Memory of weeks of misery.

Jim was yelling.

'Get him off! Get him off, for God's sake, get the brute off!'

The van had been driven into the yard and two police cars were now outside. Headlights flooded the scene. Liese was desperate. She had to get Shadow away, but if anyone helped her the dog might turn on them. Roger solved the problem, throwing her a small joint of meat he had cooked for that night's supper and then put away until another day.

Shadow adored meat, which he had been fed in his first home but not been given since. Liese took him up the steps and shut the door on him. The fat man stared at them.

'I'll sue you. That dog's dangerous and needs to be destroyed. You'd no right to set a trap with a police dog.'

'I'd think twice,' Don said, putting Venn to guard the man, although he did not think there was much chance of him being able to move for some considerable time. Falling backwards down five steps with all that weight could have done him little good. He looked down without sympathy and then radioed for an ambulance.

'He's not a police dog. You bred him. Now you can see what your treatment of your pups produces. He's typical.'

The other two men were driven away. A policeman accompanied Jim to the hospital and Don, Bill and Colin began to investigate the van. Nan was safe in Roger's sitting-room with his own dogs, who had welcomed her. The policeman who was sitting with them thought he had the best part of the bargain that night. She would stay with the five until her pups were almost due.

There were eight dogs of various breeds asleep in the cages, one of them a greyhound. Don found their collars, all with tags, in the glove box of the van. Fitting the dogs to the owners would not be possible, as no collar specified the breed of dog, but each family could be contacted and asked to claim their pet.

'Doped,' Don said in disgust. 'I don't imagine they'd give them enough to do harm, but we'd best get Dick out in the morning, to check on them all before we let them go home.'

The bitch lying on the floor looked up at them anxiously.

'That's their bait,' Colin said. 'She's in season. Probably belongs to Jim.'

Liese had come out to see if she could help. After carrying two of the smaller cages into the main block, where sleepy dogs woke and barked, she went back to her own quarters and looked at the hole in the wire. Back to the leash for Shadow in the morning.

The dogs were left in the cages as they were all asleep. Dick, when telephoned, doubted if they would wake till morning. The silver and trophies were discovered. Don looked at them.

'Grey Ghost. He's a well-known dog. He'd probably have been black by tomorrow and renamed Black Prince or Black Bomber, or something like that, and brought out as a newcomer.'

When they had gone Liese took Shadow into the enclosure. He was used to being sound asleep at this time, and it was a quick foray for which she was thankful. She seemed only to have been asleep herself for about five minutes when the telephone woke her.

She leaped out of bed, stubbing her toe, and Shadow

barked. Frankie! No one else would phone her at this time. What had happened now? Suppose she had had a heart attack after all the stress?

She lifted the receiver, afraid of what was to come.

It was Roger.

'Liese. They found Khan. He's just come back, but he's filthy. Everyone else is busy tidying up after the night's work. They found the holding area, just in time, as apparently the dogs were due to be sent south in the next few days. Frankie's dogs are there, safe, and Bill's taking them back today. Can you come and help me? With luck he'll look as good as new by the time his owners come.'

She glanced at the clock. Half-past five. She felt a sudden rush of excitement. The curse was lifted. Had there ever been a curse? She didn't know. Maybe God had listened this time and felt they had suffered enough. She pulled on her clothes and hurried as fast as she could. She was startled when headlights flooded the scene. She had forgotten the strategically parked cars.

Khan greeted her with joy. He was used to bathing, as he needed it every time he was shown, and stood quite still, occasionally licking Liese's hand as she held him steady. He looked so thin when he was soaked with water that she was shocked.

'He couldn't get like that in a few days,' she said, horrified.

'He's mostly coat when we look at him normally,' Roger said. Relief had given him back his colour and his enthusiasm. 'Just look at this filthy water. Don said he'd never seen anywhere quite so squalid as the barn where they hid the dogs. It was a good quarter of a mile from the house and when people heard barking they thought it came from either Jim's place or the hound kennels which are not far away.'

'How did they find it?'

'Mrs Jim showed them. She couldn't cope with all those

extra dogs with Jim away, and in any case she wasn't involved in their disposal. Apparently there are a number of men down south who take a dog and sell it in a pub, saying they're off to work abroad, or getting divorced, or there's a new baby. Surprising how many people fall for it.'

He went on talking as if he was wound up.

'Half of the barn contained about ten brood bitches, all in stalls, all whelped every six months. I'd think that was where Shadow was born. They'll be reported and probably closed down. Don sent for the RSPCA inspector, and he was busy there when Don left.'

It was three hours before the silky coat was dry and Khan stood before them in all his splendour. He ate as if he had been starved for a week, and clung to Roger as if afraid that he might be stolen again if left on his own.

'I don't think my dogs will object to him and he's good with other dogs. Let's have some breakfast. I could eat an elephant!'

After an initial examination the dogs settled down. Khan lay at Roger's feet, his eyes following him anxiously if he moved across the room. Once the food was served and both humans sat down to eat, he relaxed and went to sleep.

Roger had cooked bacon and eggs, mushrooms and tomatoes and two huge slices of fried bread. Liese, sure she couldn't eat at all, discovered she was ravenous. She, like Roger, had scarcely eaten anything for the last few days. She kept looking at Khan to make sure he was really there and she wasn't dreaming.

He was greyhound thin, with the brown and white silky coat shining after their hard work. His ears drooped across the floor, and whenever either of them moved the dark brown almond-shaped eyes opened and looked up at them, willing them not to leave him alone.

'It's a lovely breed,' Roger said. 'They're such gentle

dogs. In the desert they hunt alongside the falcons. Desert tribes carry them on their saddles or on camels, as the hot earth scorches their feet. Not many breeds have such a romantic origin.'

'Not everybody's dog, I'd think,' Liese said, with memories of a lurcher her aunt had once owned that needed a ten-mile gallop round and round the field every day.

'They need space and free running, but what a dog to own . . . there's nothing like watching them move. A well-made dog just flows over the ground. We'd better exercise him. On lead today . . . I feel I need a police escort until he's safely home.'

'It's over,' Liese said, as a surge of overwhelming relief washed through her.

'I'm not so sure,' Roger said. 'Those places can harbour all kinds of bugs, and if they've had any epidemic there . . . we'd better suggest all the dogs see their vets and are quarantined. I've known of several pups that died of distemper or parvo a few days after being bought from there.'

Roger took Khan with him into the office. Liese went home briefly to shower and change and feed Helmet and Shadow, and then took the dog out into the run for a short walk around. He wanted to run but she could not risk it until the wire was mended. She would ring Hanson as soon as she returned to the office.

She took him in and rang Frankie, who was overjoyed.

'Bill brought them. Luckily he knew them as he'd seen the pups when he visited here. Bonus is snappy and they all need cleaning up, but Petra's still feeding her pups, and they haven't suffered. Jim was aware of their worth and took more care of them than I expected. Must go, love. It's going to take hours to sort them out and clean them up.'

Dealing with the post, which still contained cancellations, Liese suddenly realised she would miss Bill. His assignment was ended and he'd be on duty back home again. He was fun to have around and invariably left her feeling happier. Colin would be gone too. He cheered everyone.

Roger was exercising and feeding his own dogs, and she was alone with Khan who leaned against her, anxious for contact, and followed her even to the coffee percolator. When Spike came into the office at coffee time, with his usual rush, the dog cowered to the ground. Roger, following, stared at him in dismay and then knelt beside him, stroking the soft fur.

'It's OK, feller. None of us will hurt you.'

It was some minutes before the dog relaxed and allowed Spike to come and speak to him, soothing him, reminding him that he was among friends.

'Damn, and damn, and damn again,' Roger said, pouring coffee, while Liese stroked the dog and petted him, soothing him. 'If only we'd had him for a few more days. I don't know what they did to him. He flinched when I picked up his lead to bring him over here.'

'I'd like to curse them,' Gregory said, overhearing as he came into the room. 'Give them a taste of what they gave us. Not that I think . . .'

'I'd rather not think,' Liese said. Evan, told the news on his way in, had driven off to the village and raided Mrs Hodge's stores.

'Need to celebrate,' he said. 'It's been a long time.'

The knock on the door startled them. When it opened in response to Roger's call, Khan leaped to his feet and launched himself in a frenzy of crying and tail-beating, almost knocking his owner over. The man knelt beside him, hugging him, and was near to tears.

'We got home last night. Our neighbour said you'd lost him. He'd been stolen. The kids haven't stopped crying, nor has my wife . . . was he stolen?'

'Yes, but we moved heaven and earth to find him. The

'police've been wonderful,' Liese said, as Roger looked too bemused to answer.

'Can I ring home? I must tell them . . . oh, Khan, Khan, lad. We thought we'd lost you for ever. I came to find out what had happened. The rest of the family were too distressed. My wife wanted to sue you for negligence.' He was hugging the dog, who had him almost on the ground and was still leaping all over him, licking his face and hands, whimpering with pleasure. The man was laughing with excitement, and unable to utter a single coherent sentence.

Roger still seemed to have lost the power of speech.

Liese looked in the book and dialled the number. She handed over the receiver, not daring to announce herself.

'Mo . . . Mo. It's all right, he's here, he's fine. Tell the boys. I'll be home with him by lunchtime . . . no, we're not going to sue. They did all they could . . . I'll see you.'

He rang off.

'We had a dreadful night. My wife wanted to come here at once and find out what had happened. If we had, we could have taken him home.'

'He didn't come back till early morning,' Roger said. 'It's a long story. Coffee? Cakes? Let him settle before you take him back.'

He listened in silence as Gregory told him what had happened. He was still in pain from his cracked cheek-bone, but his eye had faded to an odd yellow colour. Roger explained the action the police had taken.

'It worked,' he said. 'I only hope that the full story gets into the press as we've had so many cancellations since Khan's loss was in the news. We couldn't keep it quiet . . . we wanted everyone to be looking out for him.'

'I'll make sure it gets reported,' Khan's owner promised. 'You couldn't have done more. I'll make sure people know what really happened.'

Everyone went out to see them off. Khan, fastened on to the passenger seat with a dog harness and seat belt, gazed at them regally.

'One thing,' Evan said, biting thoughtfully into a jam doughnut, 'we had empty kennels for the dogs they had in the van. They're beginning to come round.'

'The police are contacting their owners. They should all, hopefully, be collected today.' Roger too was exploring the cake tin.

'Shouldn't the vet have seen Khan before he went home?' Liese asked.

'Dick did. He came to see Khan the moment he arrived and also had a look at the doped dogs, to see if he knew what had been used. He wasn't sure, but said they'd not be much worse when it wore off.'

There was only half the usual number of dogs in kennels, even with the eight that had been rescued from the van. Nobody seemed able to settle. Liese brought her sandwiches to the office at lunchtime, after she had given Shadow a run in the newly repaired enclosure. She needed company.

They were all surprised when Sue walked in. Her face brightened at the fervour with which they greeted her. She looked a different girl. She was walking with stick crutches.

'Just come to say I'll be moving out. Got a new job . . . I ought to have said before, only I wasn't sure it was going to happen. I felt if I told anyone, it wouldn't. Don't really think I could walk dogs for a long time anyway,' she said.

Roger had brought Kaos into the office. Sue looked at his plastered leg.

'I know just how he feels, poor old fellow,' she said.

She had a parcel under her arm. When she opened it for them it revealed a painted plaque which bore the legend 'COTTER'S KENNELS' surrounded by ten pups of different breeds, running, jumping, scratching, playing, and one chasing his tail. It was beautifully painted, and varnished to protect the picture.

Roger looked at it and Sue, seeing his expression, smiled. She sat down and took a sandwich. Liese had pooled them, putting them all on one plate so that everyone had a choice and a change from their own usual fillings.

'Didn't know I could draw,' Sue said. 'I found out in hospital when they brought me paper and crayons as a joke. I'm living in Gran's house now. She's moved in with Mum. Me and Caro and Tone have her home now. The baby's here, a little boy. Born two days ago. They've called him Ray.'

And you won't be able to abbreviate that. Or is it Raymond? Liese wondered.

'Tone shaped the plaque, and varnished it when I'd finished. We've both got jobs now with a sign-writer, and I'm going to art school next year. Going into business with Tone when I finish. We're getting lots of orders.'

'You can do one for me,' Evan said. 'Make a present for my Mam. Ivy Cottage, they live in.'

The door opened again.

Liese stared in astonishment as Bill walked in.

'Party time,' Spike said, with a grin at the newcomer.

'You the new boy, in my place?' Sue asked.

'He's one of the policemen who helped us with our recent problem,' Roger said.

'I read about it. Rotten luck.'

A horn sounded in the drive.

'That's Tone. He brought me over. He wants to see Caro and the baby. We had to pass the end of the lane on the way to the hospital. Promised I wouldn't be long. See you.'

'That was hail and farewell,' Bill said, laughing as he helped himself to coffee and food. 'Chinese takeaway for everyone on me tomorrow. I'm celebrating too.'

276

'Celebrating what?' Liese asked, stifling a desire to run and hug him. She hoped he wouldn't be going back too soon. If only Shadow would tolerate him, she could give him a meal.

'I asked for a transfer. Just come through and I'm posted here. Don's offered me a permanent lodging in his house. You'll be seeing a lot of me in future.'

He looked at Liese.

'I promised Frankie I'd bring you over when I visit my parents. We'll have to fit around that monster of yours at first, but maybe he'll improve with time. You never know.'

Don, who had followed Bill in, looked at Liese.

'He did well last night. The makings of a good dog there. I misjudged him. A villain would never have let go, even with meat offered to him. He had good reason to hate that man. He's responsible for the dog's behaviour, not the people who first had him. Though they didn't help as they didn't know how to overcome his problems.'

'Why did Jim come up to my place? Was he after Shadow?'

Don, who had also joined the party, laughed.

'He's talking now. He was too clever by half. He worked out that the bitch was in your house at night and that was the reason for the enclosure, to make it doubly safe for her. The whelping kennel was a distraction, due to our being wary after Khan's abduction.'

'Why did you open the door?' Bill asked.

'I fell asleep watching TV. Didn't wake till then and Shadow needed to go out. I reckoned no one was really likely to come, and if they did it wouldn't be just that moment.'

'Maybe the gods were watching over us,' Roger said.

'I'm kidnapping Liese, and taking her out for a meal tonight,' Bill said. 'So don't keep her too long.' He looked at her as if daring her to refuse. 'You can feed Shadow early. Won't hurt for once.'

They ate in a restaurant overlooking the river, where swans glided and ducks spent much of the time with their tails up and their heads down, reminding Liese of a childhood poem that she could not recall to mind at all, which vaguely irritated her.

'The story of Khan was on this evening's news,' Bill said. 'It ought to go a long way to restoring confidence in Roger. So many other dogs were stolen. They've been operating for several years, but mostly in other places. They wanted to interview Roger but he refused. They did interview Khan's owner and had a shot of the dog himself, looking magnificent.'

'If only my affairs could be settled as easily,' Liese said.

'What has Edward left you?'

'Absolutely nothing, when I think about it.'

'So if he's left everything to this mistress of his and the kid, what are you losing?'

Liese stared at him.

'Absolutely nothing.'

'Right. Don't even consider it's a forgery. If it is, she'll have all she deserves. If it's not, she still gets what she deserves and you're free ... penniless maybe, but you don't owe anybody anything.'

'Can I do that?' It sounded too easy.

'Edward did it ... not you. If he did make that will. If he didn't, then this Anita whatever her name is has done it to herself. Let her enjoy it. No house ... no property ... nothing whatever.'

'Dr McDowd was right,' Liese said. 'Life is odd. Nothing's quite what it seems. He says if we're good inside then evil can't harm or corrupt us. I don't know what to believe, do you?'

'At the moment, full of good food and a little good wine, I feel that life is meant for living and that the future is waiting for both of us ... I hope together. I'm not your brother, Liese. I'm the bloke next door who's been hankering after a ghost woman for years . . . I have been faithful to thee, Cynara, in my fashion. Nobody else has ever taken your place. I tried . . . it never worked.'

'I don't know . . . I'm so tired,' Liese said. 'It's gone on so long . . . I don't want to give up on Shadow, but sometimes I wonder . . .'

'I'm not giving up on either of you,' Bill said.

She rang Michael Dutton in the morning.

'I'm not contesting the will,' she said. 'She can have it . . . all of it.'

'I'll tell her,' he said, and she had an odd feeling that he was laughing. 'I'll send her my bill for the settlement of the estate and ring Laycock and tell him to do the same. You can't possibly be responsible when none of it was yours.' Liese was not sure if he was joking.

* * *

Gradually, over the following months, everything returned to normal. One morning in early October Bill came into the enclosure, holding out an outsize garlic sausage. Shadow ran across to him, looked at him and, after some thought, took it and ate it. He collected his kong and offered it to Bill, who threw it for him. He played with the dog for some time. When the man followed Liese up the steps, Shadow looked at him and gave a deep sigh, as if acknowledging that others had a right to his home too.

'Come for your evening meal tonight,' Liese said. 'You're not on duty?'

Bill looked at her, and took both her hands.

'Giving up the big brother idea?'

Shadow was watching them. People now fascinated him. He barked at strangers, but accepted everyone in the kennels and Sue too, who had begun to visit. Memory was fading.

'Frankie wants to be Matron of Honour,' Liese said,

279

feeling mischievous. She and Frankie had joked on the phone about a possible wedding.

Bill stared at her and then whirled her round and hugged her. Shadow, startled, barked.

'Don't rush it. He's a long way to go,' Liese said. 'I need a year and so does Shadow, but that's a promise. Unless you give me cause to change my mind. I can't face another disaster.'

'Trust me,' Bill said. 'You've known me a long time.'

He held her closely for a moment, and then kissed her hair.

'No pressure,' he promised. She smiled as he went out of the door.

That night, after Bill had gone, she wrote down Shadow's progress. He could now be walked down the lanes, and run in the paddock and was no longer barking at other dogs. He greeted Roger with a waving tail. Bill was a frequent and welcome visitor.

Her leaky ship had made its way to harbour, and she felt as if she was, at last, in a safe haven, with a happy future ahead. Edward's ghost was laid.